WINNING MY BEST FRIEND'S GIRL

PIPER RAYNE

D1731781

Cover Design: By Hang Le

Diversity Editor: Renita McKinney

1st Line Editor: Joy Editing

2nd Line Editor: My Brother's Editor

Proofreader: Shawna Gavas, Behind The Writer

Imagine lying in a hospital bed and the doctor who pulls the curtain back to treat you is the one who got away. Even if you never really had her in the first place. She's not only your high school crush, she's the ex-girlfriend of your ex-best friend. The one girl you've always wanted.

Here's a step-by-step list to finally win her over...

Key to win #1: Try not to take offense that she snuck back into town without telling you—six months ago.
Key to win #2: Rekindle the friendship to ease the awkwardness. But... DO NOT enter the friend zone.
Key to win #3: Ignore the fact that she went speed dating the night before. Take it as good a sign—maybe she's looking for a relationship.
Key to win #4: Attempt to keep the two of you out of the town gossip blog and away from your large family.

Make sure you don't let this last one throw you off your mission.

Key to win #5: Don't get deterred when you find out the past is about to repeat itself. Because the man she met at the speed dating night is your best buddy from work.

Just remember, you sat back and let her slip away once, you won't do it a second time. Failure is *not* an option.

Winning my *Best Friend's Girl*

The Baileys

Austin Bailey - 37 years old
(*Biology Teacher/Baseball Coach*)
Savannah Bailey - 35 years old
(*Runs Bailey Timber Corp*)
Brooklyn Bailey - 32 years old
(*Runs Essential Oil Company*)
Rome Bailey -30 years old
(*Chef*)
Denver Bailey - 30 years old
(*Bush Pilot*)
Juno Bailey - 29 years old
(*Matchmaker*)
Kingston Bailey - 28 years old
(*Smokejumper*)
Phoenix Bailey - 24 years old
(*Singer*)
Sedona Bailey - 24 years old
(*Travel Writer*)

ONE

Kingston

I'm an easygoing guy. Not a lot gets under my skin.

My dad was a man of many quotes. At least when it came to me. Looking back, I think it's because I was the sensitive one in the family. He'd say he wasn't clever enough to come up with them on his own, so he never recited one without giving the author credit. "Winning means you're willing to go longer, work harder, and give more than anyone else by Vince Lombardi was his favorite to use when I was struggling. Didn't matter if it was sports or academics, he'd say that quote to me. I didn't figure out the meaning until years after his death, and even then, my oldest brother, Austin, had to explain it to me.

There was a time in my life when I didn't fight the battle because I was more afraid of losing something than winning something. I promised myself I'd never make that mistake again.

Which is most likely why the battles I pick now are fires. Whether I'm jumping out of a plane and parachuting into a forest fire, or carrying someone out of a burning house, I always win. These fights feel safer than the ones that could break my heart.

Lou climbs into the firetruck right after me, sitting across the way. The sirens go off as the truck rolls out of the station. Lou and I attended the fire academy at the same time—which was right around the time I lost my childhood best friend and the girl I love.

"Romeo, tell your sister thanks for me," he says, winking.

A woman once referred to me as her knight in shining armor after I used the Jaws of Life to free her from a wrecked car. She'd plowed her car over an embankment because she was intoxicated. But it was her repeatedly asking me to be her Romeo that earned me a nickname that makes most people—and by people, I mean women—think I'm a player. I'm not, in case you're wondering.

"Why is that?"

"For the blind speed dating thing she's doing over at Tipsy Turvy." His perma-smile says he met someone.

"Oh, yeah, I missed that. I had to work."

Lou's eyebrows raise. "Is that what we're calling it? Work?"

Monk blares the siren because people are shitty and can't take a second to pull their car to the side of the road for us to get through.

"I have no idea what you're talking about." I glance out the window because I'm in a crappy mood. Lou is riding high after his speed dating night and I just don't feel like hearing about it. I'm a shitty friend.

"Proby wan Kenobi was at the hospital and overheard Samantha talking about a date you two went on."

I roll my eyes. Samantha's a flirt, and yeah, I went out

with her because I was horny. I know that's not a noble thing to say, but my dick is starting to get excited any time it sees my hand. Doesn't matter though. Nothing happened.

"We went out," I admit.

"And?"

Lou's the kiss-and-tell guy. I'm not. "Nothing. We had some drinks."

For most of the night, Samantha and I discussed this Adventure Alaska Expedition she's interested in. I guess she does Spartan races all the time and the next thing she wants to conquer is some seven-day adventure race where you're with three other people and have to navigate with only physical maps. I will say her excitement, and adrenaline, is a high for me. She didn't wince when we talked about me heli-skiing and speed riding down a mountain. She said it sounded thrilling and she'd love to go sometime. The fact that she loves crazy shit like I do upped her attractive level by ten.

"Bullshit," he says. "I'm not asking for specifics, but a 'I banged her over the kitchen table' would suffice."

"Jesus, Lunchbox, one day you're gonna meet a woman who will make you second-guess sharing all the details," Greasy says, shaking his head from the seat beside us.

Lunchbox is Lou's nickname because the man eats all the shit out of the fridge. Lou's the one always asking if he can have one fry or if you're going to eat all that. He's lucky his side job of carpentry helps him keep the weight off.

Lou flips off Greasy. "We're not all married with fifty kids."

"That's offensive," I say with a grin.

Greasy only has five kids, though they're all under six, so when they visit the fire station, it's like a daycare—but the sappy love look on his face when his exhausted wife walks through the garage doors is pretty awesome. I guess he won his battle.

Lou waves off my comment. "Your parents had nine kids, not you." We sit in silence for maybe a minute because Lou hates quiet. "Aren't you gonna ask me?"

"Ask you what?"

Now he's the one sporting the insulted look. "The girl from speed dating. Your sister didn't tell you?"

"No, she lives with Colton now. She's moved out."

He nods as though he didn't remember.

"So she's amazing," he says without me asking for more information or really paying attention.

I love the guy, but this is same old, same old for him. This girl will have morphed into a blood-seeking piranha by next week. As much as I don't do relationships, Lou thinks he wants one. He doesn't. He just wants regular sex.

"Okay, boys, hate to interrupt the locker room talk, but we have a fire to fight," Captain says from up front as we pull up to a burning apartment building. The fire isn't out of control yet by the looks of it, but it will be if we don't get in there. "We're first on the scene. Since you're so chatty, Lunchbox, you get to go in first with Romeo behind you. Greasy, you get the hose connected..." The Captain continues to rattle off responsibilities, and we file out of the fire truck.

After getting our gear together and pulling out our axes, Lou and I head in to investigate the fire. My adrenaline kicks into overdrive the closer we get to the building.

Once we're inside the smoke-filled stairway, Lou talks again. "So this girl, she's like no other girl I've ever met. She's smart and gorgeous. She thinks I'm funny."

"Then she must be a keeper," Captain says over the radio. "Concentrate on the fire."

Lou kicks in the door of the first apartment, and we walk through, scouring the rooms for people who might be trapped or too afraid to run.

"Tank is coming in now with Greasy," Captain tells us.

I press the button for my radio. "Apartment one is clear. Filled with smoke, no flame."

"We went to the bar for drinks afterward. Turns out she was there once before when I was, but we must not have written each other down because we didn't connect," Lou says as we walk up the stairs to the second floor.

"Cool."

"I'm thinking of taking her to your brother's restaurant," he says.

"Why would you come to Lake Starlight?" I ask.

"This is the type of woman you wine and dine, not take to Tipsy Turvy to play darts and drink beer."

"I'm not sure any woman is the kind who'd prefer to be taken to Tipsy Turvy on a first date. That's more of a 'we've been dating for a while and there's a big game on, want to go for wings and a beer' kind of thing." I head to the stairs to climb up another floor.

"Are you dissing my game? I've got better game than you."

"Captain, I'm not sure this building is occupied. Every apartment is bare of furniture," Tank says over the radio.

"Hold on. I've got Sergeant Blecker," Captain says.

I stop on the stairwell in case our instructions change.

"You're right, the place is empty. Shift our search for source at this point."

Tank and Greasy follow us up the stairs. "We'll go to three," they say, walking by us as we stop on the second floor to check behind the doors.

"I'm telling you. This girl is a game-changer," Lou says.

Tank and Greasy laugh.

"You guys wait and see. You'll be getting wedding invitations in the mail within a year. I promise."

"You know all this from one night?" I ask.

"When you know, you know."

I kick open a door and a cloud of smoke billows out into the hallway, making me unable to see an inch in front of me. I can't deny I too believe you just know when you know. I felt a pull in my heart the moment Stella Harrison walked into my classroom in the fourth grade—her brown skin, pigtails and big dark eyes drew me in. My crush continued for years until she and Owen started to date. Then I tried to ignore that pull—which is when everything crumbled around me.

"Nothing on level two, we're going to four," I say into the radio.

We bypass Tank and Greasy on the third, where they're outwardly laughing at Lou.

"I'm going to prove you all wrong," Lou says, and there's a conviction in his tone that makes me believe that this mystery girl could very well be a game-changer for him.

I mean, doesn't that happen to everyone at some point if they're lucky? A man finds a woman who makes him believe in marriage and makes him ready to push away the possibilities of all other women?

"Does she have a name?" I ask as we finish climbing from the third to the fourth floor.

"Stella."

I turn back to face him. A two-by-four crashes down between us with flames across the length of it. I step back and my head hits something hard and unforgiving and I crash to the floor.

TWO

Stella

"Morning, Stella." Allie's at the nurses' station when I arrive at Memorial Hospital's Emergency Room for my shift.

"Afternoon actually," I say, snapping on my badge.

"I've been here too long. Winter is still approaching, right? I didn't miss it because I've been here so long?" She forks her salad while clicking buttons on the computer. One thing I've discovered about Allie in my first week here is that no one multitasks like her.

I chuckle. "You're good. But thanks for the reminder. I'm worried I've lost my ability to drive in the snow." I check out the board to see which patients we have in-house and what sort of issues I'll be dealing with.

Transferring hospitals in the middle of my residency left me feeling uneasy. Someone was looking over me when I sneaked into town without anyone knowing. I've kept up with Kingston Bailey enough to know that he works for the Anchorage Fire Department, so there's a possibility I might run into him here. My only saving grace has been that he smoke jumps in the spring and summer, which allowed me to have a false sense of security these past months. But that's done with now that we're deep into autumn. I still sneak in and out of Lake Starlight like a thief in the night.

I'm not scared of Kingston Bailey. Well, okay, I am, but not in terms of my physical safety. Kingston and I shared an attraction that terrifies me, yet we never even explored a relationship. He's the one guy who made me forget the consequences of my actions—and I most definitely prefer to stay in control. I stayed away from Lake Starlight for eight years, and I'm only returning now because of my mom's lupus diagnosis.

After I talked to her doctor—a phone call she still doesn't know happened—I decided to move my residency from a crowded New York City hospital, where I'd treat anything from gunshot wounds to pneumonia, to Anchorage, where the cases are usually less life-threatening. I won't get the experience here that I would've had in New York City, but I never saw myself as a big city lifer anyway.

"It's like riding a bike. Just make sure you get snow tires." Allie chomps down on her salad. "How are you adjusting here?"

I shrug. "So far so good."

No one knows that every time a paramedic brings in a patient, a knot forms in my stomach, worried that the medic on duty might be Kingston. I never told him I was transferred to the hospital his fire station transports patients to. I even stood across the street from his apartment like a creeper, but my bravado fizzled when he stepped out of his apartment with Owen. I watched the two men whose friendship I destroyed once upon a time, and all that turmoil festered back up inside me. They laughed as they slid into a truck, and I didn't want to ruin that. Kingston's new truck suggests he's no longer a boy who has to drive his brothers' hand-me-downs.

"We like having you here. The nurses talk about you more than Romeo." She stabs her fork into the salad. "And believe me, we discuss Romeo all the time." She rolls her eyes.

"Romeo?" I chuckle.

I've met a lot of new people over the past week, and I've always thought of myself as good with names. I never wanted to be the doctor who didn't refer to her patient by name, so I practice with the association game. There's no way I would've forgotten a Romeo.

"You haven't met Romeo?" Allie leans back in her chair and fans herself. "He's one of those men who should be a model in a magazine or a cologne commercial or something."

Having five more minutes before Ralph runs me through his patient list, I sit down next to her and laugh. "That sounds a little far-fetched."

She shakes her head, eyes wide. "Just wait. You'll know him when he comes in."

"Okay, but feel free to point him out to me in case I miss this amazing guy."

She waves her finger in front of my face. "You just wait. You'll be sighing the first time you see him."

"Okay." I roll my eyes with a smile.

She laughs and picks up her salad bowl to face me. "Are you married? Engaged?"

I shake my head. "Neither."

"I figured. Most doctors in their residency haven't been in the dating circuit for a while." She piles another forkful of lettuce into her mouth.

"Well, I did meet a promising guy last night."

"Where at?"

I look at her left hand and see no wedding ring. "My friend is obsessed with this blind speed dating thing and I met him there. We had a drink together after the event and exchanged phone numbers, but..."

"But what?"

I shrug. "It's not like I have a ton of time."

She quirks her eyebrow.

Yes, I have a lot more time than if I was in New York, but I'm not up for a serious relationship.

"Tell me about him."

"He's tall and good-looking. Bit of a flirt." I bite my lower lip. "One of those guys you have a hard time reading. You don't know if he's flirtatious with just you or with every girl he comes into contact with."

"I always go by how they act with the waitresses. If he's too flirtatious with them, then I'm out."

I rack my brain for how he acted but remember that he went up to the bar to get our drinks.

"What does he do?" Allie asks.

"He's a carpenter. He was talking about this house he's working on, about the woodwork he's doing with the banister. It sounded amazing." Which it did. Made me want to drag him to my mom's B & B and see what he'd suggest to spruce up the place.

"A man who's good with his hands." She winks, and I laugh.

"Dr. Harrison, are you ready for rounds?" Ralph says behind me.

I quickly stand to face him. Allie turns to her computer as if we're two school-aged kids getting scolded by the principal. But Ralph isn't my boss. He's just another resident who thinks he's a bigger deal than he is. But I guess when your family donated the pediatric wing to the hospital, you think you stand taller than the rest.

"Ralph," I say. "Good afternoon. I already looked over the board."

He takes his own dry erase marker out of his pocket because he only uses his. The shade of blue is a little darker than the community one the rest of us use.

"Dr. Harrison," he says and waits because he wants me to call him Dr. Teller. Usually I would refer to my fellow residents as doctor, but I kind of like getting under his skin. When I only smile at him, waiting for him to continue, he huffs and marks up the board. "I'm waiting on labs to confirm, but I think it's just a gallbladder in room five. Room four is a case of the flu, so we're waiting for the test to come back while we rehydrate him on an IV. When we discharge him, we should discuss the urgent care clinics he could use rather than the emergency room."

"So it's slow tonight," I say.

"You should be happy you weren't here last month with that pile-up on the interstate." He's mentioned that one instance more times than I can count in the week I've worked here. It's like he's proud. People died and were injured in that pile-up.

"We got a few of the patients over at County." I was at County hospital first, cycling through my labor and delivery, surgery, and cardiac residencies before I came to Memorial.

"Well, you didn't get the triage patients. We got the ones hanging on by a thread."

I smile, although I'm sure my eyes are rolled so far back in my head, he's wondering if I need medical attention.

An ambulance calls in on their line, and Allie picks up the phone.

"Have a great night, Ralph."

"You as well, Dr. Harrison. If you need me, you have my cell."

I smile at Allie. "Oh, I'm sure we'll be fine. Plus, you know Dr. Anderson is here."

He nods and says nothing because Dr. Anderson is our Chief Resident and the person I would call if I needed anything, not Ralph.

I decide to visit the patients and make sure everyone is comfortable and to let them know I'll be taking over for Dr. Teller. The first room I come to is room five, so I knock and walk in. A woman lies in the bed with her husband at her side, on his phone.

"Hello, I'm Dr. Harrison. I just wanted to check up on you."

"Margie," she says, "and this is my husband Mark."

I think of M&M's and repeat their names in my head once more. I smile and nod at them both.

"That other doctor said they were waiting on labs, but it's been hours," she complains, which isn't uncommon when people are in pain. In high school, my mom had a gallbladder attack that had her keeled over in agony, and that woman can handle pain like a UFC fighter.

"Let me look at your chart. How is the pain level?"

I go through everything with her and see that her labs aren't back yet, so I send them a quick note to see what the holdup is. We talk for a little while and I promise her we'll get some stronger pain meds in right away. Allie's walking by as I leave the room.

"Can you get the patient in room five—"

"You're in luck. Romeo just came in," she says.

"Well, I have patients to see."

"He's a patient." Her eyes widen. "Got injured on the job."

"Okay, Allie, this isn't *The Bachelor*. Can you please put the patient in room five out of her misery and get her some more pain meds? The notes are in her file."

She nods. "Okay, but I suggest heading to room eight." She shrugs like I'm stupid if I don't.

I shake my head and continue on my path to room six. If I get to eight, then so be it, but I have a feeling whoever this Romeo guy is, he doesn't hold a candle to some guys I've seen walking the streets of New York.

"Hello, I'm Dr. Harrison," I say, walking into room six.

Twenty minutes later, I'm outside room eight, and for some reason, butterflies hit my stomach. I don't even know if this guy is actually good-looking or what he does that they know him so well at the hospital, but he was injured on the job according to all the details Allie gave me. I really need to get better at asking more detailed questions about people who aren't my patients. Life in Anchorage is slower than New York. I can take a moment to breathe here.

I knock and walk into the room, my hand reaching for the antiseptic dispenser. It shoots cold liquid onto my hand.

"Hi, I'm the resident overseeing you today." I scribble my name on the board. "How's the pain? Anything I can get you?"

I look up to finally get a good look at this Romeo guy, and my heart skips a beat. I should have guessed he'd be their Romeo.

"Stella? Jesus, how hard did I hit my head?" He puts his hand on his head.

I step back. "Kingston."

But even I hear the lack of surprise in my tone. I feel a

sudden wave of relief that the moment I've been anticipating and dreading is over. It will come out that I've
returned. Now I just have to pull up my big girl panties and
be clear about the reasons I returned—and they weren't
for him.

"Stella, dear." Grandma Dori hugs me, her arms tight
and welcoming. She never judged me as the girl who tore
two best friends apart. She's treated me almost like a grand-
child—to the point of sending me birthday cards while I was
away.

"Hi, Dori," I say, my eyes unable to pull away from
Kingston's. I'm not even close to prepared to see him again.

His gaze holds mine, and a soft smile crosses his lips.

"I'll be right back." I leave the room and press my back
to the wall outside the door, inhaling deep breaths.

Allie whistles as she passes me. "Told you the minute
you saw him, you'd be sighing."

I say nothing but continue to mentally give myself the
pep talk I need to go back in there and be a professional.
Get through this, Stella, and it's smooth sailing from here.

THREE

Kingston

I try to get up but cringe when my brain feels like scrambled eggs in my skull.

Savannah pushes me back onto the pillow. "You can't get up."

"But—"

"I'll go so someone else can come in." Colton bolts from the room as if someone screamed fire.

"I think this is wonderful. She's a doctor. Did you hear that?" Grandma Dori says.

I say nothing. I knew she was going to medical school. Following her on Instagram allowed me to know things about her that aren't my business. Nothing on her Instagram feed alluded to her being back in Alaska though.

Then what Lou said earlier clicks. "Fuck!"

"What?" Savannah puts her hand on my head like a mother. "Are you okay? Do I—"

"How popular of a name is Stella?"

"Last year it was in the top fifty. When we were looking

for Brinley's name I remember seeing it, so it's not terribly uncommon." Savannah throws out facts only she could remember months after having her daughter.

"How about Stella's in Anchorage who frequent Tipsy Turvy? The bar most of the hospital staff, firefighters, and police officers go to?"

Juno steps away from the bed, pulling out her phone. "I should go too, let someone else come in." Juno heads to the curtain just as Austin walks past.

He thumbs toward the door. "I swear I just saw—"

"Yep, it's her," Savannah says.

"She's a doctor," Grandma Dori says with pride.

Austin nods at Grandma Dori as if that isn't important right now.

"Juno," I say, stopping her before she can escape. "Last night you held a blind speed dating thing at Tipsy Turvy, right?"

Her mouth moves in a million different directions, as do her eyes, which never land on me. "I might have."

Juno is a horrible liar, but she's better than I thought because she's not nearly surprised enough at seeing Stella. How long has she known she's back? How long has she been keeping it from me?

"I'm not sure I understand. Why are we talking about the blind date thing? What does that have to do with Stella?" Grandma Dori asks.

My gaze meets Juno's and she slowly nods, a tear slipping from her eye. "I wanted to tell you." She steps toward the bed. "But she asked me not to and..."

I close my eyes, trying to control my anger over the fact that she kept Stella's return from me for who knows how long. "Did she talk to someone after the event last night?"

Lou's compliments about the woman he met last night

all fit Stella. She is beautiful. She's wicked smart, and she *is* a game-changer. The one you'd change your life for.

Juno nods. "I'm sorry, King."

"Can I have a moment?" I ask everyone.

Juno doesn't waste a minute, rushing from the room.

"Yes, you probably need your rest. You all go, and I'll stay with him," Grandma Dori says, grabbing my hand.

Before they can leave, the curtain draws open and Stella stands there. Her dark hair is in smooth and pulled back, and her face only has a light layer of makeup on—some red lipstick and maybe a little mascara from what I can tell. Her deep umber skin still radiates a glow of beauty like it did the day she first walked into my fourth grade class. The white coat with her name embroidered in blue thread looks perfect on her. I always knew she'd be successful, achieve her dreams. She's always been out of my league, but she's *way* out of my league now.

"Sorry. But..." She sanitizes her hands again and sits at the computer. After scanning her ID card, she types away. "What did they bring you in for? Are you burned?"

"They think he has a concussion. The last doctor said something about an MRI," Grandma Dori says.

She purses her lips and reads the notes on the screen. "Probably not necessary. They don't often show anything unless it's severe which given your state is unlikely, but let's do one to be safe."

"Can we please not do this?" I say in a strangled whisper.

Stella turns away from the computer, swiveling in her chair to face me, her dark eyes holding a tinge of sadness and a lot of apprehension.

"Everyone give me a moment with Stella," I say.

Savannah and Austin have some silent conversation as

if they're my parents. Which they kind of are in a weird sort of way.

"Come on, Grandma, Brinley was just about to say your name the other day. Maybe if she sees you, today will be the day," Savannah says.

Grandma Dori's eyes light up and I mouth a thank you to Savannah as she leaves the room. Her great-grandkids are about the only thing that could get Grandma Dori to leave us alone. Once the room is clear, I attempt to sit up straighter.

"You can't do that. You have to relax," Stella says, standing from her chair but stopping before coming all the way over to the bed.

"Can we not be doctor and patient right now?"

Her tongue slides out along her bottom lip. The same move that pulled me to her like a fly to a trap when we were younger. I can't help but be reminded of the way she tasted when I kissed her all those years ago. "I should have told you I was back."

"Yeah, you should have," I say. "Why didn't you?"

She lets out a huge breath. "You know how it is, Kingston. You would have pushed, and I wouldn't have had the energy to push back. I'm not going to get between you and Owen again."

"To hell with Owen," I say. My friendship with him is complicated. We've never truly gotten back to where we were before teenage hormones took over and we fought over the girl we both fell in love with. The girl standing in front of me right now.

"Don't say that. The only reason I'm back here is because of my mom." She glances toward the door. "She's sick."

"Selene is sick? I just saw her."

She smiles briefly, but then her lips press together. "It's lupus. It's an autoimmune—"

"I know what lupus is," I say. "How long and how bad?"

"She was diagnosed two years ago, and it's been okay so far. But I talked to her doctor and you know how she is... she only wants holistic medicine, so I'm trying to push her into taking this other drug that might help her more. Her being ill just reminded me that I couldn't stay away forever."

A part of me always knew when she returned, it would be because of her mom. It shouldn't hurt that I've never been enough to keep her here, but it does.

"Then why not come to me and tell me?" I ask.

She dodges eye contact with me. It's clear why she didn't. I have no part in her future. I'm only part of her past.

"Never mind. Don't answer that."

"But—"

I shake my head, not ready to hear her say it. I can play this two ways. Do what I did to drive her away in the first place and never have her in my life or have her in my life in a different capacity. The way she was before I fell head over heels in love with her. "It's fine. Honestly. But I'd like to at least be friends."

"Friends?" Her tone is one of surprise and disgust mixed together.

"Yeah, remember that's how we started off? I work at the fire department, so we're going to see each other a lot. I don't want it to be awkward."

She nods a few times, her eyes meeting mine. "Are you sure?"

I chuckle although it's fake. "Yeah, I'm positive. If you need any help with your mom, let me know. Or is it a secret?"

She shakes her head as though she wasn't expecting this

reaction from me. But she made her decision about us as soon as she snuck back into town. I wasn't important enough to tell, and although it hurts, I can't keep torturing myself. She obviously doesn't feel the same way about me as I do about her.

"You know how prideful she is," Stella says.

I do. Selene is a tough-ass woman, and she raised her daughter to be just as tough. "Then I won't say anything."

The door nudges open and Allie pops her head in. She smiles at me first then looks at Stella. "Dr. Harrison, the patient in room five's labs have returned and I need your authorization to contact the surgeon."

"Thanks, Allie. I'll be right there."

"You hanging in there, Romeo?" Allie asks. "I'll go check on your MRI. We told them stat."

I wink. "Thanks."

"No problem."

The door shuts and Stella's head tilts, giving me a glimpse of one side of her long neck. The same neck I used to always wish I could put my lips on. "Romeo?"

"It's a nickname at the station. I didn't earn it the way you think I did." Although I'm not going to tell her the details.

"Well, they sure like you around here. I heard all about you before I realized you were Romeo."

I smile wide. The nurses flirt and a few have insinuated they'd like to do more than that, but I work with these people. I'm not going to ruin our working relationship just for some ass I can get somewhere else. "What do they say?"

"I'm not telling." She smiles, and it lights up her face for the first time.

"I hope it's positive?" I say.

"I'm sure you do." Our eyes lock briefly, and her hands

grip the railing at the bottom of my bed. My mouth opens to say something else, but she speaks before I can. "I should go and check on my other patients. I'm sure Allie is on top of your MRI, but I'll be back."

"Thanks," I say.

She smiles softly and turns to leave.

"Stella?" I stop her before she can escape.

She glances over her shoulder at me.

"You look really good."

"So do you, King." She pushes the curtain back and slides out of my view.

My fingers grip the sheets on either side of my hips.

Friends. I must be delusional to offer that option. Look how that ended up the first time. The worst part is, she doesn't even know that she's talking to one of my good friends. The person who has been essentially my best friend since I joined the department. And I'm the jackass who didn't tell her that dating the guy she met last night puts us right back to where we were when she left Lake Starlight eight years ago.

Austin walks through the curtain a couple of minutes later. My oldest brother is the one who tried to guide me through the tangled vines of Stella and Owen and mine's friendship. He's seen me at my worst, yet he never throws it in my face.

"So what's going on?" He takes the chair to my left. "Did you talk to her?"

I nod. "We agreed to be friends."

"Friends?" His voice sounds just like hers did.

"We were friends once."

He runs his hand through his hair. "King, you were friends when you were adolescents, before puberty hit and feelings developed. She's the girl you've always loved. How can you possibly just be friends with her?"

Obviously, Juno kept the fact that she knows Stella is talking to Lou to herself. "Last night at Tipsy Turvy, she met Lou and they exchanged numbers."

Austin's jaw drops, but he recovers before he thinks I've seen his reaction. "You've got to be kidding me. It's all happening again?"

I nod, unable to really process that I lost her before I even knew she was back. Then again, she decided to keep her return a secret. She went to a blind dating event to meet someone new, knowing I was a short drive down the highway. I'll be damned if I look like the lovesick puppy dog following after her with my tongue hanging out—again.

"No, it's not happening again. Because I'm gonna move on with my life." I grab my phone and click on Instagram, unfollowing her with the tap of my thumb. "It's time I move forward in my life without the name Stella Harrison haunting me."

"What do you mean?" Austin leans back in the chair.

"I'm going to start looking ahead to my future."

"I'm proud of you. It takes guts to do that." He smiles, happy because he believes, like the rest of my family does, that I don't care about the future or value my life all that much.

Maybe I'm just the last one to know that Stella Harrison and Kingston Bailey aren't meant to walk away into the sunset and live happily ever after.

FOUR

Stella

The following Friday after seeing Kingston live and in person, Lou knocks on my apartment door. I've tried to push Kingston from my thoughts all week, but it's proven to be easier said than done.

A seed of guilt sprouts every time I talk to Lou on the phone. I've had boyfriends since high school, but nothing that turned serious. Only one guy ever called me out on my need to keep my emotions close to my chest. But I think that was because I allowed our relationship to continue when I should have ended it weeks earlier.

But Kingston was so quick to suggest that we just be friends, what am I supposed to think? Not to mention I purposely didn't tell him I was in town. The anger I saw in his eyes isn't unwarranted.

I open the door to find Lou dressed in a pair of nice jeans and a button-down shirt. He's attractive, and I'm sure a lot of women admire his broad shoulders and tall frame.

Pushing Kingston out of my head, I grab my purse from my kitchen table and join him on the other side of the door.

"You look stunning," he says.

I smile. "You look great too."

The typical awkward silence of a first date blankets us as we walk out of my apartment to his truck. I keep having to remind myself that I'm back in Alaska, where the truck to car ratio is two hundred to one.

He's a gentleman and opens the door for me, waiting for me to be situated before shutting it slowly to secure me. He rounds the hood of the truck and climbs in next to me.

"Are you hungry?" he asks.

"I am."

"Me too. I had no time for lunch today, so you'll have to excuse me if I look like a starved animal at the dinner table."

I laugh. "You're already forgiven."

He heads onto the interstate. Once we're driving for a few minutes I figure someone better know where I'm going and who I'm with. I pull out my phone and text my mom.

Me: *I'm on a date with a guy named Lou and he drives a red pick-up truck. He's a carpenter from Anchorage and we're going to dinner.*

The three dots appear right away.

Mom: *Okay, license plate would be nice next time. LOL*

Lou glances over.

I shut off the screen and shove my phone back inside my purse. "Sorry."

"Don't apologize. I'm sure that being a doctor, you're on call a lot."

We talk about the differences between my job in New York compared to here. I find out Lou is actually from a smaller town up north, and to him, Anchorage is a big city. He's been here since he graduated high school and has no desire to go back.

As we continue heading south, we pass a sign saying *Lake Starlight - 5 Miles*. A knot forms in my stomach.

"Where are we headed?" I ask.

He never takes his eyes off the road. "Lake Starlight. Have you been there before?"

I laugh. "It's where I grew up."

He glances over. "I figured you came here for your residency. I didn't realize you grew up here."

I recall all the things I told him the night we had a drink together. I was ambiguous about my past. Probably because I stopped telling people I was from Alaska when I was in New York. They all asked the same questions about moose, dark winters and sunny summers, crab, and the cold weather. At first, I would negate all their assumptions that we live in igloos and hunt for our food, but after a while, talking about all the great things Alaska has to offer made me sad because I missed it. But I didn't know how to come back without causing strife.

"Yeah, I lived here until I left for college."

"That's crazy. I have a buddy from here. I'm actually taking you to his brother's restaurant. I've had his food a few times at family get-togethers and he's mad talented."

My gut churns. I glance at his back window. There it is. How did I not notice that earlier? "Lou?"

"Yeah?"

"You said you're a carpenter."

"Yeah. Remind me to tell you about this house I'm doing with this beautiful stained glass—"

"And this is your truck?" I glance around the interior.

He nods. "Yeah." Glancing over when we get to the stoplight, his forehead wrinkles. "Why?"

"What's with the firefighter sticker?"

He smiles but tries to stop himself. "Yeah, well... I was kind of keeping that to myself because you know how women are with firefighters."

"How is that?"

"Obsessive. Some of them date us just so they can say they're dating one. But I was gonna tell you tonight. Next week I'm taking some paramedic shifts and you'd probably see me around the hospital anyway."

There's so much I want to say right now. I'm upset that he held back information that's important for reasons he has no idea of. So instead of addressing his lack of transparency, I focus on the most important thing at the moment—finding out if it even matters.

"Who is your friend from Lake Starlight?" I close my eyes.

There's no way this is happening. They must work at different engine companies. Surely there's another brother duo who lives in Lake Starlight where one's a firefighter and one owns a restaurant. It has to be someone else's brother besides Kingston's brother Rome, who owns Terra and Mare. This cannot happen twice in my lifetime. It just can't.

"Kingston Bailey. You know him?"

My throat closes and I cough, even though I knew in my gut it was him.

"Oh shit, were you guys, like, enemies or something? He's pretty cool now but kind of conceited. Is that how he was when you knew him? Is that why you don't like him?"

Lou rambles on while I wrap my head around the news, pushing away the assumption Lou has that we don't like each other when it's always been the complete opposite.

"We went to high school together. We were... close friends."

"Oh shit, did you guys date?" His eyes are wide now. He pulls over by the curb in downtown Lake Starlight, where Rome's restaurant is their version of nightlife.

"We never dated." Which is the truth. We never *officially* dated.

He lets loose a long breath. "Thank goodness. That'd be awkward."

Oh, Lou, you have no idea. "Did you tell him about me? I mean..."

Seriously, Stella, I doubt he's gushing to his best friend about the great woman he met days ago.

"I mentioned you, but he's been out because of his concussion." He glances at me, and the streetlight glowing into the cab reveals his questioning eyes. "I sense there's more."

This isn't something I can hide from him. When Kingston finds out I'm dating... actually, I have no idea if they're even good friends. "How close are you and Kingston?"

"King? We've been tight since the academy."

My head falls to the headrest. "Oh, Lou, I'm not sure this is a good idea."

"What am I missing?"

"Kingston and I never dated, but we share a past just the same." Instead of looking at Lou, I scour the people walking into Terra and Mare. The people I'll have to address if I walk in there with this man.

"What kind of past?"

There's no way I can fully explain the situation to him. "In high school, I was dating his friend, Owen. Kingston and I were friends—"

"High school?" He laughs, and my attention is stripped away from the patrons of the restaurant and over to him. "That was almost a decade ago."

"But—"

"Stella, I'm asking you to have dinner, not to marry me or even classify us as dating. At Tipsy Turvy, I felt like we had a connection. At least enough of one to explore, which is what spurred me to ask you to dinner."

"You don't understand."

He can't. He didn't witness the situation that unfolded. The fights in the hallways, the screaming and arguing and tears. All the nights my head wound up in my mom's lap.

"Believe me, whatever you had with Kingston hasn't stopped him over the years."

I look up from my lap, and he nods, confirming my fear that he earned the nickname Romeo the way one would assume. Which he had every right to. We were never a couple. It doesn't stop the jab in my heart though.

"Let's do this... one dinner," he says. "That's all I ask. We can eat as friends and get to know each other. But we're already out and here. Come on."

My stomach churns as I watch people walk in and out of Rome's restaurant. I fear that silverware will screech across plates and conversations will halt the minute I step inside. Whispers of "She's back. Does Kingston know?" being murmured as we're seated.

"Okay, but can we go anywhere but here?" I ask.

He turns the keys in the ignition. "Definitely."

Luckily, Lou is a cool guy and he takes me to a great

burrito place in Portage Glacier, far enough away that I won't see anyone from Lake Starlight.

And we do have a great night. Midway through dinner, I finally forget that he's close friends with Kingston. I'm not sure if he feels as though I don't want to talk about myself or if he's worried I'll end up crying over our chips and salsa, but he carries the entire conversation. Impressively enough, he weaves in sly questions about me but never stays on the topic of me long enough to go too deep.

At the end of the night, he pulls up outside my apartment and he walks me to the door.

"I had a great time," Lou says.

"I did too. Thanks for pushing me to keep it. You're really a great guy, but I have to be upfront with you. You and me dating isn't a good idea since you're friends with Kingston."

He rocks back on his heels. "So if I ditch him as a friend, you'll date me?"

I laugh, and thankfully he does too. I promised myself a long time ago I'd never get between Kingston and a friend again. "I'm sorry, but I'm definitely up for being friends."

Lou nods. "I can't convince you, huh?"

I smile but shake my head. "No. Again—"

He interrupts me right away. "You can stop saying you're sorry now. It's starting to feel like a breakup."

I chuckle, grabbing my keys out of my purse. "So I'll see you around the hospital?"

"Sure will. Friends... for now."

"Lou," I say before he thinks he can pull out all the stops and get me to agree to more. "I'm serious."

He nods. "Don't worry, I'd never pressure you too much, but we'll give it some time." He steps forward, and I stiffen. His lips press to my cheek. "Goodnight, Stella."

He walks down the short sidewalk back to his truck, and I turn to my door, inserting my key. I remind myself that I made the right decision, because Kingston and I are a web that no one ever escapes, and I won't let anyone else get tangled in.

FIVE

Stella

Ten Years Old
First day of school

I walk into the classroom and everyone stops what they're doing and looks at me. I smile and put my head down, heading to the teacher's desk. All the chaos I walked into starts back up.

Mrs. Nickelson, Mrs. Nickelson. I've repeated her name multiple times so I don't mess it up.

"Owen, I told you to stop picking up Annie. This isn't wrestling class." Mrs. Nickelson rolls her eyes, but when she spots me, her smile turns warm and welcoming. "Stella, right?"

I nod and swallow. My stomach feels like I'm about to go down the hill of a roller coaster and my mouth is so dry, I had to stop at the water fountain on my way from the office to here.

"Welcome. Class." Mrs. Nickelson snaps her fingers,

and when the boys and girls continue to mess around, she claps. There's some rustling, but the students find their desks and sit. "This is Stella Harrison. She's a new student." She sits on a stool a few feet away from me. "Why don't you tell us a little about yourself?"

I look up, and all their eyes are on me. That light feeling in my stomach quickly weighs heavy as if there's an anchor in there now. As I scan the students, my eyes rest on one boy who has his head in his hand and is weaving figure eights on his desk with one finger. He's sitting smack in the middle of the class, so I pretend I'm talking to him. It feels safer since he obviously doesn't care to listen to my life story.

"Okay... I'm Stella. Um..."

"Where are you from, Stella?" Mrs. Nickelson asks, and I turn to her. She really seems nice from how much she smiles.

"I'm from Arizona."

"Yikes, you're not used to winter at all, are you?" Mrs. Nickelson asks.

I shake my head. "The first time I saw snow was when we moved here." On the plane, when my mom pointed out the window at the snow-peaked mountains under us.

A few of the kids murmur about how crazy that sounds.

"And who did you move up here with?"

Thank goodness Mrs. Nickelson is asking the questions. I don't have a very interesting life story.

"My mom."

"Very nice. And I think I heard she's opening up a bed-and-breakfast?"

"What's that?" a boy in the back asks.

The boy I've been watching glances over his shoulder at the kid and rolls his eyes before staring at his desk again, watching his finger slide around the top of the desk. The boy looks sort of sad.

"It's like a hotel, but more personal," the teacher says. "The person who owns it usually cooks your meals, and sometimes you share a bathroom with other guests."

"Why would someone want to do that?" the kid asks.

"It's a different experience. Like I said, it's more personal and quaint."

"What's quaint mean?" another boy asks.

Mrs. Nickelson's smile falters slightly. "I'll dig out more information for you and we'll discuss it tomorrow. Let's focus on Stella right now."

No, please.

"And what do you like to do, Stella?" she asks.

"Um... I like to... play outside. My mom's an artist, so we do a lot of things with paint and clay."

"That sounds like a lot of fun. Doesn't it, class?"

The class says 'uh-huh' as if they've rehearsed it.

"Go ahead and have a seat, Stella. There's one right there between Owen and Kingston." She points at the only empty desk in the room. "Kingston, be a dear and raise your hand so Stella knows who you are."

I wish I could tell her that's not necessary, but the boy who's been doing figure eights with his finger puts his arm in the air without ever looking up at me. Kingston is the sad boy's name.

When I slide into the desk, the boy on the other side leans toward me. "You don't have a dad?"

I shake my head.

"Why?"

A year ago, I would have teared up, but I've been practicing at night before I go to bed because I knew people at my new school would ask questions and I'd have to answer them. "He died."

"Oh. I'm sorry." The kid, who was leaning back in his chair, puts all four legs back down on the carpeted floor.

Mrs. Nickelson tells everyone to open their textbooks. "Stella, you can share with either Kingston or Owen until we get you one."

I look at the sad boy and slide my desk over next to his. He opens his textbook and slides it my way, apparently not caring if he can see it or not. I push it so it rests on both of our desks, but he never looks up. Mrs. Nickelson talks about plants and oxygen, but I can't stop thinking of this boy next to me. She assigns us a project and says we can work as a team since I don't have my textbook yet.

"Are you okay?" I ask him.

He looks at me. His eyes are a soft brown. "Yeah."

We sit in silence for a while.

"How did your dad die?" he asks.

"Cancer."

Please don't ask anything else. I don't want to think about it today. Not when my mom moved us up here to get away from her memories, not caring at all what I wanted. I loved that I remembered my dad in every room of my old house, or the pool out back where he would throw me in the air. Now I'm in some town in Alaska where it's cold and snowy and miserable.

"Mine died in a snowmobile accident," he says.

"Your dad died?"

"My mom and my dad."

"That sucks," I say quietly.

His eyes lock with mine and there's something there. An understanding maybe. He nods. "About your dad too. I guess at least I don't have to move like you did."

An instant bond forms between the two of us. We've both experienced huge losses, but at least I have my mom.

When I go home that night, I don't tell my mom about the sad boy in class, but I think about him when I go to bed. For the first time since my mom cried over my dad's casket, I wished I could take away someone else's pain.

SIX

Kingston

L ou is laid out on his bed when I walk upstairs to the
bunks at the fire station.

"You look like you just got dumped." I drop my bag next
to my bed and sit down.

"I kind of did." He sits up and rests his arms on his
thighs. "You know a Stella Harrison?"

I lean down and open up my bag just to not have to look
at him. It's the one asshole thing I've done since we've been
friends—not telling him that the girl he met is the girl I've
been infatuated with forever. But I didn't tell him because
I'm fine with it. Maybe fine isn't the right word, but I'm
hoping that seeing the two of them together will help me
move on. Because God knows it's time for me to move on.

"Sure do," I say.

"I went out with her on Saturday." He stares at me,
waiting to judge my reaction.

"How did it go?"

"Jesus, King, how could you not tell me?"

My shoulders slump. He knows. "I don't know. My head running into a steel pipe and knocking me the fuck out?"

He stands and paces, running his hand through his hair. Lou can be on the more dramatic side when he wants. "After. Why didn't you tell me after?"

"There are a lot of Stellas, how did I know it was one and the same?"

"Bullshit." He stops and stares at me as though he wants a real answer. I'm not going to give him one. "There aren't that many Stellas in Alaska. Few enough that you should've asked more questions about her."

"I had more important things on my mind—like healing my head."

It was a blessing that I didn't have to work for a week because that meant I could dodge Lou.

"Be straight. I was going to take her to Rome's place, and then she starts saying how we can't see one another... how you two have a past and it's not a good idea."

I bite my lip to hold back the lottery-winning smile that wants to break across my face. "We do have a past, but it's been, like, eight years since she left for New York. It's fine. I'd tell you if it wasn't."

"Would you?" He sits on his bed, which is coincidentally right next to mine.

"Yeah. Since when am I a hold-anything-in kind of guy?"

He probably shouldn't answer that. I held this in when I shouldn't have let him go in blind with Stella.

"I'm serious. I really liked her. She's great, you know?"

I laugh instead of agreeing. She's one in a fucking million, as cliché as that sounds. But she doesn't feel the same about me and I'm man enough to admit defeat.

"But before I go full steam ahead, I need to know where your head is," he says.

Come on, channel drama class from high school, when Mr. Clayton told me to get into character. That I couldn't be Kingston acting like Crutchie from *Newsies*—I had to be Crutchie. I argued that I didn't know what it was like to have a disabled leg, which led to me getting looked at above the rim of his glasses. The classic look he'd give you right before he kicked you out of class and got you suspended from a game of whatever sport you played. Since I was pitching against Greywall that weekend, I did the best damn acting job I could and kept my mouth shut. Which is what I plan to do right now.

I stand and clamp my hand on his shoulder. "Stella is in my rearview mirror, man."

"You sure?"

"Jesus, Lunchbox."

He quirks an eyebrow at me. I never use his nickname because I sense he doesn't much like it. "Okay, subject closed."

"Good. I'm going down to eat something. You in?" I ask.

"Yeah."

Finally Lou stops harping on the Stella subject and we head down to the kitchen to find Greasy cooking. Might as well take my Tums now.

"What's up?" I fist-bump Greasy and grab a bottle of water before sitting at the table.

"Did you see this?" Lou pulls a piece of paper off of the corkboard that's supposed to be for important news but is usually filled with business cards for the firefighters' side businesses. Most of us have a second gig, except for me.

Greasy looks over his shoulder. "Yeah, we did that when we were younger. Of course it wasn't that nice of a place.

We had to take a shit in an outhouse. I froze my ass off that year, but we had good times."

Lou slides the piece of paper across the table to me. It's an ad for a rental for first responders to use all winter long. You go up on your days off.

Greasy wipes his hands on his apron and hovers over my shoulder. "I might have to leave the missus and sign myself up. That's right by Alyeska." He nudges my shoulder. "They're doing that death skiing with the helicopter up there."

Lou chuckles.

"You mean heli-skiing, and it's not death," I say, shaking my head.

"It's not safe either," Lou says, mostly because he's too chickenshit to fly up a mountain on a helicopter and ski down. If he only knew I plan to speed ride this winter— skiing with a parachute. Lou picks up the paper again. "I think we should do it. Guy days. We'll have a blast."

It's tempting. Especially now that Stella's back. Get out of Lake Starlight and Anchorage on my days off. Plus Greasy's right. Being by the mountain will let me do all the crazy shit I want. "Yeah, I'm—"

Tank walks in. "You guys saw the flyer? There are a few openings, but the nurses are taking them like they're One Direction reunion tickets, so you better grab your spot if you want in." Tank pulls a Gatorade out of the fridge and straddles the chair.

"I thought it was a firefighter thing?" Lou inspects the piece of paper as if there's some fine print somewhere.

"It says first responder." Tank points at the bold block letters on the top of the page. "It's actually one of the doctor's houses, I guess. He's renting it out for the entire winter because his wife is pregnant, and they can't go that far away. I'm not sure of the whole story, but it's a quick way to find out who's single in our small circle." He waggles his eyebrows.

"Which nurses?" I ask.

Tank's gaze falls on me. "Samantha is one."

I roll my eyes. Of course, I do want to pick her brain about the Alaska Adventure Race she was talking about when we went out.

"Who else?" Lou presses.

It doesn't take a genius to realize Lou wants to know if Stella is going in on it. Although she loves to ski, I'm not sure if she would want to be away from her mom.

Tank shrugs. "Don't know. It doesn't really matter since you have no idea, with the schedules, who you'll be up there with."

"I'm not signing up for some shit where I end up sleeping on the floor with, like, fifty people." I sip my water.

Greasy laughs, stirring what I think is chili with a layer of grease on top. Hence his name.

"Nah, spots are limited. It's not a free-for-all. Although I'm not sure I see the downfall if it was," Tank says.

I shake my head at the big guy. He should be the one called Romeo.

"Come on, Romeo, let's do it." Lou looks at me.

I'm not sure. I mean, what if he brings Stella up there? I said I was cool, and I'm hopeful that seeing them together will hopefully turn off that section of my brain that still sees her in my future, but any sort of swimsuit on her as she dips into the hot tub will make that almost impossible. Not to mention, listening to sex noises coming from their room? Hell no.

"Yeah, I got a lot of shit to do this year," I say, standing.

"I'll be checking the truck to make sure we're good when we get a call."

I leave them in the kitchen because Lou will try everything in his power to persuade me. He's persistent, but if I give in, my winter will suck. Instead of pausing to feel how much I care about this turn of events, I restock the rig.

———

"WE'RE ABOUT TWO MINUTES OUT," Lou says over the radio to the hospital.

I'm in back of the ambulance with a woman who fell. I'm hoping she didn't break her hip, as I fear she may have.

"It doesn't even hurt. I think I can go. Just drop me off," she says, smiling sweetly as though she's about to give me a butterscotch.

"Ma'am, you really should get it checked out. I've given you a small dose of pain medicine, so that's probably making you feel better than you should." I wink and pull out my clipboard, propping it on my knee to start my report. The last place I want to be is the hospital.

"All right, fine. But just because you're cute."

I glance up and give her a smile, shake my head and look back at my keyboard.

"I have a great-niece you might like."

I glance at her and chuckle. Lou laughs harder up front. It's not an unfamiliar occurrence for one of us to get hit on or have someone know someone who would be perfect for us.

"She's a teacher and so kind and sweet. Easy on the eyes, like you," she says.

"Oh, I'm seeing someone," I lie, which is also a common occurrence. It's a polite way to brush people off.

She exaggerates looking at my left hand. "I don't see a ring."

"Not yet, but..." I can't lie that well. I'm not going to tell the woman I'm engaged or some shit like that. "We haven't gotten there yet."

"Then I say you should give my great-niece a chance."

I laugh and shake my head.

"We're here," Lou says.

The older lady pats my hand. "Think about it."

We roll her out of the ambulance. Samantha is the nurse who meets us at the sliding doors. I relay all the information to her and she nods, helping us roll her into a room. Lou and I are picking up the patient and putting her on the hospital bed when Stella walks in, sanitizing her hands and running them along one another before looking up.

She introduces herself to the patient. Our eyes catch as the woman tells her what happened, but Stella doesn't miss a beat, taking the patient's hand and telling the woman they'll get it all squared away. She's as sweet and caring of a doctor as I always knew she'd be.

Clearing my throat, I take the stretcher and wheel it out of the room. Samantha comes out a minute later, and I'm all too aware that Lou hasn't followed.

"Hey, I was thinking maybe we could have a drink at Tipsy's tomorrow?" Samantha bites her lip.

I have to decide right now whether I'm going to pursue this. Just as I'm about to refuse and say I have plans, Lou and Stella walk out of the room, Stella laughing at something Lou said. Her smile fades as our eyes catch when they walk by.

"Sure," I say. "I'll be there at seven."

Samantha's face lights up and she bounces on the heels of her shoes, walking toward the nurses' station. "Great. I'll see you then," she says loudly, as though she's trying to make everyone around aware we have a date.

Stella is at the computer, not paying much attention to Lou, who's now involved in a conversation with Allie.

"Samantha?" Stella calls her over. "We need to order an MRI, and can you get a geriatric orthopedic doc on the phone? I have a bad feeling she broke her hip."

Samantha smiles and turns away from me.

I smile back then bury my head in my paperwork before handing it to Allie.

She signs it and hands it back to me with a smile. "What's up, Romeo? Are you really going out with Samantha?"

"It's just a drink," I say.

"Uh-huh, I've heard that before."

Stella glances at me and smiles.

"Did you know that these two know one another?" Lou thumbs at both Stella and me.

Allie tilts her head, taking a bite of a sandwich that looks as if it came from the cafeteria. She steadies her gaze on Stella more than me.

Stella smiles and looks up. "We went to high school together."

"Really?" Allie turns her attention to me. "Huh."

Although she's said nothing much, it feels as though she's said everything.

"Let's go, Lou," I say and walk over to the stretcher. "Bye."

I wave to Allie and Stella, who looks amazed by my politeness, and push the stretcher from the emergency room. I turn the corner and ignore the fact that Lou isn't following me. After all, I agreed that it wouldn't bother me if they date. I might as well deal with it.

SEVEN

Stella

I'm getting changed out of my scrubs when Allie comes into the locker room. "Spill."

"What?"

"You went to high school with Romeo?"

I pretend it's not a big deal. Which it's not. I went to high school with a lot of people, right? "I did."

"The fact that you didn't tell me after I so kindly told you about his nickname says you're hiding something. What gives?" She sits on the bench, crosses her legs, and stares at me.

"Privacy? I'm changing."

She waves me off. "Please, I'm sure you're used to this environment. And if that's the best you can do to try to deter me away, then you need some new tactics."

"It's nothing." I sit next to her to put on my shoes. "We grew up in a small town together. I didn't know Romeo was Kingston Bailey."

"Lake Starlight?" she asks, and I raise my eyebrows.

"What? Anchorage isn't huge. He told me once where he was from. Did you know there's this thing called Lake Starlight Buzz Wheel?"

"Uh-huh," I say, tying my shoe.

"It's awesome. I religiously check that thing all the time now."

Great. Not that I didn't find myself checking it in New York sometimes on the nights when I missed home. My mom always filled me in on the town gossip, but she kept out anything having to do with Kingston. Every time I clicked on that page, I feared I'd read about his upcoming wedding.

"Yeah well, don't believe everything you read on that thing."

"I went to Lake Starlight once. You guys have the cutest downtown. Tell me." She elbows me. "Did you and Kingston walk hand in hand through that gazebo area when you were just youngsters and fall in love?"

"You're delusional." I stand and grab my watch out of my locker, securing it around my wrist.

"Am I though?" She waves her phone.

"What have you read?"

She holds her phone in front of her and clears her throat as though she's about to give a speech. "'Rumors are flying that two of our own have reconnected up in Anchorage. Kingston Bailey suffered a concussion last week during a fire, and the entire Bailey clan rushed up to the hospital to make sure he was okay. Which he thankfully was, but...'"—she peeks at me and I groan—"'the surprise was on everyone when Stella Harrison pulled back the curtain to announce that she was his doctor.'" Allie's eyes widen as if she's recapping a soap opera episode. "'Now I think we all figured they role-played doctor and patient when they were younger, but it's been eight years since Stella Harrison was a permanent fixture in Alaska. Anyone else worried that history will repeat itself? I think I speak for us all when I say that I can't bear to see either of them broken apart all over again.'"

Allie clicks off her phone and drops it in her lap, staring at me silently, waiting.

I sit back on the bench and put my head in my hands. "I can't believe you follow that thing and I can't believe they're talking about us. How did anyone find out?"

"From what I've read over the years, whoever writes this should work for the FBI. They know so much shit."

I peek up at her through my fingers. "Feel like going for a drink?"

She hops up and rushes to her locker. "I never thought you'd ask."

Five minutes later, her purse is crossways around her body and we're walking out of the employee locker room toward my car. I need a friend right now, and Allie's the first one here to truly try to befriend me. I love Cami from my time working with her at County, but we never clicked enough to become close friends. I feel that spark of female kinship with Allie. Like we fit. I'm willing to trust that she'll keep my secrets. Because I do not want Anchorage Memorial Hospital to turn into Lake Starlight High School 2.0 and have the gossip drive me out.

"CAN I have a quesadilla with guacamole and sour cream, as well as..." Allie's eyes scour the menu. "Oh, truffle fries." She glances at me over the top of the menu as if I should be jumping up and down. She really is cute. "And an order of truffle fries. And I need a water as well as the beer please."

The waitress nods and heads to enter in our order.

"Okay, I've patiently waited for us to get here and sit down. Then I waited for the waitress to come over and take our order. I will not wait for the meal to arrive before you start to spill. I need at least a morsel of information."

I lay the cloth napkin in my lap and glance out the window at the snow that's floating down. You know how horrible it is to have snow always remind you of someone you lost? It sucks.

My mind travels back in time through my history with Kingston. "Owen, Kingston, and I were friends when we were kids from the time I moved to Alaska. In a town the size of Lake Starlight, you have no choice but to be friends with everyone. But then high school started, and all the hormones kicked in. Kingston would always flirt with me. Putting his arm around my shoulders in the hallway or leaning his shoulder on the locker next to mine. Owen kind of kept his distance, which surprised me. Owen was always the in-your-face, over-the-top personality and Kingston was the shy guy.

"They both played baseball. Kingston was a great pitcher while Owen was the catcher. They were best friends. The kind where they retold stories again and again about the stupid shit they did at parties when they were younger and everyone would laugh. People were envious of their friendship. It was thick and woven deeply through their lives. They balanced one another. When Kingston got too crazy with his stunts—"

"Stunts?" Allie interrupts.

The waitress arrives with our drinks, and we thank her.

"Kingston is, for lack of a better word, a daredevil. He loves the thrill of teetering on the line of sanity. You know he's a smoke jumper, right?"

She nods. "It's one of the things that makes him sexy." My immediate thought must show on my face because she quickly places her hand over mine. "I'm not interested in him though. He's hot, but I've been through the type. Not that he's a bad type, but I'm glad I never wanted him because the tension at the nurses' station earlier was intense."

The truffle fries arrive and Allie picks one up and slides the basket to me. "Carry on. Their friendship was the kind everyone wants to have." She waves for me to continue.

"Owen asked me to homecoming junior year, and I accepted. We started dating right after and that changed everything." I can feel the anxiety ramping up in my body all over again. "It was as quick as a snap-of-a-finger. Kingston stopped coming to my locker between classes. When it was time to pick partners for an assignment in social studies, he didn't even glance my way. He started hanging out with other guys, and by the end of junior year, he sat at a completely different lunch table. But the big rumor that made the rounds was that he asked his brother, who was the baseball coach, to not have Owen catch for him."

She dips her fry in the aioli sauce and stares at me. "That's a big deal?"

"Well, before then, Kingston wouldn't use any other catcher besides Owen. They just had a connection, and it worked well for the team." It's hard to explain the disaster it all turned into to someone who isn't from Lake Starlight, who didn't bear witness to the downfall of their friendship. All because of me.

"Did you know Kingston liked you?"

I shake my head. "No. He was kind of flirty with a lot of

the girls at school. I didn't realize he actually liked me until..."

"Finally you're going to give me the good stuff," she says, dipping another fry. "These will make you feel better, I promise."

I pick up a fry. "I should tell you, my dad died when I was nine, which spurred my mom to move to Lake Starlight. She took the life insurance money and bought a bed-and-breakfast for us to start over. I don't know if you know, but Kingston's parents died in a snowmobile accident when he was ten."

Her face softens like most people's do after they hear the tragic news. "I'm sorry for both of you."

"Thank you, but the fact that we both lost people close to us, we bonded over that. Our senior year, I was walking through downtown Lake Starlight and it had just started to snow. It was reported we were going to get a heavy storm and school would be canceled the next day. I wanted to be alone because it was the anniversary of my dad's death."

Then I'm transported back to that scene, and I'm not just telling the story to Allie but experiencing that moment all over again.

"Stella?" Kingston asks, as if he's not sure it's me under my big coat and hat, when he walks out of the bookstore.

"Hey, Kingston," I say and weave past him. We aren't really friends anymore and I'm sure he wants to continue on his way.

"You okay?" He follows me, dipping his head to see in my eyes. "Did something happen with Owen?"

I shake my head. Owen has no idea where I am right now. A tear slips down my face, and Kingston's hand lightly grasps my upper arm. He detours us off Main Street to the shore of Lake Starlight. We walk down the long wood dock in silence, and he takes his book out of the bag before placing the plastic bag down for me to sit on. Our feet dangle off the dock over the freezing water.

He doesn't pry for me to tell him the reason for my tears, but the silence is too uncomfortable for me. "It's the anniversary."

"I'm sorry," he murmurs.

For some reason, the fact that I didn't have to tell him specifically what anniversary, that he just knew, reinforces the bond I've always felt with him. Like he knows a secret. I guess he does.

"What do you do?" I ask.

He shrugs. "You won't do what I do." He moves the book in his hands, fanning out the pages.

"Why?"

He huffs. "We're different. You're walking the streets of Lake Starlight crying and I... well, I'd be unleashing my anger."

"You're still angry?"

He huffs. "I think I'll always be angry. Aren't you?"

I haven't been angry in some time. Sure, I'm upset and feel as though life isn't fair, that my dad was taken too soon, but anger isn't ever a part of it. "Not really. I'm sad. Especially for my mom. She locks herself in her art room, and tomorrow she'll come out and act like everything is perfect. She's so disciplined with her grieving. I'm jealous."

"Sometimes I think it's best that my parents went together. That's what my grandma says. Even though it's one of those bullshit lines people say. I wish one of them was here for us, maybe for them, it was meant to happen that way. I'm not saying your parents didn't love one another the way mine did."

I shake my head. "I didn't take it that way."

We sit in silence while he fiddles with his book and I sway my legs back and forth.

"What would you do, Kingston?"

"Hell. I'd probably jump in the lake or do some other crazy shit."

I peek at him, the moonlight reflecting down on his dark hair and boyish grin. My gaze casts out to the dark lake. It hasn't frozen over yet, and the light sprinkle of snowflakes disintegrate when they touch the water's surface. A sudden urge to feel the cold water hits me, maybe it will numb the pain.

Standing, I shed my coat, hat, and mitts, then kick off my boots.

"What are you doing?" Kingston glances beside him then back in front, trying to be the polite boy he was raised to be.

"I'm going in."

He springs up, shaking the dock. "No, you're not. You'll die. It's too cold."

I smile and jump in with my skirt and blouse still on.

Oh shit. The cold water feels like a vise squeezing the air from my chest. I emerge from under the water to a splash in front of me. Two arms wrap around me and pull me to the edge of the dock.

"You're crazy," he says.

"I can swim, Kingston." I slide out from his hold and we both climb out of the water.

"Come on." He picks up my clothes and boots. "My truck is around the corner. You've got to warm up."

We run to his truck, shivering the whole time, and a laugh bubbles out of me, quickly turning into hysteria. "I can't believe I did that. I get why you do it. I've never felt so alive."

"Never do anything like that again," he says, pulling

blankets from the back of his truck and starting the engine. "You have to strip down, I won't look." He turns his back, and I watch him peel off his own shirt.

I quickly undress and put my coat back on. When we're wrapped in blankets, he ushers me into his truck and we sit in silence with our hands in front of the heat vents. The windows fog up and it feels as though we're in our own private igloo.

"You can't do crazy shit like that," he says, turning his eyes on me.

"Why? I loved it."

When he faces me, the sexual energy between us ignites. It's always been there, but I've ignored it until this moment. For the first time, I feel as if someone really sees me. Not as the good student or the dutiful daughter. As the girl who's carried on with the scars of losing a parent. He recognizes my grief because he bears the same pain.

"Because you're better than that," he says. "You'll do something good with that pain."

I sink into his truck seat, his words knocking me off my axis. I have to remind myself he's not mine to reassure of his own worth. I'm dating Owen, and their friendship has already been slowly chipped away because of that. I can't make it any worse.

"King," I whisper, and he turns away from the heater. "You know how amazing of a person you are, right?"

He laughs. "Of course. Don't get all Psych 101 on me, Harrison."

I smile and let him deflect because I'm scared what will happen if I don't.

"So you kissed?" Allie interrupts.

I wake up from the memory, staring at the plates of food in front of us. "No. We didn't."

"So you jumped in a lake. That's all." She sounds disappointed.

I smile, remembering the feeling of the cold water hitting my skin. "I guess you had to be there."

"I will get it out of you eventually!" She points at me with her quesadilla in hand.

I laugh because I'm not sure anyone understands the bond between Kingston and me. All anyone sees is a guy who fell in love with his best friend's girlfriend, but we're so much more than that.

EIGHT

Kingston

Samantha's already at Tipsy Turvy's when I arrive. As soon as she spots me, her hand is in the air, flagging me down. Her enthusiastic wave is unnecessary since it's a weekday night, and the bar isn't busting at the seams or anything.

I shrug off my jacket and slide onto the bar stool beside her. The waitress comes over and I order a beer. Samantha says she's good with what she's got right now. I eye her drink to see it's some kind of cocktail.

"So how was your shift?" she asks.

"Good. Nothing major." My attention goes to the football game on the television.

"Remember that Adventure Race I was talking to you about?" she asks.

I look at her and nod, thanking the waitress when she brings over my beer.

"The sign-up is next week. Are you still interested?"

I know right away that I need to be straight in this situation. "I am, but there's something we should talk about first."

She leans back and her lips wrap around the small black straw.

"I'm not looking for a relationship right now."

A loud and annoying laugh erupts out of her, and I look around to see how many people are staring at us. Thankfully, it's a weekday night. "Well, thanks for the disclaimer, but I know you're not a relationship kind of guy."

I'm so sick of this reputation I've been given. "Why do you say that?"

"Because you're... you, Romeo."

I sip my beer then cross my arms. It's not like I'm gonna tell her why I'm not looking for a relationship. I thought maybe I could give it a try, but I can't string someone along when my mind is one hundred percent on Stella. It's not fair to anyone. "I'm not who people think I am. Just an FYI."

She laughs. "It's okay. I'm not looking for anything serious either. I figure we can have some fun." Her eyes widen as if she's just thought of something. "Hey, I snagged a spot at that house. Did you?"

I shake my head.

"No worries. I can bring you up as my guest. You know how you were talking about speed riding? I found out we can do it up there. My brother has a friend who did it and..."

I drown her out because yes, I want to ride down a mountain on my skis with a parachute, but Samantha is wrong. She's not a friends-with-benefits girl. No girl ever is. They say they're okay with it at first, but slowly it turns into wanting more dinners and less sex, then before I can stop the snowball from rolling down the hill uncontrollably, she's talking about feelings and the future and crap.

"Yeah, I'm not going up there," I say to stop her line of thinking.

Her gaze shifts to the door then back to me. "Because of Stella Harrison?"

I sip my beer as a distraction. "What?"

"Someone said they overheard that you guys knew one another in high school."

"We did."

"And is she the reason why you went cold as a dead fish on me?" She slurps her drink down to nothing.

"Samantha, we went out once."

"Yeah, and I thought we had a good time, but as soon as Stella came into town, something changed. Did you guys date?"

I roll my eyes. How did my life in Lake Starlight follow me to Anchorage? Oh yeah, because Stella is here now.

I don't even have a chance to answer before Samantha nods toward the door. "Oh look, here she comes with Lou."

I glance over my shoulder and my gaze locks with Stella's. Fuck. This is the last thing I want right now. She raises her hand halfway in the air. Lou nods to me, looking as uncomfortable as I am over the fact that neither of us mentioned we both planned a date after we were on shift together.

"Should we invite them to sit with us?" she asks, and I get the distinct impression this is a test.

"No." I sip my beer, my eyes straying to the television once more.

"Maybe you could use me to make her jealous?"

I narrow my eyes at Samantha. I'd love to take the time to lecture her about her self-worth but... actually, no. I *am* going to tell her, so she demands more of the next guy.

"Samantha, you're a great girl. We're so much alike, I

think we'd be better friends than lovers. The fact that you want to speed ride with me says we'd have a blast doing crazy shit together, but I'm not emotionally available. Stella and I never dated, but I'm hung up on her. And that's not fair to you. Never ever volunteer to make someone jealous by using yourself as the pawn. You're worth more than that and you're going to make some guy a lucky bastard. Maybe I could've been that guy if someone didn't steal my heart years ago. I'm sorry, but like I said, this isn't gonna work." I slide off the stool, throwing some money onto the bar and grabbing my jacket.

"Wait." Samantha puts her hand on mine. "No one has ever said such nice things to me. I get it." She glances at Stella and Lou. "And I won't tell anyone. Truth is, I just had a horrible breakup and I want to forget him, but maybe we can be in misery together?" She pats the bar top. "Sit down. Enjoy your beer."

"I don't lead women on," I say, still unsure if I should stay or not.

"Relax, Romeo. I might be good at petting your ego, but I'm not really into trying to convert a guy who has a hard-on for someone else."

I laugh, hang my jacket on the back of the chair, and slide back onto the bar stool. "So just friends?"

"Friends." She smiles and waves down the waitress. "I'll have the Philly cheesesteak wrap, the truffle fries, and a beer?"

I laugh as the waitress looks to me for an order.

"Now that I won't be sleeping with you tonight, I'm going to eat my feelings," Samantha says.

"Nice. You could've done that anyway." I order hot wings and carrots and celery with ranch.

The waitress takes our orders and leaves.

"Guys say that, but they're not up for a woman eating whatever she wants without judging."

"I think you'd be surprised."

She waves me off and peeks over at Stella. I'm trying to pretend they aren't here, but it's not working.

"Let's talk about the Adventure Race thing. Maybe since we agreed to being friends, we can make it work," I say.

Her face lights up. "We need two more team members."

She pulls out her phone and I hover close, watching the videos of last year's expedition race. The experience needed for the seven-day challenge means only one thing—I have to recruit Denver unless I plan on dying up on the mountain.

We eat and laugh, and I enjoy my evening with Samantha. I'm not sure I've ever had a girl as a friend. Other than Stella, but I guess if I'm honest with myself she was never really just a friend. My heart beat out of my chest the first time she walked into my fourth grade classroom, even if I hid it well. Then my heart shriveled and died when she left Alaska.

THAT SUNDAY, I'm heading to Terra and Mare for a family dinner planned by Grandma Dori. Sedona popping back into town pregnant was a shock, and I think maybe Grandma is in fix-it mode.

As I'm driving down Main Street, I spot Stella walking down the sidewalk—similar to how I found her almost a decade ago. Racking my brain, I calculate the date. Shit.

I park quickly then run across the street, holding my hand out for traffic to stop. The sound of a horn honking spurs Stella to look up.

"Hey," I say.

"Hi." Just like that day all those years ago, she's bundled in a coat and a hat, but she's not crying. Thank God, I'm not sure I could handle that.

"Today's the day?"

She nods.

"Selene locked up in her art room?"

She nods.

"You're not going to jump into the lake again, are you?"

She shakes her head.

Usually I'd make a smart-ass comment about her not having a voice but today's not a day for jokes. "Want to forget for a little while?"

She nods.

"Come on. A classic Bailey dinner will make that happen. You can listen to us all argue." I tug on her coat sleeve, but she stays in place.

"That's not a good idea."

"Please, my family loves you more than me." I tug again and she steps forward.

"Are you sure I'm not intruding?"

"Not at all. Everyone would love to see you. Besides, Juno has Colton working on last-minute wedding stuff, so they won't even be there tonight."

She nods, still seeming unsure. "Okay."

I don't dissect whatever made her agree. I've been where she is. I'm familiar with the desperation of wanting to think of anything but the what-ifs that still plague you.

The silence that falls over the room when we walk into the restaurant suggests they're stunned. Savannah's eyes zero in between us to make sure we're not holding hands or something. Liam smiles with Brinley in his arms, rocking her to sleep.

Sedona gets up from her chair. Holy shit, her belly grows bigger and bigger every damn day. "Stella, I missed talking to you at the hospital. How have you been? Come and sit."

"Congratulations," Stella says, staring at Sedona's swollen stomach.

Sedona runs her hands down her baby bump. "Thanks. And before you ask, no, Jamison isn't here. He's not up for the challenge."

I stop shaking hands with Wyatt and look at the two women. Did they keep in contact?

Sedona smiles nicely to me to suggest that they might have gotten together a few times in New York. I guess I shouldn't be surprised.

Stella grips my sister's hand. "I'm sorry."

"Nothing I can do about it. His loss." Sedona puts on a brave smile, but I can see the sadness underneath.

That asshole Jamison better watch out if I ever see him again.

"So true."

"Stella Harrison!" Grandma Dori comes out of the back of the restaurant and her arms are wide and welcoming, enveloping Stella.

While she questions Stella on everything she's missed, my siblings eye me with their own questions. I shake my head.

Finally, Stella sits down next to me at the table. Rome comes out of the back with the food, Calista helping him with the bread baskets.

"You're late," Calista says to me.

I tickle her and pull her onto my lap. "Say hello to my friend, Stella."

"Hi." She waves.

"This is Rome's daughter, Calista, and that's Dion and Phoebe."

Harley walks in with a belly as swollen as Sedona's.

"And our fourth is due soon," Rome says with a proud grin.

Harley kisses her husband on the cheek. "Not too soon."

Harley and Sedona talk about swollen ankles and not fitting into booths anymore while Austin glares at me across the table. He nods toward the door. A minute later, he says he forgot something in his truck and leaves the restaurant.

Since he left me no opening to follow without being obvious, I just announce to everyone that Austin wants to lecture me, stand, grab my coat, and head out the door.

He's leaning on the side of the building when I come out. "What's going on?"

"Nothing. Stella needed a friend today and I figured our family has always loved her."

Austin nods. "Are you two a couple?"

"No. She's dating Lou."

"Really? And you're okay with that?" He shakes his head.

"I told you I was pushing her out of my life." I do my best to have my poker face on, but I don't know if I succeed.

"Doesn't look like it." He nods toward the restaurant. "We can't repeat the past."

"Not gonna happen. I'm cool. Promise."

Austin nods. "And you'll talk to me should things change?"

"I've got this handled." I clamp him on the shoulder and squeeze.

The thing about having Austin as an older-brother-turned-guardian is he isn't as strict as a parent. He trusts me to a point, but the last thing I need is for him to have to bail me out again.

We walk back in, and I'm happy to find Stella enthralled in a conversation with Holly.

"Hey, Denver, remind me to talk to you about the Alaska Adventure Race Expedition," I say.

Denver peeks up from eating his pasta. "Why?"

"That's super dangerous," Cleo says, looking at Denver. "Last year, that one guy died."

"Again I ask why?" Denver says.

"Because I have an in and figured I need you if I want to make it out alive." I chuckle.

"What's this?" Stella asks, joining our conversation.

"It's a ridiculous week-long race where you travel through the Alaskan wilderness—ice mountains, raging rapids, you name it. There're pit stops, but you only have access to the things you pack," Cleo says.

Cleo's clearly not a fan, so my only hope is that she doesn't have Denver by the balls and he'll still agree to join me. Surely, she doesn't have an impact on his decision.

"I'll have to look into it." Denver piles another heaping spoonful into his mouth.

"Absolutely not. You're not doing it." Cleo's voice is louder than I've ever heard it.

Denver looks thrown back. "Babe, I'm an expert," he says with a wink.

"I'm in." Griffin raises his hand.

I point and nod. He's done more than enough survivalist excursions to be an asset.

Phoenix takes his arm and pulls it down to his side. "No, you're not."

Cleo and Denver argue next to me, and Griffin and Phoenix argue across the table.

"Why do you still do all this crazy crap?" Stella softly asks next to me.

When Sedona turns her head, I know she heard, but she tries to act as though she's having a conversation with Maverick about some new video game.

"What do you mean?" I ask Stella.

"So you still don't care whether you live or die?" Stella asks.

It's not her words as much as the disgusted look on her face that takes me aback.

She doesn't speak to me again for most of dinner, and when the night ends, she's off with a quick goodbye and not even a backward glance.

NINE

Stella

"Mom?" I knock on her art room door.

"Come in."

Luther Vandross plays behind the door, which means she's in the zone. I have a feeling I'm going solo to Juno and Colton's wedding. I love my mom, but she has a tendency to get wrapped up in her work.

As I open the door and step into the room, I find her in her pajamas with her apron on. I guess I have my answer.

"Am I going to the wedding by myself?" I ask.

She picks up the remote for the stereo I bought her. The one she fought me hard on, saying she needed to listen to vinyl if she wants to feel the music. But after she started using the stereo, she learned how much better her flow is when she's not interrupted by having to change out records constantly.

I peek around her canvas and stop dead in my tracks. I'm always struck by my mom's talent with a paintbrush, no matter how many times I see her work, but this is not what I want to see right before I go to a wedding.

"I'm sorry, sweetie. I got inspired a few nights ago and it just kind of flew out of me."

"Mom." It's a painting of my father. Not how I knew him though—how he would've looked had he still been alive today.

"I know. I'm sorry if it upsets you, but it just kind of happened and I went with it." My hands land on her shoulders, and she pats one. "He would have been gorgeous with salt and pepper in his hair against the dark hue of his skin, still with that gentle look in his eye. He was a fine man then and he would be now."

I ignore the Kleenex on the table nearby and take a moment to soak in the painting. "Yeah, he would have." After a moment, I sit on a nearby stool. "Mom?"

"Yeah?" She picks up her paintbrushes and heads to her sink.

"How come you never got remarried?"

She never so much as went out on a date with anyone as far as I know. There aren't a ton of African Americans in Lake Starlight, and if she's attracted to only black men, her options are limited living here. But I don't think she's ever even entertained the idea of dating.

She turns off the faucet and comes and sits on the stool across from me. "I was lucky. Some people take a lifetime to find their perfect match. Some never find it. I found it with your dad. To date again was just senseless." She shrugs.

"But you might have found a companion. Maybe you wouldn't have loved him as much as Dad, but you could have loved him in a different way."

She laughs and pats my knee. "What are you really asking me, baby? What's this about?"

I shrug, running my hands down the skirt of my dress. "I just wondered. I hate you being here alone."

"I'm not alone. I have my guests and my art." She motions to the room around her, which is packed with her paintings and sculptures, some finished, some still works in progress.

"But—"

She waves her finger between us. "You and I are two different people."

"What does that mean?"

"It means you hate being alone and I enjoy solitude. Sometimes I'm so lost in my head that I expect to find your dad outside that door, waiting for me to finish."

I stand and turn around. "That's what I'm saying. There could be a man on the other side of that door. One to massage your shoulders and feet after a long day of sculpting. One who will make you dinner and make you feel special."

"Stella?"

I look over my shoulder.

"Is this about Kingston Bailey?"

My hands twist around one another, knotting and pulling. She always could figure out when something was on my mind. "I'm dating his friend. Well, not really dating. I've been on two dates with the guy, but he's super nice."

"But?"

"It's complicated."

"There are so many men in this state, why are you always choosing his best friends?"

I turn around to make a sharp comeback, but when our gazes collide, my bravado fails. She's right. How do I keep finding myself in these situations? "I told the guy I couldn't date him, but he didn't accept no for an answer. Besides, Kingston was adamant he doesn't care."

She laughs. "Do you see this ending like it did with Kingston and Owen?"

I shake my head. "No, I don't think so. Kingston says he only wants to be friends with me. But still, he just has this way with me. And it's still there after all these years."

"What do you mean?" She tilts her head.

"When he's in the room, I feel so transparent. Like he knows every single thing about me, every thought in my head. He knows what excites me, what I hate, what I love."

She nods and smiles. "So why aren't you dating Kingston?"

It's a valid question. One I don't have an answer for—except for the excuse of what happened our senior year. It's my fault the course he'd charted for his future had to change. My fault he never attended college. I'm the reason he's jumping out of airplanes into burning forests.

When I say nothing, my mom speaks up. "Go have fun at the wedding. Try not to go down that wormhole of the past. Each day is a fresh start." She nudges me. "My present is on the table. Give my regards to them, but if I go to that wedding, I'm going to lose my vision for this piece and it's important for me to finish it."

I nod and step in to hug her, but she's smarter than me, keeping me at arm's length so I don't get paint all over my dress.

I climb into my SUV to drive to the church, and it's like the universe wants to dig that rusted knife into my gut to make sure I remember what happened, because Tracy Chapman's "Give Me One Reason" plays on the radio. I'm there at that party our senior year when everything that had been simmering for years finally boiled over.

"Want anything to drink?" Owen asks, already stepping toward the keg in the kitchen.

"No, I'm good." I scour the living room of the house party. This is the third party that we've been to tonight, but this one makes my heart thump harder because Kingston's truck was parked along the curb.

"Hey, Stella." My friend Jenny comes to my side. "Aren't you dying to get to New York?"

I nod. I've been accepted to NYU for the fall semester, and although I hate to leave my mom, I can't stay here and become the kind of doctor I want.

"I thought you and Owen weren't a thing anymore," she says, following my vision to him now doing a keg stand.

"We aren't, but we're still friends."

We've already decided neither one of us wants a long-distance relationship. At first, we agreed to take it day by day, but I know Owen well enough to know that after I get on that plane, I won't be on his radar anymore. The breakup is probably too amicable for us being together for a little over a year, which says a lot.

I talk with Jenny for a bit about how she's going to Idaho, along with a few of our classmates. Owen is sticking around and opting for community college. Kingston hasn't told anyone where he's going, but my assumption is he'll stick around too.

Owen never returns, but I catch him standing by the keg, talking to some guys from the baseball team.

"I'm going to go to the bathroom," I say to Jenny.

I weave between people dancing in the hallway, but my feet freeze when I spot Kingston, a beer held to his lips and Renee Quayle at his side. She's caging him to the wall.

I slip past by them to the bathroom. "Excuse me."

"Hey, Stella," Kingston says, nodding at me.

"Oh, hey, Stella," Renee says.

"Hey, guys." I smile and grab the doorknob to open the door, but it's locked. So I lean against the wall to wait, wishing I could disappear.

"Come on. My parents aren't home." Renee probably thinks she's whispering, but my guess is the Solo cup of spiked punch in her hand isn't her first drink.

"Nah, we're graduating soon. Don't you want to hang out with everyone?" Kingston asks.

"I only care about hanging out with you."

I glance at them from the corner of my eye and see her slide closer to him, her hand running down his chest.

"I'll just come back later," I say, sliding past them to escape the feeling that someone has their hand gripped around my throat, squeezing.

"Hey." Kingston grabs my wrist. "Hold up. I need to talk to you about something."

"King!" Renee screeches.

He looks at her as if she came out of thin air, and I wonder how many beers he's drank tonight. "Give me a sec and then we'll continue this conversation."

Renee smiles, appeased. "Make it quick." Then she bounces off down the hall.

The bathroom door opens. Kingston grabs my hand, saying a fleeting hello to whoever was in there, then drags me inside and locks us in the bathroom.

My gut knots. "We can't be in here alone."

He shakes his head. "I don't give a shit about Owen. I have a surprise. You still going to New York?" He puts his arms on either side of my waist, pinning me against the counter and my heart rate picks up. He doesn't look drunk.

I nod.

"I just got a partial funding to Bentley University. It's

division two, but they want me to pitch for them. It's, like, four hours away from you."

I haven't seen him this happy in forever. His energy and excitement burst out of him like the popped cork of a champagne bottle. "Okay..."

"Okay? We can finally be together, on our own. You told me last week how much you were going to miss me when you left." He steps closer to me. God, he smells so good.

"What about Owen?"

"Fuck Owen. Jesus, Stella, you know how much work I did to make this happen? How many strings Austin pulled for me? I did it for you." His fingertips land on the bare skin above my waist, and shivers run up my spine. He rests his forehead against mine. "Aren't you happy? I thought you'd be happy."

I close my eyes and inhale the smell of his cologne. The same kind I have a sample of in my keepsake box at home. "I am, but this thing has caused so much trouble already."

"What has?" He inches closer and my body aches for him to kiss me, to touch me.

"Us. You and Owen are acquaintances at best now, when the three of us used to be inseparable. What will this do to him if we get together?"

"Fuck, Stella. No one gave a shit what it would do to me if the two of you got together!" He backs away from me, his hands going to his hair.

Guilt floods me like a dam burst because he's right. But he never told me he felt anything for me. I thought my feelings were one-sided and I was confused when Owen asked me out. But Owen told me that he'd cleared it with Kingston.

"I thought you wanted this like I did," Kingston finally says.

We've never had a conversation about us being together.

Sure, there's this underlying current of want that's like a live wire between us, but he's never actually said the words.

"I didn't say I don't. I don't know. I'm just surprised and—"

His lips are on mine before I can finish speaking and at first, I melt into the kiss. His tongue eases into my mouth with a gentleness I didn't think he possessed. When our tongues meet, a current rushes through my body and centers between my thighs in a dull throbbing of need. His hands skim over my ass and presses me closer to him and that's when I come back to myself and the reality of our situation.

I press on his chest and pull away. "We can't."

He stares at me for a second, betrayal in his eyes. "Forget it!" he yells, and whips open the door. "I'm an idiot."

Owen stands there with his fist raised as though he was about to knock. "What the hell is going on?"

"Nothing." Kingston slides past him and heads to the kitchen.

Owen looks at me, and I stare back at him, probably looking as guilty as I feel. "Fuck this, Bailey. Why the hell were you in a locked bathroom with my girl?" He follows Kingston's path to the kitchen, and I rush to keep up.

"Last I checked, she's not your girl anymore," Kingston throws back at him over his shoulder.

"Let's go. It's nothing." I pull on Owen's arm, but he yanks it out of my grasp and I fall back, hitting the counter and the cabinets.

"Ouch," I mumble.

Kingston whips around and asks if I'm okay. "What the fuck, man?"

Kingston moves to come back to me, but Owen shoves him with both hands and Kingston stumbles out onto the deck.

"I didn't do anything," Owen says. "You're the one who needs to explain why you were in the bathroom with her."

"It's none of your business," Kingston says. "It's between Stella and me." Kingston looks over Owen's shoulder and winks at me.

Dread fills my every cell.

"This is the way it's going to be then? You're just going to try to steal her away from me because you were too chicken-shit to ask her out in the first place?" Owen lets loose a cruel laugh.

They circle one another, their fists at the ready. The other partygoers start chanting "fight."

"Talk about stealing. You knew I was going to ask her out, but once again, you couldn't handle me having something you wanted." Kingston's charismatic smile is plastered on for the masses. The one he uses to make people believe he doesn't have a care in the world.

"This has been a long time coming." Owen throws the first punch, but Kingston ducks and jabs Owen in the ribs.

"Someone stop them," I say, busting through the crowd. I dodge and weave as they continue to go at one another. "Just stop!"

Kingston does and looks right at me, his strong facade cracking, but Owen tackles him around the stomach. Kingston is knocked back and they both tumble down the stairs of the deck. Everyone rushes to the deck railing, but it's Kingston's wail of pain that silences the crowd.

Owen stands and spits on him. "Fucking baby Bailey. Eat shit." He disappears to the side of the house.

I run down the steps, and Renee joins.

"It's my shoulder," Kingston says, looking at me and gripping his right shoulder. "Call Austin. Can someone drive me to the hospital?"

"I can." Renee raises her hand then falls on her ass.

"I haven't had anything to drink tonight," I say.

A relieved expression crosses his face. "Keys are in my pocket."

I fish them out, and two guys from the baseball team help Kingston to his truck.

An hour later, Kingston's fate is sealed when Austin walks into the waiting room, where I sit with the rest of his family.

"His shoulder is done. He won't play next year."

Savannah meets Austin in the center of the room. They whisper about something as Austin runs his hand through his hair. I catch them glancing in my direction more than once. Embarrassment floods my face, and Juno takes my hand. It doesn't help erase any of the shame or guilt though. It seems I bring nothing but misery to Kingston's life.

TEN

Kingston

I'm helping Phoebe fill her basket with rose petals when Stella walks into the church and heads over to the coat check. Once she's shed her winter jacket, I see that she's wearing a beige dress that would look plain on anyone but her. It's form-fitting and showcases her gorgeous curves to perfection. Her hair is in locs and pulled back in an updo, and my eyes fall to her exposed neck, my mouth salivating like a dog. She's stunning.

"Uncle Kingston!" Phoebe pats my cheek and points at the basket. "The petals."

Stella laughs and I strip my eyes off of her to the spilled petals on the floor.

"Do you want some help?" Stella crouches and picks up some of the petals, placing them in the basket for Phoebe.

"You changed your hair," I say. "I like it."

She doesn't respond, just gives me a small smile.

"You're pretty," Phoebe says.

Stella's smile grows and I wish I had the same effect on

her as my niece. Unfortunately, I'm realizing I make Stella more anxious than excited.

"Thank you. I love your dress." Stella touches the big puffy layers of her flower girl dress.

"I'm Cinderella." Phoebe twirls.

"Yes, you are."

Stella stands as Phoebe runs to join Calista and Dion with Rome and Harley talking outside on the church steps.

Juno and Colton kept the wedding in Lake Starlight, but no one else is actually part of the ceremony, which I'm thankful for. One less tuxedo to wear. When you have eight siblings, you end up wearing a lot of them. So it's just the flower girls, ring bearer, and them. Perfect really.

Cleo and Denver walk into the church, Cleo one step ahead of Denver.

"I'm not talking to you." Cleo points at me and walks past me into the church, snatching a program off the table.

"She'll be fine." Denver winks, catches up, puts his arm over his soon-to-be wife's, and whispers something, midway down the aisle.

"You made a lot of enemies at that dinner," Stella says.

"Go figure. That's why I'm usually MIA in this family." I put out my arm. "Can I escort you and your mom down the aisle?"

She slides her arm through mine. "My mom isn't coming. It's just me."

The words 'just' and 'Stella' should never be used side by side.

"Then you get to sit with the family and me."

She stops walking. "No. I can't do that. Just put me in the back."

I reach my hand across my body and cover hers. "You

know no one puts Baby in the corner. The same goes for you. You're not meant to be in the back, Stella."

A bronze glow fills her cheeks and I'm transported for a moment to a younger version of the woman in front of me. The one I fell for, fast and dangerously. I must've been delusional when I decided I could just be her friend.

"I see your pickup lines have improved," she says. "I guess I see where Romeo fits."

I wince. I hate the nickname but telling any one of the guys I hate it would just spur them to use it more often than they already do. "I think it's time I tell you the story behind that nickname."

"It's okay, Kingston. I…"

I follow her gaze to the guests. Guests who are staring unapologetically at us.

"I hate this," she whispers.

I think because I stayed in Lake Starlight, people have stopped thinking only of what happened to me all those years ago. The pitying stares because of my shoulder or because I lost the girl have disappeared over the years. I'm no longer seen solely as the lovesick, heartbroken Kingston. Now I'm Kingston Bailey, the smoke jumper. It's freeing. But because Stella left and never really came back much, she's never had an opportunity to shake it off.

"Don't worry, they're just curious," I say.

"Curious of what mess I'll leave behind me again."

We reach the front pews and I'm thankful to see Liam and Wyatt there. All the rest of my family are farther down, huddled together at the end of the aisle.

"Funny, I haven't seen you two without a stained shirt in a long time." I purposely sit us behind them. They can all be in the front row.

"Just wait until you have a baby," Wyatt says.

"He probably already does," Liam jokes.

I glance quickly at Stella, who says nothing.

Lucky for me, crying commences in the back and it's like each baby must have its own cry, because Liam holds up his hands. "Not it."

Wyatt stands. "That's Lance." He heads down the side aisle.

Liam turns around in the pew, his suit a contrast to everything he normally portrays. "So, Stella, doctor huh? Now you two can play doctor and patient for real now."

"So, Savannah, huh?" Stella asks. "She finally gave in to you."

Liam and I laugh.

"Touché," Liam says. "But you guys are Buzz Wheel news now. You missed when I was front page news. Once you've been outed, it's like being recruited into a fraternity."

"You and Savannah were making out in a car like you wanted to get caught," I remind him.

A cocky grin splashes on his face as though he's remembering it all over again. "The good ol' days before night feedings. I will say though, your sister's tits look fantastic in the dress she's wearing."

I roll my eyes. "Thanks for the warning. I'll make sure to keep eye contact with her."

Stella laughs next to me. "I see nothing's changed since I've been away."

She crosses her legs and her high heel dangles off her painted toes. My gaze takes a journey up her firm leg, imagining if she were mine so I could have them wrapped around my waist.

"It's Lake Starlight. Not much changes." Liam glances toward the back. "Seriously though, a doctor. That's impressive. Congrats. After your residency, where do you see your-self settling down?"

Stella clears her throat, and I look at her intently, trying not to seem eager for her answer. Could she be back in Alaska for good?

She wiggles in her seat. "I'm not sure yet."

Liam nods. "You know Lake Starlight needs our own doctor, right? After Dr. Coleman retired and moved to Maine, people have to go to Greywall now."

"My mom mentioned something about that."

"So if you open a family practice, it'd be an instant success." Liam smiles.

Dr. Coleman retired two years ago, so I'm not sure what Liam is trying to get at. Sure, if Stella wanted to start a prac-tice here she'd be successful, but even I know that's a long way off.

"I'll think about it," she says as if Liam offered her the job.

"Oh shit, it's about to start." Liam nods toward the back of the room.

Stella weaves her head, bobbing to get a view, and I realize I'm blocking her.

"Here. Switch spots," I say, standing, but she stands too and so I sit.

Both of us change course so many times, I end up sliding over and she sits down right on my open palm. Her ass is in my hand and I resist the urge to flex my fingers. *Do not feel her ass without permission.*

"Sorry." I slide my hand out.

She glances at me, biting her full lip, before turning her attention to the center of the room, where Savannah, Brook-lyn, and Holly all walk the babies down the aisle.

Wyatt returns to his pew with Grandma Dori, sliding in

right in front of Stella. She reaches back and squeezes Stella's hand, and Stella smiles as if she's just as excited as Grandma Dori to see Juno get married.

My two sisters and Holly all come and stand near the pew, rocking their babies, who are more interested in their mothers' necklaces and earrings than anything that's going on around them. The music continues as Phoebe and Dion walk down the aisle. Dion's almost dragging Phoebe, who's suddenly shy and not moving. Rome steps out of the pew to go help.

Harley slides in next to me, carefully because of her belly. "I knew she was going to freeze. She's not like Calista." Her forehead falls to my shoulder.

Rome squats in front of the preacher and waves at Phoebe to come to him. The guests all quietly laugh, which makes Phoebe's cheeks pink more. Dion finally leaves her and walks down the aisle before sitting down next to his dad in defeat.

Calista starts walking but stops when she sees Phoebe standing there.

"I can't look. Tell me what's happening. Are my kids ruining the wedding?" Harley groans.

"They're stealing the show," I say with a chuckle. "But Phoebe isn't moving at all."

She looks over my shoulder. "Oh crap. Come on, Calista, be the big sister you need to be right now. Take her hand," she whispers.

Rome's waving and blowing out a frustrated breath, his eyes venturing from Harley to Phoebe. Calista just stands there.

Phoebe sticks her two fingers into her mouth. I'm about to hop over the pew until Phoebe stares in our direction. But it's clear she's only looking at Stella. Then Stella does a little twirl and acts as if she's throwing the petals. Phoebe laughs and twirls down the aisle a step or two. She stops, so Stella does the same thing and Phoebe twirls. It's the longest walk or dance down an aisle ever, but Phoebe finally reaches Stella. Instead of walking to the front and her dad, she walks right into our pew, sitting on the floor between Stella and me.

"She's amazing," Harley whispers in my ear before bending down to get Phoebe, who rips her arm out of Harley's hold.

"I sit here," Phoebe says.

Harley holds up her hands. "Whatever floats your boat."

Calista walks down, doing a great job of sprinkling the petals on top of the ones Phoebe did. Then the music changes. I glance at Colton waiting at the end of the aisle. He smooths his shirt under his tuxedo jacket and inhales a deep breath.

Juno and Austin step into the room and the women all 'ooh' and 'aah'.

"She's beautiful," Harley says behind me.

Stella turns to me, but she nods to Harley in agreement, slyly wiping away a tear.

"The dress is kind of big, no?" Rome asks from where he now stands on the other side of Harley.

Juno looks beautiful. Her dress is just really poofy. I open my mouth to respond but Stella shoots me a look.

I hear Rome say, "Ouch." Phoebe steps up on the pew between Stella and me, but she still can't see, so she leans forward to peer down the aisle. Stella's hands instantly fall to my niece's hips so she doesn't fall over, and my heart thumps. That move, which I've seen my sisters and sisters-in-law do a million times, comes from such a motherly instinct. It shouldn't hit me the way it does, making me imagine her doing that with our own child.

We all sit down, and Austin sits next to Holly, taking Easton in his arms. I slide over to make room for Phoebe, who spends the majority of the ceremony staring at Stella and sliding her hand in and out of Stella's.

Colton and Juno say their vows, kiss, and are announced husband and wife. I watch my sister start her happily ever after with the man she's been in love with her entire life.

A pang of jealousy hits me because I'm not sure I'll ever experience what she's got. If I look around at my family these days, all I find are couples. Holly and Austin, Liam and Savannah, Brooklyn and Wyatt, Phoenix and Griffin, Cleo and Denver, Rome and Harley. They're holding one another, kissing and sharing something that couples in love do. Then there's me and poor Sedona, who's rubbing her hands over her belly and watching Juno and Colton with a smile. I don't know how she's smiling after what happened with Jamison.

We all file out of the pews after the happy couple, and once we're in the vestibule of the church, everyone goes to get their coats. I ask Stella for her coat check number since Phoebe is still attached to Stella.

At the coat check, Harley slides up next to me. "I like her, and I'm not just saying that because she managed to keep my kid quiet for the entire ceremony."

I glance at her, and based on her level of giddiness, if she wasn't so pregnant, I'd think she was drunk. "Thanks. I like her too." I pass the coat check guy my tickets and my gut twists.

I'm doing it again. Taking care of Stella because it's

second nature to me when I should just be leaving her to do her own thing.

"Are you going to win her back?"

"Nope." Yet another reason I should keep my distance. Everyone thinks being nice to Stella means something.

"I can see the sexual tension between you guys. It's clear you two still have a thing for one another." She nods and grips her stomach.

I glance down. "You good?"

She shoos me. "Fine. It's my fourth, I know the signs of labor."

I nod. She knows more than anyone here probably, the way her and my brother keep popping out kids. I tip the coat check guy.

"Ask her to dance tonight? Start slow," Harley says.

"Okay, thanks for the advice."

I head back over to Stella and my niece, Harley joining me.

"And maybe you should drive her home? Or is that too awkward?"

I walk a little faster, hoping to lose her because there are already enough people up in my business.

"Here's your coat." I hold it out to Stella. "Want to ride together to the reception?"

Jesus, I just can't help myself.

"Sure," Stella says, which surprises me.

Harley gives me a thumbs-up behind Stella's back.

"Me too!" Phoebe yells and raises her hand.

"Oh no, you come with me and Daddy." Harley reaches for Phoebe's hand, but she runs and hides behind Stella.

Then there's an awkward game of "catch me" between Harley and Phoebe that occurs around Stella, but Rome comes over and swoops Phoebe up in his arms, pretending she's a plane even though she's crying and screaming "Stella" as though she's in the cast of *A Streetcar Named Desire*. If we weren't the focus of everyone's attention before, we are now.

We're finally free to go, so I escort Stella down the stairs. As is typical of my luck, we run into the worst possible person we could—Stella's ex-boyfriend.

ELEVEN

Kingston

"Owen," Stella says. I hate the way her voice sounds breathless.

"Well, look who I found." Owen smirks at my hand on Stella's lower back.

I retract my hand as if we're back in high school again, but I have to remember, she's not his anymore.

"Juno and—" I start, but he cuts me off.

"Colton. Yeah, I heard." Owen rocks back on his heels. "You're looking great, Stella."

Is it bad that I'm happy she's covered up with her coat? That he doesn't see her stunning figure in the dress she's wearing?

"So do you. What do you do now?" she asks.

"I own my own fishing boat."

She nods. "That's awesome."

"I heard you're a doctor now?" Of course he heard. It was all over Buzz Wheel.

"I'm in my residency."

"Congratulations. Tell Juno and Colton I said congratulations, okay? I gotta go. I'll call you next week, King." He heads down the sidewalk before either of us can respond.

Whatever level of comfort Stella and I had reached vanishes, and just like that, it's awkward and weird.

After senior year, it took a while for Owen and me to find our way back to friendship, and even then, it's never been the same. He blamed himself for my shoulder, and I blamed myself for hitting on his girlfriend—even if she wasn't technically his girlfriend in that moment. There's still this level of competitiveness between us that wasn't there before we both fell for Stella.

Stella glances at me. "Awkward."

"Come on." I guide her down the remaining steps and to my truck, which is around the corner.

After I close my passenger door and round the back of my truck, I spot Owen sitting on a park bench, watching us. I act as though I don't see him sitting there and climb into my driver's seat. I'm not sure what he's thinking, but we can talk about it later. Maybe by then my head will be on straight and I'll remember all the reasons I promised myself I'd get over Stella.

We ride to the reception hall in silence. Unless you count Radio Ralph's show from Sunrise Bay's local radio station. He's busy arguing with people who say they liked a band before they became popular. Stella laughs a few times. For some reason, it feels safer to listen to Radio Ralph than to turn the station to music. A lot of songs pull me back to that vortex of our high school years, and though I have no idea if it's the same for Stella, I'd rather not chance it.

We park outside the reception hall, and I walk her across the parking lot, her arm in mine. Her perfume stirs up a craving for that scent to be soaked into my bedsheets.

To know she was in my bed and my hands were on her. Jesus, I sound like a fucking creeper.

We pick up our table assignments, and sadly, she's in the back with Greta from Sweet Suga Things and a few other locals, people Selene would have wanted to sit with. I'm at the family table up front.

"I guess we'll find one another after dinner?" she says, tapping her place card against her full red lips.

I swallow deeply. "I guess. Maybe you can score the donut recipe from Greta."

She laughs, and we part ways. I watch her walk to her table and put down her place card. The people at her table all stand and welcome her home, which makes her ebony eyes shine with happiness.

"You're swimming through murky waters," Austin says, clasping me on the shoulder.

Easton lies asleep over one shoulder. Austin's suit jacket is gone, and his sleeves are rolled up. I guess when you're a parent, you don't really give a fuck what you look like as long as you're comfortable.

"It's nothing. Just gave her a ride." I shrug.

Austin huffs. "I'm not gonna give you advice. The heart isn't something you can negotiate with." He looks at Easton. "All I ask is that if this doesn't go as you'd like, don't lose it. Okay? Just come to me and we'll work it out."

I nod, my eyes never straying from her.

"Forget it. I can already see that look in your eyes." He walks away, and I briefly hear him talking to Holly about love and recklessness and no control.

At the bar, I grab a drink and think about grabbing one for Stella, but that's weird. She's not my date and I've already glanced over enough to know she's drinking the wine on the table. And she's holding her own at the table. She doesn't need me to intercede.

"Hey." Phoenix pokes her finger into my chest. "We have a problem."

Sedona waddles up—there's no other word for it—alongside Phoenix, laughing and asking for a club soda with a lime.

I brush my hands down my suit. "Hands off the suit, okay?"

"You bring up this ridiculous adventure race and now Griffin's ready to train all winter in order to be prepared. He and Denver are talking about it nonstop. You better hope that Cleo or I don't put a hit out on you."

Sedona laughs.

I run my hand through my hair, chuckling. "He doesn't have to do it if he doesn't want. It was just me putting the opportunity out there."

"And you think my survivalist boyfriend wouldn't want to go? You'd think that him almost dying would knock some sense into him, but nooo, he still went out with Cleo and Denver for that stupid reality show." She knocks on the bar. "Give me the strongest thing you have."

"Phoenix," Sedona says.

Phoenix doesn't glance in her direction. "What?"

"This isn't like a movie. You have to tell them exactly what you want."

I fist-bump Sedona behind Phoenix's back as Phoenix says, "Fine. Give me a Shirley Temple."

I quizzically look at Sedona as she does me.

"Shirley Temple?" I ask.

"I'm getting it for Maverick, okay? He loves them."

"Speaking of the big man." I raise my hand up as Maverick comes to the bar. He hits my palm, but not with the gusto Dion does. Hell, Phoebe might smack harder. "Phoenix is getting you a Shirley Temple drink."

His nose scrunches. "I'm not drinking that, Phoenix."

"What? We can ask for extra cherries in it. I thought they were your favorite?" Her lips turn down and she glances at Sedona.

"That was last year." He's probably way too used to events with fancy clothes and bartenders who serve you whatever you want, thanks to the celebrity status of both his dad and Phoenix, not to mention his own mom. "I'll have a Coke."

Phoenix leans against the bar and sips the Shirley Temple like a sad little girl. Maverick gets his Coke and leaves, pulling his phone from his pocket.

"He's gone. I've lost him," Phoenix says.

"You have not." Sedona wraps her arm around her twin's shoulder. "A change in drink preference doesn't mean anything."

But it's clear Sedona's words don't convince Phoenix.

"I need to talk to Griffin." Phoenix pushes off the bar and weaves through the party-goers, a woman on a mission.

"What do you think she's gonna do?" I ask Sedona.

She runs her hands over her swollen belly. "I'm afraid she's going to make one of these."

"That wouldn't be a bad thing, would it?"

Sedona looks lovingly at her stomach. "No, but I'm not sure Phoenix is ready. It changes a lot."

"Hey, you want to talk?" I knock my shoulder to hers.

She sips her drink and never looks at me. "No. Nothing is going to change. He's not capable of being her father."

"Her?" I ask in surprise. In the months since she's returned, I haven't spent nearly the time I need to with my little sister.

"Yep. A girl." She punches me in the arm. "You better be a damn good uncle to her. It's the only reason I came back here. She'll need a father figure and here she has loads of uncles who will look after her."

A tear slips and falls on her dress, darkening the light pink fabric, then another.

I pull her into a hug. "Oh, Sedona, I'll be the best damn uncle I can be, I promise." I draw back. "Those father-daughter dances?" I point at myself. "Count me in. Those camp-outs and whatever else dads are responsible for?" I point at myself again. "I'm there."

I see why she doesn't think I'd be available—I tend to stay away from Lake Starlight as much as possible. But that has to change. I need to man up because Sedona needs me. Hell, I don't want to be the weird uncle no one truly knows or feels comfortable with. Staying away from here was easy before my siblings had families. Although I lost my parents young, it was etched into us all that family is first—always. It's time I figure out what I really want my future to look like. I can't keep avoiding the past. Seems it will always rise up to haunt me anyway.

"Thanks, King." She wipes her face. "I swear I'm okay with it. My job as a freelance writer has the flexibility, but I want to find an apartment and Phoenix won't even talk about me leaving her and Griffin's place." She runs her hands over her stomach again. "She's coming soon, and I don't want to be that mom who relies on others for everything. And Phoenix has her own life, her own family with Griffin."

Harley chases Dion across the dance floor, catching him right before he runs into the cake table. Nearby people laugh, but Harley's anything but amused. Dion looks a little scared for his life.

"Have you thought about talking to Harley? She's the only one who really knows what you're going through."

Sedona nods. "You're right. That's probably what I should do."

"And as for having your own space. Move in with me. I have Juno's old room empty and I'm barely there. It's just me there so you don't have to worry about feeling like you're invading someone else's family. Even if it's not permanent, maybe it's a better solution for you in the short term."

"I don't want to impose. I'm sure you don't want to bring women home to see a pregnant girl sitting on the couch with a pint of ice cream on her belly."

"Why does everyone think of me as this player? I don't sleep with random women."

She shrugs and purses her lips as though she has to think about it. What the hell? "I'm not sure. I guess I assumed..."

"Listen, I'm no saint, but I'm not a player. Hell, I'd be off the market if one woman would put a sold sign on me." I look across the room and find Stella's gaze on us. A small smile on her lips. But I know better than to read into any of that.

"I know." Sedona rubs my upper arm. "Maybe this is a second chance for you guys."

"I don't think so, since I told her we could just be friends and she could date my best friend at the station." That decision stings every time I think of it.

"You didn't?" Sedona shakes her head at me, a frown on her lips.

"I did."

"King," she says, sighing.

"I know, I know. But seeing her back here caught me off guard, and she clearly doesn't feel about me the way I feel about her. I'm becoming that clingy loser guy who can't stop loving someone who clearly doesn't fucking love him back."

"She's stupid and crazy if she doesn't love you. But I think you might have it all wrong." She turns to the bartender and asks for a lemon-lime drink. "Screw it, I'm having the sugar."

"I don't have it wrong. She snuck back here and never told me. She was here for six months and not one word." I put a tip in the jar for Sedona. She needs to save her money right now.

"I think the two of you need to talk. You might have read the entire situation wrong."

I shake my head.

"Oh shit!" Harley walks by, holding her stomach, Rome at her side. She looks at me and points her finger. "Don't you dare say a thing. This is Braxton-Hicks."

I raise my hands.

"There's a lot of hostility coming your way tonight." Sedona laughs.

Stella rises from her chair and heads over to us.

"I can't walk. Rome." Harley grabs his arm and drags him down to sit with her. They both fall into a chair. Well, Harley falls onto a chair. Rome falls on his ass.

"Hey, Harley, are you okay?" Stella crouches next to her.

"Stella!" Phoebe jumps at Stella.

I snatch up Phoebe and hand her off to an approaching Phoenix for the baby fix she needs.

"Let's go into the lounge bathroom," Stella says. "Sedona, can you make sure there are no women in there? Rome, you go and get your truck. I'll just examine her really quick and see where we're progressing."

Grandma Dori must sense something is amiss because

suddenly she's there. "She's a doctor, everyone. No worries. Oh, this is so great to have a doctor in the family."

Stella looks at me and I roll my eyes.

After Sedona gives us the all-clear, we move Harley into the bathroom and position her on the couch. Stella washes her hands and situates herself to look under Harley's dress, removing her underwear.

Stella swallows hard and looks at me, eyes filled with trepidation. "Harley, you're going to have this baby right here."

"Excuse me?" Harley tries to sit up on the couch but winces and grabs her stomach.

"It's okay. I'm a doctor, and we have a great paramedic right here." Stella motions to me.

Rome walks in, oblivious to the turn of events. "Come on, truck is running."

"I'm sorry, Rome, but she's going to have the baby here. Someone call an ambulance to come for transport."

"On it!" Sedona says and leaves the room.

Harley groans and Rome falls to his knees at her side, taking her hand in his.

"It's early," she cries to Stella.

"Just sit tight. I'm going to talk with Kingston for a sec and get some supplies. I'll be right back." Stella nods for me to follow her out, so I do, and she leads me into the kitchen. "I need clean anything. Towels, tablecloths, whatever we can find. Do you how many weeks she is?"

I shrug. "I don't really know."

"When did she announce that she was pregnant?"

Again I shake my head. "I'm not always around, okay? I think at the baby shower."

"Okay, let's just grab what we need, and you can come back and help me."

Once we've quickly gathered everything, we return to the bathroom and Stella positions herself between Harley's legs.

"You're sorely mistaken if you think my little brother is gonna see my wife's pussy."

"Rome," Stella says. "Do you want a healthy baby?"

He frowns and points to me. "Eyes closed." He slides onto the couch to hold his wife's back to his front.

I leave the room and a screaming Harley to make sure that ambulance is on the way.

TWELVE

Stella

Kingston not knowing how far along his sister-in-law is confirms my suspicions that he hasn't been around Lake Starlight nearly enough. That saddens me since his entire family has found their way back here to start their families.

"Okay, Harley, when was your due date?" I ask.

"I'm, like, four weeks early."

I nod, really hoping that ambulance is here before the baby comes out. The baby should be fine if he or she is four weeks early, but any labor has risks. Even the easiest delivery can change course quickly with a simple complication. I'd rather she have this baby in a hospital.

"What could go wrong?" She looks at Rome, who looks to me for reassurance.

But I know better than to guess what we're dealing with here. Many a lawsuit has been filed based on some doctor looking into their crystal ball and trying to predict what may or may not happen.

Kingston comes back into the room, Grandma Dori right behind, dragging Sedona with her.

"Don't you dare think I'm not coming in, Kingston. Sedona needs to see this to prepare herself," Grandma Dori says.

"The baby is crowning," I say.

We get towels situated underneath her and some extras ready. By then, Harley lets out an anguished cry.

Grandma Dori touches Harley's hair and pats Rome's shoulder. "How are we doing?"

"Having a baby, G'Ma D," Rome says, a bitterness to his voice almost none of them ever have with their grandmother.

"I don't think I want to see this," Sedona says, standing at the end of the couch with a horrified expression.

"Nonsense. You need to know what you're in for," Dori says.

"Okay, she's ready to push. You have everything?" I look to Kingston, who has a tinge of green coating his cheeks, but we're doing this together. We have no choice.

He nods and positions the bowls, one with water and one without. "Want me to tear up the tablecloth?"

"Sure."

He pulls it apart with ease, the muscles in his arms and chest bunching with the effort. I'm flabbergasted that I can actually be aroused when I'm about to deliver a baby.

"Shit, Hercules," Rome says.

Once we're all ready, I inhale, praying I don't do anything to mess this up. There's added pressure when you're surrounded by people you know.

Another contraction starts.

"Okay, push, Harley," I say.

She puts her hands on her knees and pushes. Her red

face says she's doing everything she can. The only good thing is she's had three kids already, so this should go fast. The head comes out with ease, and Kingston hands me a towel to remove the membranes from the little one's airway.

"Oh my God," Sedona says. I take a quick glance at her, who looks as if she might puke.

I massage the skin around the shoulders, helping to ease them out one at a time. "One more push on the next contraction."

"I really wanted to be present for the birth, but the things I've seen happen on that sofa." Grandma Dori cringes. "It's been here for ages. Your grandfather and I made out on it once, and then he always did this thing with his—"

"Thoughts to yourself," Rome yells at his smiling grandma, who's reliving another time on this couch.

Harley's head moves side to side on Rome's chest. "I cannot believe this is happening."

But she pushes one more time when the contraction hits, and the baby slides out. I hand what I see is a little boy to Kingston, who has a clean towel available.

"I'm scarred for life! Thanks, Grandma!" Sedona races from the room as fast as her belly will allow her.

"Unbutton the top of her dress," Kingston says to Rome.

"Um, hell no," Rome says with a scowl.

"I'll open it." Grandma Dori reaches forward.

Harley looks petrified and she just gave birth to a baby in a bathroom.

"Skin to skin is best," Kingston says. "Jesus, I don't care about Harley's tits, Rome."

"Especially because he's early and won't have as much fat on him as he would otherwise," I agree with Kingston, but Harley's already opening her dress.

Kingston places the baby on her chest, pulling the towel over him. Sirens sound from outside and Kingston rushes from the room. Paramedics come in a few minutes later and there's still no placenta, so I give them the lowdown on everything that's happening.

"Thank you, Stella." Harley grips my hand. "And Kingston, you too." Tears well in her eyes. "Thank you both."

"You're welcome." I smile and watch while the paramedics leave the room, along with everyone but Kingston. I wash my hands then sit on the sofa, my hands still shaking.

After cleaning up the blood and mess, Kingston washes his hands. "You were amazing."

"I was terrified." I clench my hands to try to stop them from shaking. "When I found out she was in labor early, I was worried." I blow out a breath.

Kingston sits beside me on the couch, putting his arm around my shoulders. "No one would've guessed you were scared. You handled yourself like a pro, and because of you, they have a healthy baby boy." He squeezes my shoulder.

My muscles were so tight with anxiety that my appreciative moan slips out before I can stop myself.

"Turn around."

"No." I shake my head.

"Yes. A massage as a thank you for delivering my nephew isn't even close to payback."

I smile and position myself so my back is facing him. His hands squeeze and mold to my shoulders, and all the tension that's been taking up residence like a squatter disappears. I close my eyes and enjoy the sensation. If his hands can do this, I wonder what else they're good at. I mentally reprimand myself.

"Hey, Stella."

The room is so quiet, and the tone of his voice is so serious that I fear what he's going to ask me. "Yes?"

"How come you didn't tell me you were back?"

I let out a long breath. He wants to do this now? But I guess if he had the guts to ask, I should have the guts to answer. "Honestly?"

"All I've ever wanted from you was honesty."

"You scare me, Kingston."

His hands stop momentarily but continue a second later. "I scare you?"

I put my hand on his to stop him and turn around. "We live our lives very differently. I play it safe. You play it crazy. I lost my dad when I was nine and now my mom is sick. I get that I'll lose my mom before I die. It's all part of the cycle of life. But if I lost you because you fell off a mountain or you get swept into an avalanche... I couldn't bear it. It would have been preventable."

"But..."

I know he wants to argue. I've tried to prepare myself the best I could for his arguments about why we should be together. Still, when I look at him, it's hard to deny this burning feeling inside me that's only there when he's around. The one that makes me want to hop in his truck and have him take me anywhere, as long as we're together.

"It's hard enough for me to love someone else to begin with," I say. "To bring them into my life without the fear of experiencing that loss again. But to allow you in feels like I'd be waiting for the inevitable. The wild way you live your life... it works for you, it's how you cope, and I never want that to change. Ever. It's part of who you are. But I can't expose my whole heart to it because believe me, Kingston, if I'm still alive when you die, I'll grieve you no matter what. But if I allow myself to make a life with you and have kids with you? I'm not sure I'd ever recover. I've watched my mom's life sit at a standstill since my dad passed and I don't want the same for myself. So keeping you out of reach is how *I* deal with it the best I can."

I suck in a breath, thankful I didn't break down and cry even if I feel like sobbing. I want to beg him to change his ways. To not want to do all the dangerous shit he does that puts him at risk for no good reason.

"Anything can happen to anyone at any time," he says.

I stand. I'd love if we could see eye to eye on this, but I know we won't. "But you increase your odds. If someone did a risk management analysis on your life, you'd probably be ten times the risk factor other people are."

He leans forward and puts his forearms on his thighs, looking up at me. "So that's it, huh?"

"That's the reason I didn't tell you I was back. I was resisting temptation."

"And if I didn't live my life doing crazy shit like helicopter skiing and smoke jumping, you'd give us a shot?"

I crouch and put my hand on his. "No, because then you'd resent me down the line and that would kill me too."

His knuckles graze down my face and I close my eyes. "So that's it?"

I gather the strength I need to walk away. "That's it."

When I reach the door, he calls my name and I turn around.

"You know I love a challenge." His cocky smirk I know well appears, and my stomach flips.

"I'm not trying to be a challenge."

"I just have one more question. Do you think about me?"

I shake my head. "King—"

"Just answer the question. Do you think about me when

you're alone? When you're in bed at night. Am I the man who fulfills those fantasies of yours?"

My cheeks heat. "Stop it."

He laughs. "I think I am." He walks over to me and cages me against the door. "I think you have it all wrong. I think you like my wild streak. I think it turns you on when I do crazy shit, because if I didn't, I wouldn't go after my best friend's girl. I'd sit back and let him win." His chest radiates heat that makes me want to tear his shirt open and run my hands down those hidden abs.

"You're crazy," I say, my voice sounding too breathy even to my own ears.

"Am I?" He inches closer.

I could push him out of the way and walk out, but I stay put because the truth is, I like the feel of him this close.

"You're thinking too practically for love," Kingston says. "Sometimes the heart wants what it wants regardless of the consequences or whether it makes sense. Maybe it's time to test my theory."

I inhale, and all I smell is his cologne. "My decision is final." I push back with my ass and open the door.

He grabs my wrist. "I didn't fight for you once. I won't make that mistake again."

I pull my arm from him and walk out, hoping to escape this entire wedding before I change my mind and jump in his truck.

THIRTEEN

Kingston

After the reception finishes, Sedona, Denver, Cleo, and I take Rome's other three kids home and tuck them in. Denver and I are downstairs in the living room while Cleo and Sedona are upstairs reading bedtime stories.

"What's up with you and Stella?" Denver asks, wiggling his tie from his neck. He's already shed his jacket and hung it on the back of the chair in the living room.

"She thinks I'm too dangerous to love." I sit down in the chair.

He sprawls out on the couch, kicking his feet up on the table. "What are you, Maverick from *Top Gun*?" He chuckles to himself, grabbing the remote for the television, but he doesn't turn it on.

I shake my head because of all the reasons she could have given me, the one she did cracked me in two. If what she said is true, it means maybe she does love me, but she loves me too much to risk heartbreak.

"Seriously though." He glances over as if he's worried

Cleo will overhear him. When we hear Phoebe run down the hall and Cleo call after her, he continues. "She's worried you're going to kill yourself?"

I shrug. "I guess so."

He clicks on the television. "I can see her point. She lost her dad, so she's probably fearful of losing someone else she loves. Can't say none of us have felt that way."

"That's the thing." I lean back into the chair. "It's always been Stella for me. I was invested so young, I never really feared loving and losing someone. Not losing them to death anyway."

He lays the remote on the armrest of the couch. "Have you ever tried to figure out why you do the stupid shit you do?"

"What do you mean?"

He chuckles and holds up his hands. "Listen, I'm a survivalist. Have I found myself in shitty situations? Yeah. But I trained to get out of those. It's not the thrill I'm seeking, it's the challenge. Now that I have Cleo." He glances at the ceiling and a sly smile crosses his lips. "I'm extra careful. That doesn't mean I plan on just sitting around on my ass. I love the uncharted territories, but you bet my ass I'm gonna do anything needed to make sure I return home to her. Can you say the same?"

I roll my eyes. "I'm not trying to kill myself."

His eyebrows draw up. "You sure about that? Because from where I stand, I agree with Stella—you have no regard for your life."

"Says the man who picked fights, raced cars, and did how many other stupid things back in the day."

He pats my knee and stands. "Back in the day. When I was stupid and young. You're twenty-five now. Eventually you'll need to figure out your priorities and where they lay."

He disappears into the kitchen and returns with a beer for me. "I don't know, King, maybe Cleo just settles me. I still have the urge to do the Alaska Adventure thing you talked about. But you can bet your ass I'll make sure I'm trained and ready for anything we'd face, because coming home to her is my first priority."

I crack open my beer and guzzle down a hearty amount.

"Do you love her?" he asks. "Like *really* love her? You're sure this isn't because of Owen and some sense of competition between you guys?"

"Hell no." That's one thing I know for certain. My feelings for Stella have not and never did have anything to do with Owen. They were there before he ever asked her out and he knew it.

"I'm just making sure because you and Owen's competitiveness is next level. You do know Stella could be thinking the same thing—that she's the prize for winning the fight."

"No." But shit, he might be right. That's what it always appeared to be from the outside. It's what the townspeople thought. Stella in the center and Owen and me always tugging from either side.

"Maybe it's time to find some neutral ground. When you offered friendship, I thought you'd finally grown up. Don't get me wrong, I get the 'fight for the one you want until you win her' thing, but you and Stella have always had such an intense relationship, even as friends growing up. I think friends is where you should start, if you want my opinion."

Cleo walks into the room with Sedona and slides onto the couch. Denver wraps his arm around her, pulling her close. Sedona sits on the other free chair, and I think we're both staring at them with envy.

Maybe Denver's right. Maybe if I really want Stella, I

need to calm all this down and get to know the new Stella. The one she's grown into over the past eight years.

"Cleo, do you know you're engaged to a brilliant man?" I say before tipping back my beer.

Sedona narrows her eyes as Cleo laughs. "What advice did he give you? I might have to rebuke it."

Sedona laughs and Denver mocks offense, so Cleo kisses his cheek.

"I told King he should just concentrate on being Stella's friend right now." Denver points the neck of his beer at me.

"Isn't that what you were already doing?" Sedona asks, adjusting on the chair to try to get comfortable, which with the size of her belly, seems like an impossible feat.

"Yeah, but for real this time," I say. "Put the past behind us and just get to know one another as adults."

"Well, well. Sounds like Denver gave you some good advice. You really have matured, haven't you, babe?" Cleo kisses him again.

"So can he go on the Alaska Adventure Race then?" I ask.

Cleo whips around so fast, her blonde hair sticks to her lips. "Ugh. That race. I'm getting a glass of wine." She stands. "Are you hungry, Sedona?"

Both women head into the kitchen and Denver switches the channel to a football game. "She's breaking slowly. I'm in if you want to register," he whispers.

I shake my head and chuckle quietly. Is this really the guy I should take advice from?

———

THE NEXT DAY, Lou and I wheel an elderly man exhibiting flu-like symptoms into Memorial Hospital. Allie takes the particulars and walks in with us, getting the man set up in a room. She's adjusting the oxygen mask on his face, but her eyes are on me.

"What?" I finally ask.

"Nothing." She smirks.

I drop the clipboard on the bed and stare at her.

The man removes his oxygen mask. "Did someone tell my girlfriend I went to the hospital? She'll be looking for me tonight."

Allie's eyebrows rise.

"What's her name? I can call Healthbridge Nursing Home," I say.

He leans in closer. "It's a secret. She's kind of a shy girl and doesn't want anyone to know we're... you know." He waggles his eyebrows.

"Awesome," Lou says behind me, getting the stretcher ready to go back out to the ambulance. "Never too old for some reverse cowgirl action."

"Lou!" Allie rolls her eyes.

He holds up his hands. "How am I in the wrong here?"

"Her name is Marge, and she's on the fourth floor," the man says.

"Okay, I'll say that you two are friends and you don't want to worry her." I pat his shoulder.

Stella walks in a second later and the room suddenly feels crowded. Our eyes meet and it's clear, at least to me, that she's uncomfortable with the two of us here.

"Hey, Stella," Lou says, way too cheerful and way too familiar.

I haven't asked him if they're still seeing one another for a reason—I'm concentrating on building a friendship with Stella.

"Mr. Glassman, you were just in last week. Are you still

not feeling well?" She pulls her stethoscope from around her neck. "Let's listen to your lungs."

Allie helps Mr. Glassman sit up, and Stella glances our way before placing the stethoscope on Mr. Glassman's back. "Thank you, Lou and Kingston. We've got it from here."

We nod and leave the room. Once we're in the hallway, we sanitize the stretcher and I get the sense that he's stalling, waiting for Stella to come out, the same way I am.

"You missed your shot at the house?" Lou says, pointing at the flyer on the wall by the nurses' station.

"Guess so." Though I want to ask him who else is going, I don't.

"Samantha's in. I heard Allie took a spot. Tank and Stump are both going. It'll be a lot of fun."

I nod, continuing to wipe down the metal on the stretcher, willing myself to keep my mouth shut. Oh, who the hell cares at this point? Lou knows my history with her. "Is Stella going?"

He dodges eye contact. "No. She said she couldn't this year."

I nod. Now that I've asked and I know Stella isn't going, I'm envious of the ones who took the spots.

"So what are the two of you going to do?" I ask as we roll the stretcher out to the ambulance. "If you're gone every weekend?"

"We're not, like, exclusive, Romeo. We're just talking, nothing big. Plus sometimes she'll be working while I'm up there."

I nod and we load the stretcher. I don't know why I asked. It's hard to act as if I don't care, and I'm over talking about it right now.

"*Lou!*" Allie runs out of the hospital doors.

He crosses the short distance to her while I climb into the ambulance to get it ready for our next patient.

"Fuck, seriously?" Lou says. "That sucks. No, he's been out for a while. Sure, yeah. I'm cool with it. I tried but..."

A loud truck with a bad muffler pulls in making it impossible for me to hear their conversation anymore.

He climbs into the truck. "That fucker Dr. Tiller pulled out of the house because he found his own rental. I never understood why he took a spot to begin with." He starts the ambulance to drive us back to the station.

I secure myself in the passenger seat. "So what does that mean?"

"It means we each have to pay more. We were already short one person so unless we can find two people to fill the spots it's gonna cost us. Someone mentioned something about renting out the spots for the weeks we don't have as many people there or something, since we're all on different shifts. I don't want to deal with the specifics. I just want to drink, ski, and hot tub."

I laugh, and we pull up to the fire station a few minutes later. Tank and Stump are sitting in the kitchen, playing cards.

"Slow night?" I ask, pulling a Gatorade out of the fridge and sitting down with them.

"Yeah." Tank looks over and shrugs.

The fact that these two are close friends is comical. They're like Danny DeVito and Arnold Schwarzenegger from the movie *Twins*. They act alike but look nothing alike.

"Did you hear about Dr. Tiller?" Tank says to Lou.

"Yeah, I heard." Lou's cell phone rings. "Give me a minute." He puts up his finger and jogs upstairs.

"Why aren't you coming?" Stump asks me. "You could

be the meat the women come for, and then when you turn them down, they'll come looking for some consoling. And these arms are like magic." He holds out his arms.

"What can you fit in them? A Smurf?"

He throws a chip at me, and I laugh.

"That's the difference between you and me, Romeo. I've perfected my game because I have to. You get by on those good looks, but your game is pathetic." He puts his cards down face up on the table. "Gin Rummy, motherfucker."

Tank shakes his head and brings all the cards into reshuffle. "Seriously though, Romeo, come on. I was all up for speed skiing and I can't do that without you."

Tank's a smoke jumper with me in the spring and summer. The two of us are probably the biggest daredevils in our group. The entire summer while we fought forest fires, we talked about going speed skiing.

"Well..."

I mean, Stella won't be there and Denver's right. I shouldn't go full steam ahead in my pursuit of her. Just figure out how to be friends first. Fuck, my mind is such a clusterfuck right now.

The only thing that really ever clears it is jumping out of a plane or something equally as crazy, so I look at Tank and say, "I'm in."

"Fuck yeah, that's awesome." He smacks my hand with the handshake all the smoke jumpers have.

"Now you need to give all the women our address and tell them you're single," Stump says.

"I am single."

"That's not what I heard." His eyebrows practically hit his hairline.

Lou comes barreling down the stairs. "Guess what?"

He clasps Tank's shoulder and Tank shakes it off. The man hates being touched for some reason.

"I found us someone to take the spot. Well, *I* didn't. But now we just need one more. Say thank you, Lou," he says.

Tank laughs. "I found someone too."

"Who?"

"I—" I'm about to tell Lou when Tank shakes his head.

"You'll find out when we get up there," Tank says.

"What the hell?" Lou sits down and eyes me to fill him in.

I put up my hands.

"This is so childish." Lou shakes his head in annoyance.

Stump laughs, picking the cards Tank is dealing him up off the table. Lou grows more agitated throughout the game, and eventually we get a call to head back out. He leaves the kitchen first.

"Why aren't you telling him it's me?" I ask Tank.

Tank shrugs. "Because it's fun. He gets so uptight when he's in the dark."

I shake my head and chuckle because he's right. I stand from the table. "See you guys later."

Stump points his stubby finger my way. "Don't be a dick and say anything either."

I hold up my hands. "I'm gonna plead the Fifth."

Leaving the kitchen, I head out to the ambulance. Lou's face is red as he starts the bus. I can see why they think it's funny.

FOURTEEN

Stella

"You do understand we're in the mountains and it just snowed this morning, right?" I grip the holy shit handle above my head in Allie's SUV.

"Relax, I was born and raised in Alaska. I know how to drive. Plus, the snow's already melting." She takes a bite of the burrito she picked up when we stopped for gas. "We're going to have so much fun! Are you a stay in and read a book girl or do you ski?"

I glance into the back since it should be obvious because I brought my skis. "I ski, but reading isn't so bad either. I'll probably do both."

She nods, swallowing another bite of her burrito. "And your plans with Lou? He was on the schedule for coming up this weekend."

"Isn't everyone?" I haven't seen the schedule yet because I joined at the last minute and the person in charge put in my email wrong. Who spells Stella with one l? Allie said she'll straighten it all out today. Luckily, she's kept me in the loop, so it hasn't mattered.

"Yeah. I think everyone took off the first weekend so they could come up, but from here, it'll be scattered. I'm hoping for at least one day up here by myself." She crumples her wrapper and tosses it into the back seat of her car.

My eyes follow the wrapper to see it land among a sea of empty food bags. "Don't take this the wrong way, but do you live in your car?"

She pushes me with her hand and I laugh, my body swaying toward the window. "Stop avoiding the question. What are your plans with Lou?"

"I'm not sure yet. You and I are sharing a bedroom, right?"

She nods. "Yep."

"I guess I'll just take it as it comes."

"Okay, let me ask it this way." She puts a bottle of soda between her legs to open it up. I pick it up and open it for her. "Thanks."

"Just ask me if you need help. I'm your navigator."

She shakes her head and playfully rolls her eyes. "Again with changing the subject. What I want to know is, do you have feelings for Lou?"

Do I? He's a nice guy, attractive, funny. But he's not Kingston. He doesn't make my body buzz whenever I'm near him. When Kingston touches me, shivers cascade across my skin. And none of that is Lou's fault or within his control.

"Things with Lou are nice, I enjoy spending time with him, but I can't put him in the middle of Kingston and me."

"You're not with Kingston."

Her words feel like a slap in the face, regardless of their truth. "Still, I think I have to have the friends talk with Lou again. Especially since we might end up at this house together. Even though I explained the situation, he's still pretty flirty with me and I get the feeling he thinks I'm going to cave and change my mind at some point."

"Okay. We're about one mile up that hill." She pulls over to the side of the road and looks at me, appearing panicked as if something's wrong.

"What are you doing? You can't just pull over on the side of a mountain road! Allie?"

She places her hand on my knee. "There's something I've been hiding and I'm really sorry, but I didn't want you to bail."

"What?" I glance through the rear window, hoping not to see a semi-truck barreling toward our backside. "Can we please discuss in the driveway of the house?"

"Um... don't be mad, okay?" She presses her lips together.

"Allie?" The little time I've known Allie, I've never known her to overstep. She doesn't seem to be mean-spirited, but my stomach flips like a pancake on the griddle anyway.

"And remember, you're here for *me*. That's what sold you—wine nights and relaxation. To get away from the stress of your job and the situation with your mom."

And Kingston.

"Okay, okay, sure." My heart races every time her small SUV shakes on the shoulder when a car passes us. "Can we move this along?"

"Well, you took one spot and..." Her words trail off when a black truck rounds the corner, passing us and heading farther up the hill. The firefighter sticker on display in the rear window catches my eye. I know that truck.

"You're kidding me? Is this the reason you were so insistent about driving? Hell, Allie, I can't spend the weekend with Kingston in a cabin in the mountains."

She bites her lip and puts the car in gear.

"*No!*" I screech, my hand landing on her leg. "Turn around."

My breathing labors for a minute and I inhale deeply, letting the air stream out slowly since my body feels so out of control.

"Don't be silly. I have your back." She drives up the hill, following Kingston's truck.

"Does he even know I'm coming?"

She shrugs. "I'm not sure. Lou was bothering me the other day at the nurses' station because he said Tank found someone to take the last spot but was keeping it from him. They all love to keep secrets from Lou, so he doesn't even know Kingston's coming. I told Lou you were coming, but if that got back to Kingston, I don't think he would've joined." She shrugs again. "But I could be wrong. Your relationship with Kingston is already causing drama like we're in junior high."

"Me?" I scoff. "How about the fact that you all are purposely keeping things from Lou? Childish much?"

"Keeping a secret from Lou is like when you had a younger sibling and they wanted to hang out with you and you kept telling them no. Lou gets himself so worked up that it's funny to watch. You just don't want to tell him."

I shake my head. The fire guys I get—the jokes and razzing that goes on when a bunch of men are thrown together—but the fact Allie went in on it too? I'm surprised.

She pulls into the driveway. Kingston's truck is parked already, Lou's truck right next to his. It feels like history is about to repeat itself all over again and nausea swims in my gut.

"How did I get myself into this situation?"

She pats me on the back and turns off the ignition. "We got this. I'll be your bodyguard."

"You did this all because you wanted to make sure I came?" I ask her once we reach the back of the SUV and she opens it.

"Yep." She leans her hip on the back. "I like you, and I feel like we could be great friends. No? Am I being too clingy?"

I can't help but chuckle. She's so open, how could anyone not love her? "No, I feel the same about our friendship. But I don't want to play games and I don't want everyone up in my business. Next time, you tell me." I point at her and widen my eyes.

She hugs me and leans in to grab her bag.

"Allie!" Kingston yells, and we both look over to find him jogging down the stairs. He's wearing jeans, boots, and a heavy jacket and looks like he should be in an Outdoorsman catalog.

When he spots me, he stops short, one foot slipping out from under him, and he slides down three of the steps before hitting the bottom where he masterfully recovers. Only Kingston could manage to make me swoon with a fall.

"Shit, Stella." He runs his hand through his dark hair. "How did..." He looks behind him. "Does Lou know you're coming?"

I nod. "Yeah. He never told you?"

"Well, in truth, he didn't know *I* was coming." He heads over to his truck. "He's already in the hot tub, so I snuck in and out of the house." He lifts two cases of beer out of the bed of his truck. "Come on, you guys are gonna love it here."

How can he act so unfazed when I'm about to throw up all over the driveway?

"Is Samantha part of this too?" I ask Allie once Kingston disappears into the house.

She nods, lips pressed together. "Yeah."

"Oh, Allie." I shake my head. I don't know what Samantha and Kingston have going on, but I better prepare myself to find out.

She swings her arm around my shoulders. "This is going to be fun. F.U.N. Fun. Look, Kingston wasn't fazed in the slightest that you were here."

"He fell down three stairs," I deadpan.

She laughs. "Oh, don't get a big ego. He probably just slipped." But the look she gives me spurs laughter out of both of us. "We're not in Lake Starlight anymore, Stella."

"Cute," I say, and we climb the stairs.

The worst part about this situation is that there's a growing excitement in my belly at the prospect of being with Kingston for an entire weekend. God help me. Will this pull toward him ever go away?

FIFTEEN

Kingston

"Fuck," I murmur. Stella is the other person who took a spot. And no one told me. Here I thought we were playing a game on Lou, but someone fucking played me too. Tank and Stump were on shift last night, so they said they'd meet us up here later tonight. It's just us for the time being.

I talked to Allie and Samantha two nights ago to get everything squared away and no one said shit to me about Stella being here. Allie might act like she doesn't know anything about Stella and me, but she does. The sly looks she's been giving me every time I drop off a patient and the fact that she and Stella are close makes me think she knows more than the fact we went to high school together.

I load my beer into the fridge and grab two cold ones Lou brought up. He's already in the hot tub on the deck, steam rising into the cold air. The deck speakers, which are hooked up to the stereo in the house are blaring music. His head rests back and his eyes are closed.

"Look at you, lazy ass," I say.

His eyes spring open and I toss him a can of beer. He's so surprised to see me he doesn't catch it and it sinks to the depths of the hot tub. I crack my beer open while he fumbles around in the bubbles, looking for his.

"What the hell?"

I open my arms. "I'm the guy. Sorry, but Tank said he'd push me out of the helicopter if I told you." I sit on the ledge of the deck, the snow-covered forest surrounding the house at my back.

"I thought you said no way?" He pulls the beer out of the hot water and cracks it open.

"Changed my mind. Tank promised me he'd do all the crazy shit I want out on the mountains. How could I pass that up?"

He glances into the house, but the windows are tinted to keep out the sun during the summer. I'm not an idiot— he's checking to see if Stella is here. Might as well get this out of the way.

"Yeah, Stella's here."

He bites his lip and doesn't directly look at me. I can't blame him for not telling me Stella took a spot. I haven't pried about what is or isn't going on with those two. And I wasn't supposed to be up here anyway.

"She is?"

"Yep." I pop the P and take a pull from my beer. "She and Allie just got here. Tank and Stump are coming later tonight, and I'm not sure when Samantha's coming."

As though lightning struck him in the hot tub, his face transforms into a wide smile and he walks to the side closest to me, putting out his hand. "It's awesome that you took the last spot. We're going to have a killer time."

He's bullshitting. I've ruined his plan to be with Stella without my interference and only someone who knows what it's like to lose those opportunities with her understands how pissed he must be.

Regardless, I smack his hand and fist-bump him. "Yeah, I can't wait to get out there tomorrow." My gaze strays to the mountains over my shoulder. Samantha said she arranged the helicopter and guide. My adrenaline was picking up the entire ride up here.

"Well, I'll be on the regular slopes."

"Pussy," I cough.

He rolls his eyes. "You act like I'm on the bunny hill doing the V formation. I'm shredding it on a double black diamond. Let's remember who the loser riding down on skis is."

"Loser? Try OG of the skiing world." He thinks because he snowboards, he's better than me.

"Try snowboarding and get back to me."

"Try heading down a mountain with a parachute on your back. Oh, that's right, you're too much of a pussy." I point at him and snap my fingers.

The sliding door opens and Allie steps out, a beer in her hand, gawking at the view. "Holy shit." She hooks her arm through Stella's, dragging her to the edge of the deck. "See, aren't you glad I convinced you to come up?"

"Hey now, you weren't the only one," Lou pipes up from the hot tub.

Allie turns around, resting her back on the railing while Stella's gaze remains on the view and my gaze remains stuck on Stella. She's dressed in a pair of black yoga pants and a long sweater and boots. Her black hair is still in locs and pulled back into a ponytail. She's adorable and cute and sexy all wrapped up together. If only I could tear my eyes from her neck.

It's torture to want a girl for so long that eight years

later, you're still imagining what it's like to be with her. I have no idea the sounds she makes when she comes or how long it would take me to find the perfect spot on her body to drive her mad. Does her back arch? Does she moan? Is she vocal and would she tell me to do it again? I've imagined all of it as I beat off over the years, but I still don't *know*.

"Yeah, yeah. Lou helped too." Allie rolls her eyes.

"Well, I love it. Thank you both for the push." Stella sips from her wine glass. Sick fuck that I am, I watch her swallow. She must sense my eyes on her because she turns to me briefly before moving her attention to Lou. "How's the water?"

"It's perfect. Grab your suit."

I remain quiet, just an observer. Allie's gaze darts to me, as if we're all waiting with bated breath to see what Stella will do. But she and Lou are dating, so she should be able to jump in the hot tub and spend some time with him, as much as that grates me. I could cock-block my friend and join them, but I'm not gonna do that.

"I'm going to scour the fridge and see what we should make for dinner." I jump off the deck and disappear inside.

The sliding door opens behind me as I open the cabinets. We were told there'd be essentials, but we still have to do some shopping.

"Romeo," Allie says, sidling up to the breakfast bar, holding her beer with both her hands where it rests on the counter.

"What's up?"

"Mind helping me with a cooler in my car? I have some food for tonight and Tank said he'll grab some stuff at the butcher's for tomorrow."

"I think I should go to the store anyway." I walk past her, but she grabs my arm to stop me.

"I don't want this to be uncomfortable for anyone. Stella's being all weird now."

Out of instinct, I look out the sliding doors. Lou's standing at the edge of the hot tub now, his washboard abs on display. Mine are better, but Stella will see that in good time. "It's not weird. I just only brought snacks so…"

She releases my arm and slides to her feet from the stool. "Give a weak girl like me a hand?" She flutters her eyelashes, her voice imitating a helpless Southern girl.

I can't help but smile. "Sure, let's go."

"Thank you. You have all those big muscles and everything." She keeps up with her version of a Southern belle—Allie's lived in Alaska her entire life, as far as I know.

We walk down the stairs toward the cars. "I have to say, the place is pretty awesome."

She nods. "Yeah. Dr. Anderson's family is in real estate. I think this cabin was his wedding present."

"Must be nice." I stare at the log-style cabin that also has a modern touch.

"Tell me about it." She looks at the house now too, and all I can think of is what's going on around the back of the house. "So are we just gonna stare at the house and not mention how awkward it was out on the deck?"

I nod toward her car and she pulls out her keys, unlocking it with the key fob. "Last I checked, you're the one who withheld the information from me that Stella was coming."

She laughs and pulls out the items she wants me to take into the house. "Are you mad?"

Is she kidding? I'd never be mad about getting to spend time with Stella. Even if I have to watch my friend moon over her. "I should be."

"But you're not because you and Stella are…" She leans

her back into me and makes a heart in the air with both of her fingers.

I nudge her back up straight. "Whatever. We're friends. That's all."

Allie rolls her eyes. "Tell me something, how do I meet Grandma Dori?"

Her question throws me, and I do a double-take. "Grandma Dori?"

She nods. "I read about her all the time in the Lake Starlight Buzz Wheel."

"And you wanna meet her?"

"I'm probably the blog's most faithful reader. Your entire family is in that thing all the time."

I shake my head and blow out a breath. "Trust me, you're not their most faithful reader. I wish that thing would disappear."

I place what she gave me on top of the cooler, grab both handles, and head to the stairs.

"So no one knows who writes it?"

I look over my shoulder. "You do know Stella's from Lake Starlight too? You could ask her all this."

"Oh, that girl is tight-lipped."

We reach the door and I step to the side, waiting for her to open it for me. "You're seriously telling me she never told you anything about us?"

She dodges eye contact.

I knew it. "That's what I thought."

Shutting the door, she rushes to catch up to me in the kitchen. "Believe me, whoever it is who writes Buzz Wheel knows a helluva lot more than she told me." After opening the cooler, she takes things out and places them on the counter.

"The entire town would be happy to answer any questions you might have. Set up a booth in the middle of the gazebo with a sign that says, 'Give me the gossip on Stella Harrison and Kingston Bailey.' People will share and they won't even need you to do anything for them. They like to discuss my turmoil."

She shifts her attention from the fridge to the cooler. I glance inside to see the girl has everything from bacon to chicken to eggs and wine coolers.

"Let us chip in for some of this?" I shift my weight to pull my wallet out of my back pocket.

"Who said I was sharing?"

"Interesting. I'm wondering which of us would win if the two of us had an eating contest."

She points at herself. "I would."

"You would what?" Stella comes in from the deck and Lou follows, a towel wrapped around his waist. Probably to cover up his bulge.

"Eat Kingston under the table," Allie says with a megawatt grin.

Stella raises her eyebrows at me. "He eats large pizzas on the regular."

I raise my hand for a high five. "Looks like your girl is Team Kingston."

Allie pretends to be offended. "Whatever. I know my worth."

We all laugh, and I shift my attention back to Stella. "You never told me that nosey Allie's been spying on our town gossip blog."

"Yeah, she thinks Grandma Dori is famous. For an entire hour of the drive up here, I was quizzed all about your family."

"The Baileys are fucking awesome," Lou says.

"Thanks, man. I like them." I give him an appreciative smile.

"You've met the Baileys!" Allie screams, pointing an accusatory finger at Lou and then at me. "I want an introduction."

I catch Stella's eye, and we share a moment of understanding. I didn't always appreciate my family. Stella taught me to do that.

SIXTEEN

Kingston

Eighteen Years Old

I walk down the dock. Only the lights of the small boats still out on Lake Starlight are visible on the water. Sitting on the edge, my feet dangle and I itch to jump in. Submerge myself and come out on the other side of the lake. I'd rather do anything other than what I'm about to do.

A burst of colorful light breaks through the night sky and reflects down onto the calm water of the lake. Idiots on the boats are setting off fireworks.

Footsteps sound behind me on the wooden dock, but I refrain from looking over my shoulder. Stella picked a place we both knew would be empty after all the families left the beach.

She's quiet and says nothing until she's next to me, just like she was that night months earlier when the water was freezing.

"Hi," she says. "Thanks for meeting me."

"You knew I would."

She nods, then she's quiet for a few minutes. "Have you talked to Owen?"

The last person I want to talk about is Owen.

"No." I glance at my arm.

Although it's healed now and I'm done with the sling, I won't be attending Bentley University on a scholarship. The fact that the injury happened from a fight at a party meant to them, I didn't have the character to play for them. The coach said his hands were tied—it was the athletic director's decision. Didn't help any that last year, a guy on the football team hit his girlfriend at a party, so there's a low tolerance for bullshit. Austin argued that it wasn't close to the same thing and tried to explain the dynamics of the fucked-up threesome between Stella, Owen, and me, but all they heard was drama and trouble.

"You should talk to him. He never wanted you to lose the opportunity of your scholarship."

"If he wants to make amends, he can face me."

She places her hand on my thigh and I jolt for a moment before relaxing under her touch. "He went to the hospital. You know that, right?"

I say nothing. No one told me he came.

"Austin kicked him out. Said they didn't want you any more aggravated than you already were. I kind of think he wanted to do the same to me."

I look at her, then back at her hand on my thigh. The rich darkness of her skin still contrasts with my tanned thigh, even after a summer spent in the sun. I long to touch more of her, but instead, I take her hand in mine, wanting to feel its softness and remember her touch, even if it is only just her hand. Our fingers slide along one another's, getting comfortable with the feeling since we never had the opportunity to be anything more than friends who always teetered on the line of being more.

"Why do you always paint your nails?" She keeps her nails short but always painted.

She huffs because that's not what she wants to talk about. She wants to talk about feelings and say goodbye when I just want to avoid the topic. "My mom never paints hers because she works with her hands so much. She used to paint mine as a kid and say things like, 'One of us has to be pretty for Daddy' or 'One of us needs to have nice hands so they don't think we're all a bunch of scoundrels.' It just kind of stuck and now I always have them painted."

We sit in silence for another minute while I try to memorize the feeling of her hand in mine.

"You'll be away for the next anniversary." She'll be in New York City for the anniversary of her dad's death.

"I know," she says quietly.

"What do you think you'll do?"

She laughs, probably remembering that night we jumped in the lake. A warm feeling fills my chest because I gave her that. A memory that makes her laugh on a day that will always bring her sadness.

"I'm not sure. Maybe I should find something crazy to do, like bungee jump off the Empire State Building?"

I knock her with my shoulder. "You might get arrested."

"It might be worth it."

"If you weren't so scared," I tease.

She huffs again and eventually nods. "Yeah, my wild side lives vicariously through you."

"I'll take that as a challenge." I tighten my hold on her hand.

"I should probably get going," she says without moving an inch.

That damn boat sets off another round of fireworks. The ashes sprinkle down around us and fizzle when they hit the surface of the water.

"It's so beautiful here," she says. "I'm going to miss it."

"Are you really?"

She slides her hand out from mine, probably because of the edge in my voice. "Yes, I'm going to miss Lake Starlight."

"Are you going to miss me?" I could lie and say I didn't mean for that question to fall out of my mouth, but I want the answer.

She rocks her shoulder to mine. "Of course I'm going to miss you."

"Then why don't we try the long distance thing? I know it won't be easy—"

"King, we can't." She shakes her head and looks at the water.

"Give me a few months to get things in line. I'm sure I can figure something out to get me out to New York City with you."

She blows out a breath and startles when the boat sets off another huge round of fireworks. We both use the beauty of the colors exploding in the sky as a distraction for a moment, watching the colors trickle down to the water in front of us.

"You can't come to New York. Your life is here, plus... you need to heal things with Owen. He feels horrible for what happened."

"How would you know that?" I snap.

"I saw him yesterday. To say goodbye."

I spring to my feet, the restless energy and agitation I'm so used to overtaking me. "So I'm second place once again?"

"No. Come and sit back down." She pats the spot I stood from.

"I need to breathe, and I can't do that with you next to me." My fingers weave together on the back of my head and I pull on my neck, hoping for some relief. "I don't get it, Stella. I've done everything for our future, and you keep pushing me away. Just be straight—do you not have any feelings for me?"

Her fingers run the length of the wood and I'm about to warn her about getting a splinter, but part of me wants her to feel a morsel of the pain she's inflicting on me.

She turns all the way around but remains sitting. Pulling up her knees, she hugs them to her chest. "King, you've been a great friend—"

"Fucking hell. Friend?" I roll my eyes.

"Well, if you'd let me finish instead of continuing to interrupt me."

I snap my head back in her direction. "Just tell me. Put me out of my damn misery." I'm already feeling as pathetic as they come right now.

"When I first came to Lake Starlight, I was envious of the friendship you and Owen had. You always had each other's back. He was so protective of you because you'd just lost your parents. And it only grew over the years." She shakes her head. "I never should've agreed to going to home-coming with Owen and I never should've dated him, because there was a part of me that wanted you. That wished it were you who'd asked me. I honestly thought Owen had cleared it with you. I thought I misunderstood your flirtation with me, because let's face it, you can be flirty with a lot of girls. But then as I saw the friendship between you and Owen disintegrate and then you stopped talking to me... I'd always ask Owen what the reason was, and he said that friends part sometimes and shook off my concern."

I keep my back to her, watching as the sky lights up in

white, red, and blue, listening to the sizzle of them burning out as they fall to the water.

"I'll always regret being the reason you and Owen aren't friends anymore. And that I ruined your chance to play baseball in college. It's all because of me and that will never change, King. No matter what happens between us, our past will always plague our future. Don't you see that?"

I circle back around. "All I see when I look at you is love. My heart doesn't hurt, it soars."

"All I see when I look at you is regret. Regret that I let what happened, happen. If I never would've moved here, you and Owen would still be friends. You'd be playing baseball on a scholarship at college."

"You can't say that." Owen and I are complicated. We're competitive to a degree that's borderline psychotic sometimes. If it wasn't Stella we were competing for, it would have been something or someone else.

"I can because I've been in the middle of this tug-of-war for the past two years. I'm going to go to New York City tomorrow and I'm not sure when I'm gonna return. I hope you can make amends with Owen, but I *really* hope you find something you love to do with your life. I only want happiness for you."

I break the distance and crouch to eye level with her. It's like she doesn't understand what I'm saying. "*You* are my happiness."

Her deep brown eyes lock with mine. "You can't put that on me right now."

I stand and turn away from her again. There's my answer. "Did you ever have feelings for me, or have I always been the fool?"

"I did... I do. I'd do almost anything to turn the clock back and say no to Owen when he asked me out. For us to handle this differently. But there's no time machine and I cannot live with myself knowing I've ruined your friendship *and* your future. I have to go to New York City to save myself as well. We need the distance. You need to—"

"Don't say it. If you say his name one more time, I'm gonna go ballistic." I whip around. "I don't give a shit about Owen."

"Then give a shit about your own future. Find something you love, find your calling. Baseball isn't it."

She knows me so well. I love baseball, but not like Austin did. It was his pushing to get me to play in college that led me there. But I never dreamed of the majors, and I've known enough college athletes to know it's a grueling schedule that I'm not sure I want. Still, there's no denying that scholarship would've been a good head start in life.

"You have time. You have a loving family who will help you figure it out. I've only made your life miserable for the past two years."

"So that's it?"

Another boom sounds from the water and she startles.

"Jesus, enough with the damn fireworks." I flip off the boaters.

Don't they understand? I'm getting my heart broken right now. I watch the embers of the firework fall down, and a swift current of air whooshes off the lake, rustling my hair. I watch as a glowing ember lands on her shoulder, igniting the fabric of her shirt.

"Stella!" I yell, but she's already turning her head to investigate the heat searing her skin.

I tackle her and we fall into the water. She sucks in a big breath when we pop back up above the surface.

"Thank you," she says.

I shrug.

"Your future is here and mine is anywhere else," she says. "Please understand, Kingston, it's what's best for both of us. But never think you were alone in this. The pull? I feel it too, which is why I need to leave."

I open my mouth to retort, but something catches my eye over her shoulder, and I see that there's a fire on the boat that was setting off the fireworks.

"Shit, Stella, go get help." Diving under the water, I swim to the boat, but by the time I reach it, the fire is blazing, and the people have jumped overboard.

"*Help!*" a woman cries out into the dark night. "My daughter. She can't swim."

Following the voice, I reach them and grab the young girl, whom I swim back to the shore. Once I get her onto the dock, I dive back in to make sure everyone else in the water can make it to safety.

A half hour later, a crowd is gathered on the dock, watching the boat burn. The fire department boat is nearby, spraying it down, doing what they can. I look around through the gawking townspeople, but there's no Stella.

She's already gone.

SEVENTEEN

Stella

I startle awake, looking around my surroundings. The cabin. Basement bedroom. Right.

Allie is next to me in bed, wearing her eye mask that says Rise and Grind. Not wanting to disturb her since she stayed up later than me reading, I grab my zip-up hoodie and tiptoe out of the room. But I stop as I hit the top of the stairs, hearing noise coming from the kitchen.

I debate on tiptoeing back downstairs, but a large body blocks my view of the hallway.

"Stella," Lou says. "Thought I heard something. Did I wake you?"

He's in a pair of pajama pants and a T-shirt, thank God. I feared it might've been Kingston without a shirt and I'd just faint and free-fall backward down the stairs.

"No. I'm just an early riser." I tuck the book I brought with me under my arm. I used to enjoy reading until I started med school. But Allie's always talking about her fictional characters as if they're real life people, so I grabbed a book on a whim at the hospital gift shop.

I follow him into the kitchen as Lou says, "Coffee?"

"That would be great."

He eyes my book while pouring two cups of coffee. "You're a reader?"

I shake my head. "Not much since high school, but I figure after skiing, what else am I going to do?"

"There are a lot of things I can think of to pass the time." He puts the cream and sugar on the counter in front of me.

"Which would be?" I raise my eyebrows, hoping he isn't thinking something sexual. We need to discuss where this thing with us stands, and with Kingston in the house, I'm definitely not comfortable dating Lou.

"There are a lot of beds here." He waggles his eyebrows.

I shake my head. "Lou..."

He puts up his hand. "Yeah, I know."

He keeps saying that, but yesterday at the hot tub, he asked me if I wanted to skinny dip later that night. We need to clear the air.

"Can we talk?" I ask.

"Not if it involves the word Kingston."

"You're a great guy, Lou. Some girl is going to be lucky to scoop you off the market, but I'm not that girl."

"Because you got a thing for King?" There's hurt in his eyes, and I feel badly.

From what I've witnessed, he and Kingston don't have a competitive relationship like Kingston did with Owen. They have the usual ball-busting behavior guys have with each other, but it's clear they appreciate one another's friendship. Kingston and Owen were never like that. Owen was always jealous of Kingston.

"Truth?"

"Be careful. I am the guy's best friend."

"I do, and I have no idea what to do about it. But I know that if I ever choose to move in his direction, I won't be able to if you and I have been a thing."

He winks. "I can be a great distraction in bed if you need one."

I giggle because he just won't let it go. "You're just too close to Kingston."

His hand covers his heart. "Man, day two and you stripped all my beat-off material from my arsenal."

"I don't even want to know." I lift my coffee mug to my lips.

But Lou continues anyway. "Now that I know you have a thing for my friend, if you come out in a bikini for the hot tub, I won't be able to lie in my bed at night and beat off. You're off-limits now."

"Now? What changed when you were willing to date me before?"

"Truth?" he mimics my earlier answer.

"Yeah."

"I hadn't been around the two of you enough at that point. Didn't know it was a lost cause until I felt the vibe you two give off when you're together."

"Vibe?"

"This charged chemistry. I'm a firefighter, so I'm not really afraid of much, but once the two of you decide to finally drop the barrier between you, I don't want to be within five miles." He laughs and buries his head in the fridge, pulling out a carton of eggs and bacon.

It's disturbing that we're that transparent in front of other people. First Allie and now Lou. I worry Samantha is going to feel uneasy if she senses what Lou is between us.

People mistake it for sexual tension, but sometimes it's plain old uncomfortableness because I have no idea how to act in front of Kingston. He's known these people we're in the house with, and I'm new to the group. That brings out a shyness in me I never knew existed until now. It's awkward when you're around someone who, at one point in your life, knew you better than you knew yourself and now is somewhat of a stranger to you.

"Well, I don't see that happening, so I wouldn't worry too much about it."

Lou cracks the eggs on the bowl with one hand and I find myself impressed by the maneuver. Maybe because I suck at cooking, even though my mom could be a gourmet chef. Her bed-and-breakfast guests rave all over Yelp about her mac and cheese, but I didn't get her talent in the gene pool lottery.

"Can I ask why?" he asks.

I stand from the stool and round the counter, pulling out the frying pan. To help him or hinder him, we'll see what the end result is. "Sometimes it feels like there's this invisible electric fence between us and the minute we step over, we get zapped."

He raises both eyebrows.

"There's just a long past between us. Not all good." I open up the bacon package because my sous chef skills are slightly better than my cooking skills after helping my mom in the kitchen over the years.

"It's funny, you're kind of like a secret past of Kingston's."

I stop after putting one slice in the frying pan. He takes out a fork and whisks all one dozen eggs.

"What does that mean?" I ask.

He glances over his shoulder at me. "Before you came to

town, I thought I knew everything about Kingston. I knew about his parents dying, about all of his siblings, baseball, and even his arm being injured. But I never heard your name out of his mouth. He left you out of his past. I've never seen anyone have this effect on him."

I ignore the deep gash left behind from Lou's comment about Kingston never talking about me. Even one of my med school friends knew about Kingston because I had a hard time not mentioning him when we talked about exes one day. He was never officially my ex, but he still felt like the one who'd slipped away.

"What effect is that?" I ask.

"Tortured? Or unresolved maybe? It's hard to explain. Maybe he just wanted to keep you all to himself."

I laugh. "I was in New York. He couldn't keep me all to himself."

Lou's hip lands next to mine at the stove and I feel awkward that he's this close. "I meant that he wanted to keep whatever memories the two of you share to himself. He didn't want anyone else butting in with their opinions because it might change the way he remembers things or remembers you."

I mindlessly place the rest of the bacon in the frying pan. I jump out of the way when they crackle and sizzle.

Lou takes the tongs from my hands. "Yeah, I have a feeling you're not a cook?"

"Why do you say that?"

"Because you're using a tiny frying pan and you've weaved the bacon so that it's all going to stick together into one sheet."

I step back to give him space because he's right, I'm no cook. But then I wrap my arms around his back in a friendly hug, grateful he's let me off the hook so easy and shared with me how he thinks Kingston views me.

"Thank you for understanding, Lou," I whisper.

He shakes his head and his hand touches the one I have wrapped around him. "I'm not an asshole who chases what isn't his. I just didn't know how deep you two ran."

I nod with my head on his back because he pinned it right. Kingston and I run so deep, I'm not sure either one of us will ever climb out of the hole we dug for ourselves, no matter how hard we try.

Kingston rounds the corner and freezes. I slide my hands back from around his best friend faster than a thief pickpocketing a wallet. But the quiet fury in Kingston's eyes, says he saw.

"Hey, you two." He replaces his scowl with a smile and walks all the way into the kitchen.

He isn't wearing a T-shirt and my eyes are glued to his abs as if adhesive is binding them there.

"Hey, King. I'm making breakfast," Lou says.

I clear my throat and grab my coffee. Kingston enters the small galley of the kitchen prep area and his hand lands on my hip, sliding me out of the way.

"Excuse me, Stella," Kingston says as if he touches me every day. If he did, I'm sure there wouldn't be a current circling the area he touched like a bullseye.

"Sure. How did you sleep?" I ask, doing my best to sound unaffected.

He pours his coffee, then opens the fridge and grabs the milk before tipping no more than a dash into the cup. Last night, he did most of the cooking, so he knows his way around the kitchen already, opening up a drawer and pulling out a spoon. "Great. How about you two?"

Instead of staying in his place, he squeezes by me again with his hand on my hip once more, except this time he winks. My stomach thinks we're on a roller coaster. It can't stop delving from the depths of anguish to the highs of exhilaration.

Kingston sits on a stool and sips his coffee without ever blowing into the cup.

"I slept good," I say.

"Like a rock," Lou adds, continuing to flip the bacon in a new frying pan. "What's on your agenda today? Heli-skiing?"

Kingston looks at me and his gaze dips to my chest. I follow his vision to see I'm nipping like it's forty below. I place the coffee mug on the counter and zip my hoodie shut. Kingston chuckles into his coffee.

Lou turns his attention to Kingston. "What's so funny?"

"Nothing. I was just thinking about something from the other day."

"What?" Lou asks.

I narrow my eyes at Kingston, and it spurs him to chuckle again. "You wouldn't get it. It's an inside joke."

"I see how it is." Lou pretends to be offended, then he hums a song I don't recognize.

I lean forward to grab my book off the counter, figuring I'll scatter to a secluded area of the house and enjoy my coffee since I'm not a breakfast person.

But Kingston snatches my book before I can grab it. "Whose is this?" He leans back and props a bare foot on the stool next to him.

Don't ask me why I have a thing for feet, but I do. Kingston's are corded with veins and each nail is trimmed like he just got a pedicure yesterday. It says something when a man takes care of his feet.

"It's mine." I reach for it again, but he raises it up

higher. When I round the counter, he stands, putting his palm on my forehead as though I'm one of his sisters.

"Kingston."

He holds the book in the air. "Is this what you've resorted to, Stella? Get this tagline, Lou... *Who knew my brother's friend could be Mr. Right, and not just Mr. Right Now?*" He continues to read the rest of the blurb, giving him and Lou a good laugh.

Having a little bit of dignity left, I stop trying to reach for it and stand with my arms crossed.

"Enjoy your read." Kingston winks again, and I want to staple his eyelid open.

"What has you two acting holier than thou? You telling me you don't surf the net for porn looking to get your fix? I'll bet you both have playlists arranged in order of viewing preference. At least mine has a happily ever after."

"Oh, ours have happy endings, too," Kingston says with a chuckle.

I roll my eyes and hold out my hand. He places the book in my palm. I snatch it back. "No judging."

He holds up both hands. "I'm not judging. If you want, I'm happy to read it to you."

"Why would that be?"

Tank and Stump walk into the room from the side bedroom, each of them in the clothes they wore last night, now wrinkled. Lou talks to them.

Kingston takes the opportunity of his friends' distraction to lean in close. "Because when you're horny after reading all the hot sex scenes, I'll be the closest male."

My body floods with heat as though I'm lying on a Mexican beach in the middle of summer. "You wish."

"You're right. I do."

I roll my eyes and storm out of the room, forgetting my coffee cup. Circling back around, I grab it off the counter.

Tank gives me a weird look at the same time that Samantha barrels into the room wearing her long underwear and her hair in a cute ponytail that bounces from side to side. "Today's the day, boys. Be there or be square." She runs her hand on my arm. "Morning, Stella."

"Helicopter?" I ask, forgetting for a moment what Lou was talking about a minute ago.

She smiles, accepting her cup of coffee from Stump. "Yeah, we're taking a helicopter up to the top of the mountain to ski down. I think Kingston might be using his parachute." She looks to Kingston for clarification before saying to me, "Did you want to come? I didn't figure you for an adrenaline junkie."

I'm staring at Kingston because here we go again with him trying to kill himself.

"Nah, Stella's idea of adrenaline is the moguls," he says.

I narrow my eyes, unzip my sweatshirt, and walk right past him, enjoying how his gaze falls to my swaying breasts and my nips that are out for him to see but not touch. He says nothing, and I head to the stairs and the bathroom downstairs. Shutting the door behind me, I inhale a deep breath and release it. First order of business? Extinguish the ache between my thighs.

EIGHTEEN

Kingston

What is she trying to do? I watch the sway of Stella's tits in her threadbare T-shirt and my mouth waters like a fucking faucet. Was that some sort of tease to say I'll never have my hands on those? The woman is a fucking sadist.

"Romeo?" Lou's voice interrupts me checking out her ass.

I clear my throat, crossing my fingers that Lou didn't see me gawking at the woman he's dating. Pushing Stella and her more-than-a-handful of tits from my mind, I join the rest of them in the prep area. "What's up?"

"Breakfast."

Lou stares at me for longer than a fleeting glance. Shit, he probably did see me.

"I'm so stoked. I could barely sleep." Samantha takes a seat at the table and props a leg up on the edge of her chair, eating a slice of bacon.

"You coming, Stump?" I clasp my hand on his shoulder.

He's not usually up for things like Tank is, so I'm thinking it'll just be the three of us.

"Nah. I'm heading out with Lou, Allie, and Stella. You assholes can do all that death-defying shit."

Tank smiles and forks another helping of eggs into his mouth.

"Explain the concept to me." Lou sits on the counter.

The rest of us are standing around instead of joining Samantha at the table to eat like civilized people.

"What concept?" Tank mumbles.

I'm sick of having conversations about what I choose to do with my life and body. My adrenaline needs a little more heart gallops than a normal person does to get going. So the fuck what? It's not their life I'm jeopardizing; it's mine.

"The why of it," Lou says.

Tank glances to me then at Samantha before laughing.

"It's the exhilaration." Samantha sips her coffee. "The adrenaline is a rush and when you're done..." Samantha shares a look with Tank.

He nods. "It's an aphrodisiac for sure."

Samantha nods. "Definitely."

Huh, I never get that feeling. I'm wired after and I usually want to do it all over again, but I've never felt like I wanted to have sex after. Then again, I wouldn't have complained if it was offered.

"Really?" Lou asks, hopping down from the counter and loading a plate with eggs and bacon before putting it in the microwave.

"And the sex after..." Samantha says.

Again, Samantha and Tank share a look as though they've experienced it together at one time. I've never heard any rumors of them sleeping together.

"The best," Tanks says.

Shit, I really am missing out.

"You too, Romeo?" Stump asks me.

Samantha and Tank's eyes focus in on me.

I'm embarrassed to admit the truth, but I don't lie. "I've never had sex after."

"Never?" Samantha asks, disbelieving.

"I'm usually doing this shit with buddies so..." I shrug.

"But you go to bars after, right? You've never picked someone up? Or hooked up on a group excursion?"

I shake my head. "Nope." I'm not really the guy who fucks around with random chicks. There was a time in my life, those first years after high school, when I did, but it got old really quick.

"Man, you're missing out," Tank says.

"I will say, it's best when you're both on that high." Samantha raises her hand.

Tank nods. "Definitely. Shit, you know how many times I've broken a bed afterward?"

Samantha chuckles and slides out of the chair. "I gotta go get ready. You're making me horny now, Tank. Thanks for that."

"I can always help that situation, you know?" he says to her back.

She flips him off.

"Dumbass, she's with Kingston," Lou says.

Lou saw Samantha and me at Tipsy that night and he's asked me a few questions—that I avoided answering—about what's going on. I don't want to out Samantha's history, so I never told him much, but he obviously thinks we're a thing.

"You fuckers hungry? Hello? I'm the one who bought the food." Allie walks in wearing her pajama pants, fuzzy socks, and oversized sweatshirt. She looks like a child.

"I made you a plate. It's in the microwave," Lou says.

Allie hugs him briefly. "At least one of you Neanderthals has manners." After pulling the plate out of the microwave, Allie grabs a fork, hops up onto the counter, crossing her legs to face us, and digs in. "What should we have for dinner tonight?"

Stump shakes his head. "You're so little. Where does all that food go?"

She eyes his plate. He's added a Pop-Tart someone brought, along with more eggs and bacon than any of us. "I could ask you the same thing."

"Should I put some aside for Stella?" I ask, realizing she's the only one in the house who hasn't eaten yet.

"Nah, she's not a breakfast person," Lou says.

I'm not going to lie, it's as if a jagged piece of glass just lodged itself in my chest. I finish off my meal and place my dish in the sink. "I'm going to get ready. Thanks for breakfast, Lou."

Tank is quick to follow me. He turns down the hallway to his room off the main living area while I head to the lower level where the other bedrooms are.

The bathroom door opens, and my feet come to an abrupt stop. Stella emerges, steam filling the small hallway. She's got a shower cap on, and she's wrapped in a plush white towel.

"Sorry." I step to the side, but she does too, having no choice but to walk in front of me to reach her room. I wave for her to go. "Please go ahead."

"Thanks." She ducks her head and walks in front of me.

I try to not ogle her body, but I can't deny my eyes stray a few times. Whoops. I walk by once she's at the door of her room.

I'm at my own room, two down on the right, when she says, "King?"

I turn to face her. "Yeah?"

"Can we be normal?"

"Normal?" I tilt my head.

"You know what I'm talking about. I feel like we're the buzzkills of this place."

Her shoulders slouch as though she's defeated. Ruining her fun was never my intention, but it's hard to see her with someone else. Like I'm sixteen again, watching her laugh at another guy's jokes in the hallway, and it fucking sucks.

"Yeah. I know." I could say so much. Bring up the unresolved feelings I'm starting to realize are still very much alive inside me. Why did she leave that night without finishing our goodbye? Did she not care what happened? I never would've left her. Never.

"So, truce then?"

"Stella, I don't hate you. I'm not mad. There's nothing to have a truce over."

"Can we just try to get back to that friendship like you wanted for us?"

God, that sounds like complete torture, but it's probably the best I'll get. "Sure. Want to celebrate by hopping on the helicopter with us?"

She shakes her head, but there's the start of a smile forming. "You know the answer to that."

"Yeah, I do." I turn and put my hand on the doorknob of my room.

"Be careful, okay?"

I glance over my shoulder. "I'm always careful."

I wink at her and she huffs. Once I'm in my room, I close my eyes and lean back against the door.

You got this. Friends and all that bullshit. We've been here before. Except I didn't want to be there then and I sure as hell don't want to be in the friend zone now.

———

"*HOLY SHIT!*" Samantha yells when we reach the bottom of the hill.

Tank actually does scream, and our guide, Tim—whose name threw me at first because he's roughly the age my father would be right now and shares the same name. He's also tall and lean with the dark hair just like me—laughs at Tank.

"I don't get reactions like that often," Tim says, leading the way to where the helicopter is going to meet us to take us back up.

Samantha hooks her arm through mine. "I'm so happy we did this. I've been debating it for years. Tell me what I need to do to use a parachute."

Tim glances back, obviously overhearing our conversation, but he doesn't say anything.

"I'm not sure, but you need to learn how to use an actual parachute first," I say.

One thing I've figured out with Samantha is that she's all about the adrenaline rush, but safety isn't a huge concern for her. Tank and I know how to use a parachute. We have to make sure we land where we're marked when we're smoke jumping. Otherwise we'd find ourselves landing in the middle of a forest fire.

Tank glances at me. "You wanna speed ride?"

I nod, and again Tim glances over but says nothing. He obviously has an opinion on the subject. I intended to find out from him how I can get a helicopter to take us so we can fly down. It's not unheard of. I know other smoke jumpers who did it last season.

"I'm in." Tank raises his hand, and I high five him. "And I'll give you some lessons if you want, Sam."

Sam?

"You would? That'd be awesome."

"First thing you need to do is jump out of a plane with me strapped to your back."

Her eyes light up. I think I'm off the hook if she did have any inkling to try to win me over after our conversation at the bar. "Thanks."

"I'll line it up when we get home," he says.

The helicopter lands and Tim ushers us forward, all of us carrying our skis and loading them in. Once we're seated and ready to take off again, Tank and Samantha are suddenly very coupley and I'm left with Tim. Good times.

We end up skiing down the mountain again, and the weather couldn't have been better.

At the end of the day, we take off our gear in the office where we met Tim at the beginning of the day, and he approaches me.

"I heard you talking about speed riding," he says. Now more than ever, I get that fatherly vibe from Tim. He's dressed in a long-sleeve T-shirt with his company logo and a pair of jeans with boots.

"Yeah."

"How experienced are you? I saw that you could ski, but that's only a small part of it. I saw you almost lose your ski out from under you on the second run, but you recovered quickly. Thought on the fly. So you have the calmness for it, too." He crosses his arms. The expression on his face doesn't look like he's giving me compliments.

"I'm a smoke jumper. I can parachute." The idea of strapping a parachute to my back and skis on my feet and heading down the mountain makes my heart race. I grab my snow pants and wrap them in a ball, folding them into my bag.

"Okay. But it's dangerous and I can tell you right now"—he glances over his shoulder—"Samantha isn't skilled enough for it. You and Corey, yeah." He uses Corey instead of Tank, which throws me for a second. "But if you're serious, you have to go up with someone who's going to take you somewhere safe."

"Sure, do you know a place?"

"Here. It's not something I offer, but I see it in you and your friend's eyes, you're going to do it no matter how dangerous I tell you it is. So we'll use my 'copters and set a date."

"Seriously?" I look at Tank and Samantha flirting by the vending machines. "How much does it cost?"

He studies me for a second, his arms still crossed how I imagine my father would've looked in my teenage years when I did something stupid. "Nothing."

"What?" I laugh. "You have to charge us."

He shakes his head. "No. It'll be free, but you come here first. Okay? And Samantha is not ready. If you want to come back and helicopter ski again before that and I'll see how she does, that's fine. But no novices are welcome."

Well shit, that conversation with her is going to suck.

"Why are you doing this?" I ask, unable to understand why someone who doesn't know me at all would be willing to help me get my rocks off by jumping off a cliff. He clearly doesn't look like he's excited by the prospect.

"Let's just say I'm making my own amends for something." He claps me on my shoulder and walks away.

I follow him with my gaze as he goes into an office and shuts the door.

"Let's get home. I'm starved," Tank says.

He and Samantha walk past me and he smacks her ass on the way out, but I'm still trying to figure out the puzzle of

Tim helping us. I think the dad vibe is messing with my head.

We no sooner get back to the cabin than the moans, banging headboard, and screams from Samantha's room start. I guess that adrenaline really does do it for her and Tank.

I stare outside at Stella sitting in a chair as Lou builds a fire. If I had her to come home to, the adrenaline would be an aphrodisiac for me too.

NINETEEN

Stella

While Lou builds the fire outside, I head downstairs because I'm bound and determined to read this book I bought. Right now, I'll get lost in anyone's story but mine.

When my feet hit the landing, Samantha's moaning and groaning hits my ears. The thump of the headboard in sync with her verbal declaration of how great it feels fills the small hallway.

Jealousy I've never felt before crawls up my throat and makes breathing a struggle. I bite my bottom lip. What is Kingston doing to her in there? She could be an advertisement vouching for his sexual abilities. Either that or she's a great actor because the longer I stand in the hallway listening to them, the hornier I get.

My mind drifts to images of Kingston's hands on me. I have no idea if he'd be with me like he is with Samantha right now—which sounds uncontrolled and unrestrained and a little too chaotic for my taste. Not that I don't want to be fucked good and hard. Just the thought brings a rush of blood to my face. And then I remember that he's in there with her and seething jealousy feels as if it's eating away at my insides.

I can't handle listening to him with someone else, so I grab my book from my room and rush up the stairs. I hope he takes a shower after he's done because I'm not sure I can handle smelling another woman on him even though we're only friends.

"How was skiing?" Kingston's voice startles me and I miss a stair, twirling around and falling on my ass.

"What? How?" My hand covers my heart.

He laughs and holds out a hand. "I know I'm good-looking, but you've known me almost my entire life. You should be used to these looks." He winks.

I hate that fucking wink.

I accept his hand. He's showered. Dressed in sweat-pants and a long-sleeve T-shirt with an unzipped sweatshirt over. I don't say anything, listening intently for a moment.

Sure enough, Samantha screams—or more accurately, sounds like she's howling like a wolf. If she's not careful, they're going to think she's calling the pack.

"I thought you two were…" I point toward downstairs.

"No." He laughs and steps up one step, cornering me against the railing of the stairs. "That's Tank. Why, Stella…" His gaze dips down, but I'm as covered as though I'm about to go build a snow fort. "Are you jealous?"

I scoff. "What are you talking about?" I back step up another stair, but he follows me.

"Your lip is all swollen like you've been biting it. That's usually a sign that you're upset."

I shake my head. "No, it's not."

"If you say so." He shrugs and walks by me up the stairs, seemingly unfazed.

God help me, I follow him, checking out his ass instead of telling him off.

"That's right. We're friends, so of course you wouldn't be jealous." He grabs a beer from the fridge. "Saw that you and Lou have a cozy fire out on the deck." He eyes my book. "Hmm."

"What?" I square my shoulders, grab the bottle of white wine in the fridge, and pour myself a glass.

"What?"

"Your little hmm." I slam the bottle on the counter a little too hard and he chuckles, getting the reaction he wants out of me.

"Just that if you were my girlfriend, the last thing you'd need is a book. Hell, you'd be thinking I jumped right out of those pages."

I swallow my wine. "Is that what jumping out of a heli-copter does to you? Inflates your ego?" I open my mouth to clear it up that Lou isn't my boyfriend, but he's quick to reply.

"No. I don't need to do that to know that if you were mine, Samantha's screams would sound like whispers compared to what would be coming out of your mouth." He tips the beer and I watch as his Adam's apple rises and falls.

Please, someone, save me.

"Your ego never ceases to amaze me." I walk past him with my book in hand.

"You can't deny it." He glances outside, and I follow his vision to see Lou and Allie in conversation around the fire he built.

"Deny what?" I ask.

"That you want me. Come on, Stella, when you walked downstairs, you thought that was me with Samantha and it bothered you. Just admit it."

"I thought it was disgusting, if you must know."

"But you thought it was me with her, didn't you?"

I blow out my breath and shake my head.

He looks out toward the deck again and his eyes narrow. I turn to see what's making his nostrils flare. My mouth falls open and my gaze turns back to Kingston, but he's heading to the door.

"What the hell, Lunchbox?" Kingston yells so loudly that a group of birds scatter from the surrounding trees.

Allie strips her lips off of Lou's, and I blink three times to make sure I'm seeing right.

"I'm so sorry, Stella," Allie says.

I shake my head. She has nothing to be sorry for. "Don't be."

Kingston's head whips around to me. "Don't be? Jesus, Stella, she's kissing your boyfriend."

"No," I say, but Kingston barrels across the distance and cocks his arm back.

Lou's shaking his head, telling Kingston he has it all wrong.

Kingston won't hear it. "What could I possibly have wrong? You're with Stella and you're kissing Allie." His fist connects with Lou's eye and Lou falls back into his chair, not fighting back. "You're an asshole. Do you have any idea how big you just screwed up?"

Allie rushes to Lou's side to check out the damage then runs past me inside, coming out with a steak Tank brought up last night. She places it on Lou's eye.

"Say something?" Kingston's eyes plead with me. "You cannot just let them both get away with this."

I open my mouth, but I'm stricken mute because he's being so protective.

"Fine. I will." He turns his attention back to Lou. "You're a motherfucking asshole. You had a chance with Stella. Do you understand what a fucking honor that is? And you kiss the one friend she's made since coming to Anchorage? How did I not know that my best friend is a douchebag?"

Lou stands, holding the steak to his face. "I didn't have a chance with Stella. There's nothing going on between us because she's been straight up from the beginning that she's hung up on you." He pokes Kingston in the chest. "What kind of guy do you think I am?"

Mortification heats my cheeks. Kingston turns to look at me, mouth hanging open. I nod that Lou is telling the truth.

He throws up his hands. "Why didn't anyone tell me?"

"Because we just had a conversation about it. Stella was clear with me this morning that nothing was going to happen between us. I had a great time with Allie today." He turns around and smiles, but Allie looks at me sheepishly. "We might not jump out of helicopters to get our thrills, but we got a little carried away."

"What the hell is going on?" Samantha comes out onto the deck, a sheet wrapped around her body.

Tank follows after her, wearing his boxers. "Why the hell do you have my steak on your face, Lunchbox? You owe me twenty bucks."

"Just go back to your fuck fest and do me a favor, Tank, put a muzzle on Sam." Allie waves them off.

Surprisingly, they leave without another word.

Kingston's shoulders slump. "Sorry, man, I just..." He inhales a deep breath.

"Well, at least I know if we do ever get in a fight, you've got a killer right hook." He takes the steak off his face.

Kingston winces. "Sorry, man. I just thought..."

I shake my head when he looks in my direction. It's like déjà vu all over again. I stomp into the house, walk down the stairs, and slam my bedroom door. But Samantha starts screaming again like she's in the world's greatest orgasm contest, so I snatch Allie's keys off the desk, throw on a coat, and slide into my boots.

"Stella," Allie says, rushing into the room. "You can't leave."

"I'll be back. I just need space right now." I slide past her and out the door into the hallway.

Kingston's there, sitting on the end of the stairs with his hands clasped between his open legs.

"Nope." I point at him. "I do not want to talk to you right now." I walk up the stairs, squeezing past him.

"I'm going with her," Allie says, and suddenly she's at my side at the top of the stairs. "Here, give me the keys. I'll drive you wherever you want to go."

I open up the front door and drop the keys into her hand. I turn to look behind me and find Kingston at the top of the stairs, hands in his sweatshirt, staring at me. He truly is the most gorgeous man.

"You stay here." I point at him again.

Once we're in Allie's car, I let my head fall into my hands and tears cascade down my face. Allie reverses then puts the car in drive. I glance at the house. Kingston is at the top of the stairs, watching me. I just can't right now.

"I'm sorry, Stella. I'm the worst friend ever. Did you really like Lou? Like, suddenly his lips were on mine and I kissed him back. But I thought you said you didn't like him like that and that nothing was going on with you guys anymore?" Allie rambles.

I put my hand on her forearm. "This isn't about Lou."

"Oh phew, but still, I have no idea what came over me. Why would he even kiss me?"

"Maybe because the two of you were flirting the entire time we were skiing today."

She turns off the residential street the house is on and I feel as though I can finally inhale a full breath.

"We did?" She looks at me but quickly shifts her vision back to the road. "Anyway, forget all that. So why are you crying then?"

"Because Kingston just punched his best friend because of me." I clench my shaking hands. "It's happening all over again."

"What is?" She veers into the parking lot of a small diner. "I don't know about you, but I need to eat when I'm stressed."

I laugh because when does Allie not think of food?

She turns off the ignition and holds the keys. "Pie on me?"

I nod, and we file out of the car. A nice waitress seats us in a booth by the door, and Allie orders everything—pie and a milkshake and a sundae with extra nuts.

"Okay, be straight with me, Stella. How do you really feel about Kingston?" She's looking at me with such sympathy and understanding that all the walls I've so expertly constructed in my time back here come crumbling down and the truth pours out.

"I love him."

She smiles and reaches over the table, covering my hand

with hers. "I thought so. Why the hell aren't you guys a couple then? Because that boy is crazy about you."

Over an array of sweets for the next hour, I tell her the whole sordid tale of Stella and Kingston—all the love, all the affection, all the pain, all the betrayal. All the reasons we can't be together.

TWENTY

Kingston

I made her cry. Again. What the hell is wrong with me? How could I ever think we'd be good together when all that ever lives between us is tears?

I slam the front door, heading right for the fridge, ready to drink myself into oblivion. If I'm lucky, I won't remember tomorrow what happened tonight.

Too bad Lou is prepared for me and standing in front of the fridge. "I think you need a babysitter tonight."

"I think you're wrong." His eye is purple and swollen. "Fuck, I'm sorry, man."

He touches his eye and winces. "Please, it adds to my tough appeal. But next time, why don't you start with the questions instead of the fists?"

I nod. "Can I please have a beer now?"

He motions with his head to the counter, where there's a cold beer and a shot of something dark. "You get that until I say more."

"Jesus, I'm an adult."

"Then act like one."

I down the shot and narrow my eyes at him. He's got to be fucking with me. "What does that mean?"

"It means you and Stella are acting like high school kids. This whole 'I love her, but she hurt me so I'm gonna date someone else' crap. I got caught in the middle of it, which sucks, yeah, but you told me you didn't care if I dated the love of your life. That's fucked up."

I shrug.

"Don't brush it off like it's nothing. You're miserable lately, and to tell you the truth, as soon as you and Stella are in a room together, it's awkward and weird. Why do you think I stopped asking you to come up here?"

"Because you wanted to nail Stella?" My fist clenches around my beer.

"No. Because I can tell that the two of you together is gonna be a fucking buzzkill."

I sip my beer and nudge my empty shot glass his way. He shakes his head.

"Pretty please with a cherry on top?" I say with an extra dose of sarcasm.

He shakes his head again. "If you don't want to tell me whatever happened between the two of you, fine. I don't care because it's in the past anyway. But almost a decade later, the two of you are still wrapped up in one another whether you want to admit it or not." He takes a gulp of his own beer.

"She's just the one. The one who..."

"Got away?"

I shrug. "Ran away."

He pulls a stool over and straddles it in front of me. "But you never ran after her?"

I shake my head.

"That's not like you. I feel like you run toward everything that's scary." He sips his beer. "Shit, that warehouse fire last year? You were the first one in."

I shrug again. "It's different with her."

"How so?" He pours me another shot, thank God, and I down it before he has the top back on the bottle.

"I'm not sure. She's like a fire you can't put out. One that just keeps going, but then again, I think I add fuel to the fire sometimes too."

"From what I saw, you add gasoline to the fire."

I nod. He's right. I've been a complete jackass. "Yeah, I guess."

"But I can tell you one thing, Kingston. If it were me in your shoes just now, the last thing I would've done was beat the shit out of her boyfriend because he was kissing someone else. I would've been smiling like the cat that ate the canary. Listen, I've never loved anyone enough to want their happiness over my own. Hell, I can't imagine ever feeling that way." Lou pours another shot and slides it over to me. "I think you need to be honest with yourself."

"She doesn't like the fact I'm an adrenaline junkie."

"Oh, well, I don't blame her."

My eyes snap up to meet his. Neither do I. The night of Juno's wedding when she told me it would kill her if I died, I understood. "I guess I have to change for her."

He shakes his head. "Yeah, that's not right either. You could end up resenting her."

"I wish I could remove it from me like it's one of the organs you don't really need, you know?"

"What?" His forehead wrinkles.

"My need to do crazy shit, test my boundaries. You know, get rid of it like it was tonsils or a gallbladder I have no use for. I don't know why I need it, but the thrill I get when I jump out of a plane and into a fire, or race down a mountain—it's addicting."

He blows out a breath. Lou was asked to train as a smoke jumper, but he declined, saying it wasn't his thing. "Everyone has their reasons to do and not do things. Sometimes those reasons change over time. You're not there and maybe you never will be. She'll have to accept that if you two are gonna be together. If she can't, then I don't see how it could ever work out between you guys."

I nod. The truth is crushing and feels like a weight on my chest.

I finish my beer, and for the rest of the night, we sit by the bonfire and shoot the shit. Samantha and Tank don't leave her room, but Stump joins us after he wakes from his nap. I do my best not to think about Stella, but that's pretty much impossible.

Allie and Stella don't return until I'm already in bed. Her laughter rings down the hall. I'm not upset that she's having fun. Allie's a good friend to her, and I'm happy that Stella's happy.

But early the next morning, I pack my bags, scribble a note to the group, and hightail it back to Lake Starlight. Because Lou's right—if I don't change, Stella's never going to welcome me with open arms. But if I do change, can I really be happy killing off a part of myself? It's about time I face the fact that there might not be a future for us.

———

MIDWEEK, I head to Rome and Harley's to visit my newest nephew, Linus Jacob Bailey. I'm crossing my fingers we're calling him LJ or just Jacob because how can they name him after the kid in *Peanuts* who carried his security blanket around with him?

I knock and Calista looks out the side window before opening the door.

"Uncle Kingston!" She smiles at me. "Want to take me to get ice cream?"

I pat her head. "After I see the new baby."

"Ugh." She rolls her eyes. "Fine. Everyone has to see the baby."

I swoop her up and turn her upside down. "Ice cream after. Promise."

She giggles and squirms, but I walk into the family room where toys are strewn everywhere and a passed-out Harley is on the couch with her hand inside the bassinet next to her. Little Linus, or LJ or whatever, is asleep inside. I quickly change courses and head to the hallway that veers to the kitchen.

Phoebe's twirling in the doorway and smiling at someone at the kitchen table. My guess is Rome. Dion jets down the stairs and Calista's still wiggling, but I hold her ankles firmly.

"Dion, here's your chance for payback. She's at your mercy," I say.

Dion's eyes light up and he breaks the distance. His fingers tickle his sister's ribcage.

"Stop it!" Calista screams, and Rome appears in the doorway, scowling.

"Okay, yeah, we're in trouble now." I lower Calista to the floor, and she runs as far as she can from me. I give Dion a high five.

"If you wake my wife, I'm going to gut-punch you," Rome says.

I hold up my hands. "Sorry." From what I saw, even a tornado wouldn't wake her.

Rome's wearing an apron which means food, and my stomach growls.

"What are you cooking?" I ask.

I step into the kitchen, ready to pat Phoebe on the head, but my hand hangs there when I see who my niece was showing off for. I should've known, what with Phoebe's twirls.

"Stella?" I can't keep the question from my voice.

She turns the coffee cup in her hand. "Hey, I just came by to see the baby."

I guess we're just going to pretend that her running off in tears didn't happen last weekend.

"Me too."

Dion and Calista chase one another around me, one or both of them grabbing my hands until my arms circle around me.

"I'm making granola, muffins, and easy breakfast stuff because our mornings are so damn hectic trying to get the other kids fed."

"I had gummy worms for breakfast," Dion says as if he's six, not four, and just conquered the big roller coaster.

Rome raises his eyebrows with an expression that says "See?"

I grab a piece of granola that's cooling and pop it in my mouth. "It's good."

Rome slides the rest away from me. "Of course it's good. I made it."

Stella laughs, and both of us look her way. "Are there any Bailey boys who don't have an ego?"

"No." Harley walks in with Linus in her arms. She looks like death. Seriously—baggy eyes and her clothes have stains, her hair hangs limply around her face, and she seems paler than normal.

"You look great," Stella says and stands from the table.

Is she looking at the same woman?

"You're sweet."

Stella holds out her arms and Harley passes the baby to Stella, who looks like a pro with the way she cradles his head and situates him flawlessly in her arms.

"I'm starving. He eats as much as you." Harley pokes my side.

"Your snacks are in the fridge." Rome kisses her cheek.

She zombie-walks to the fridge and takes out a container of cubed cheese, chicken, and nuts. At the kitchen table, she falls into a chair with an oomph.

"You should go upstairs and rest. We got this. I have fresh reinforcements," Rome says to her, but she waves him off.

"I had this dream that this guy came in our house and was super loud and got the kids all riled up. Oh, that's right, it wasn't a dream." Harley squares her vision on me.

I cringe. "Sorry."

Stella sits down with Linus and I peek over her shoulder. "He's a good mix of the two of you, huh?" Stella says.

"I think he's all Rome." Harley sits up to look over at him as if she can't remember what her son looks like. "Dion is more me and Rome mixed. But this guy is all Bailey, like Phoebe is, if you ask me."

"He's lucky then. Since all the Bailey men are drop dead gorgeous." I wink at Harley and she rolls her eyes.

"There's that inflated ego again," Stella says.

"I say we hand him the baby and see how full of himself he is after that," Harley says.

Stella laughs and everyone joins. It's the best damn sound in the world.

The room quiets when the three kids run into the family room to watch television. I watch Stella from the other side of the table. She looks good with a baby. I don't even know if she plans on having kids. She used to, back when we were close, but you never really know until you're actually old enough to think about these things.

I want kids and I want them to grow up in Lake Starlight. For a long time, I wasn't sure about that. The small town, the gossip, but this town built me back up after my life shattered. I hate the memories sometimes and the reminders of what I lost, but it was a good place to grow up. What could be better than being surrounded by the people you love and who love you? I want that for my own children.

But I don't want as many as Rome. That's for damn sure.

Stella's eyes catch mine across the table as Harley's head falls back to the chair and her eyes drift closed. I'd do about anything to know what Stella's thinking right now.

"Do you want to hold your nephew?" She stands and comes to my side.

As good as I thought I was with a baby, it turns out, I'm not, because the exchange is all kinds of awkward and my hand ends up grazing her boob. She probably thinks I did that on purpose.

A loud crash comes from the family room and Rome heads out to investigate. Harley startles but falls back asleep. I stare down at my brother's fourth baby. Maybe I was wrong. Maybe more is better.

Stella doesn't leave my side since my nephew has his hand wrapped around her finger. *I feel you, bud, me too.*

Her perfume lingers around us and her hair tickles my neck. If we were a couple, I'd turn and kiss her right now.

"Fatherhood looks pretty good on you," she whispers.

"Pretty good? I'd rock this job." Both her eyebrows rise at my cockiness. "I wouldn't mind a few of these."

She smiles and nods. "Me either."

I give myself approximately thirty seconds to imagine what a child of Stella's and my creation might look like. I think we'd make the cutest babies ever. I can envision our bi-racial babies now and I know they'd be drop dead gorgeous.

"I'm not sure about the name," I whisper.

Stella laughs. "It's pretty unique."

She always sugarcoats things. The sound of a phone buzzing ruins the moment, and Stella digs into her purse.

"Oh... um... it's Sedona."

Rome walks in with a pissed off look on his face. "Sedona's calling you?"

She puts the phone to her ear. "Hey, Sedona... Okay. Okay... Calm down. I'm in Lake Starlight. I'll be right over. Just sit tight and breathe." She hangs up and looks at me. "Sedona isn't feeling well. I'm going to go check on her."

I look to my right and left for someone to take the baby.

"I hate to ask this, but did you drive your truck?" Stella swiftly takes the baby from my arms and places him in Rome's hands.

"Yeah."

"I walked from my mom's place. Could you drive me?"

Is she kidding me? "Absolutely."

TWENTY-ONE

Stella

Kingston speeds through the rural streets to get to downtown. Sedona ended up taking Juno's old room in his apartment until she can figure out a long-term plan that works for her. He parks outside his apartment and we file out, him unlocking and opening the door for me. When we step inside the apartment, we find Sedona sitting on the couch with a piece of pie on a plate resting on her stomach.

"Sedona, how are you feeling?" I say, coming to her side.

Luckily, I'd packed my medical bag to go over to Harley's. In my experience of working in an emergency room, mothers have a zillion worries about their babies, and I figured Harley and Rome might want me to give the baby a once-over. But Harley's the only mom I've come across who just rolls with it. She's so chill, I'm envious.

"It stopped. It was this tightening in my stomach. But I haven't had it for five minutes, so that's a good sign, right?" She forks a piece of pie and shoves it into her mouth.

My gaze falls to a stack of Lard Have Mercy pie boxes near the trash.

"She's kind of addicted to the pies," Kingston whispers.

"I heard you. And it's called *cravings* when you're pregnant, FYI." Sedona shoots Kingston a look that could kill.

"I think I should still check you out." I walk farther into the apartment and find that it smells like Kingston. Not his cologne—he's changed that since high school—but his soap maybe. There's a game console by the television and a sports magazine on the table near the door. The space isn't really decorated in any specific color scheme. It's all man here. "Didn't Juno live here with you for a while?"

Sedona laughs. "Are you wondering because the apartment screams 'poor college bachelor' motif?"

I glance at Kingston behind me and he rolls his eyes.

"If I wasn't about to pop out a baby, I'd do something about it."

I sit down next to Sedona, and she hands me her empty plate and lifts her shirt.

"*Sedona!*" Kingston shouts.

"It's a belly, Kingston. Surely you've seen one before." She shakes her head at him.

"It's moving." He points at her with a mix of awe and agitation on his face. Sure enough, the baby must be shifting.

Sedona cradles her stomach with her hand. "She keeps doing that as if she doesn't have enough room."

"It's like in that movie *Alien*," Kingston says.

"Did you just call my baby an alien?" Sedona snips.

"No."

"Okay, you two. Let's go to your room, Sedona, and I'll examine you." I stand and hold my hand out to help her up.

She slides to the edge of the couch and, with the use of

my hand, gets on her feet. We head into the bedroom, and I feel Kingston watching me the entire time. After last weekend, we never did clear up the whole fight and everything. I guess if Sedona doesn't have to go to the hospital, now's the time.

Sedona gets on the bed and I examine her to see if she's dilated. She's not due for another few weeks, but you never know. I listen to her stomach, her heart, and search for the baby's heartbeat even though we just saw her moving.

When I'm done, I ask, "Are you excited to be having a girl?"

Sedona puts her shirt back down and slides into her sweatpants before sitting cross-legged on the bed. She looks down at her swollen stomach. "Yeah."

"Are you scared?"

She nods. "A little. I mean, I can't live with Kingston forever. He's not going to want a newborn here. I need to figure out a long-term plan, it's just scary. I always thought I'd be doing this *with* Jamison, you know?"

"I'm sure Kingston doesn't mind. Do you have any idea what you're going to do?"

She shakes her head. "I want it to just be us. I want her to know she can depend on me no matter what. That I'm strong enough for both of us and we don't need him."

Her bitter tone is understandable, though I am surprised by the situation she's in. From what I knew of Jamison back in the day, I never thought he'd be someone who wouldn't take care of his own. That said, I don't know what situation led them here.

"Have you talked to Jamison?"

She shakes her head.

"You're strong, Sedona, but you can be strong and ask for help too."

"I know. But we'll be fine." She looks up and smiles. "What about you and Kingston? What's going on?"

I stand from the bed. "I think you were just having Braxton-Hicks. You're not dilated, and I've been with you for over fifteen minutes and nothing. But keep an eye on them, and if you feel them again, we should probably go to the hospital to get you checked. When do you see your doctor?"

"Friday."

"Perfect. Let him know about today though."

She nods. "I will. Thanks."

"I better go." I glance back at the door, nervous about the conversation I'm about to have with her brother.

"So you're just going to dodge my question?"

I walk over to the door with my bag. "I'm about to face your question head-on. Mind if I steal your brother away for a little bit?"

She smiles wide. "He's all yours. Then again, he's always been yours."

She laughs as I open the door and leave, shutting it behind me.

Kingston's on the couch with his feet resting on the coffee table, and he's flicking through the channels with the remote. "How is she?"

"False alarm, I think."

"That's good." His attention remains on the television.

"Want to go for a walk?"

Seeming surprised, he looks at me and clicks off the television, his feet falling to the floor. "You want to walk around Lake Starlight with me? Rumors will fly."

I nod. "I think it's about time we have a *real* conversation. Don't you?"

He grabs his jacket that's hanging off a nearby chair. "After you?"

After dropping my bag off in Kingston's truck, we hit the downtown streets of Lake Starlight. Although winter weather is practically here, it's an unusually warm day, which is why I took advantage of the nice weather and walked the two miles from my mom's to Rome's house. Still, I button my jacket tighter and put my mittens on while we walk.

"I'm sorry about last weekend," I say. "I never should've run out. I know why you did what you did. It was sweet."

He side-glances me. "I shouldn't have hit him. He's my best friend. I'm the one who needs to apologize. I'm the one who's acting like a lunatic."

"No, you're not," I say. "This is weird. It's all weird."

"I'm so fucking happy you're home, but at the same time, I'm not. I haven't been myself since you peeled back that hospital curtain."

I nod. "I should've handled it differently. This talk should've happened as soon as I returned to Alaska."

We pass the gazebo. It would be the perfect place to stop and talk, but it doesn't feel right. There are way too many prying eyes.

"You made your feelings clear at Juno's wedding, and I haven't been respecting them. That's on me. I've thought a lot about it since last weekend, and the only solution is to make sure we're not at the house on the same days. We'll keep it professional at the hospital when we see each other. I'm thinking of putting in for a transfer."

He can't be serious. I figured we'd apologize and move forward like we always do.

"That's what you want?"

He stuffs his hands into the pockets of his jacket. "No,

it's not what I want." We stop at the corner and his eyes lock with mine. "I'd rather give us an honest shot."

"But?"

"My life choices are too scary for you, and I get it. I know you're scared, and I understand the why of it. I'm not refuting your reasons, but I can't keep pretending that my feelings for you are platonic. I love you. I always have."

I swallow, and my chest warms and my heart breaks in the same moment. We end up at the beach opening. We both stand and look out onto Lake Starlight, the long dock that holds so many memories. We're quiet for a few minutes. I'm trying to think of what I can say to him, but I don't know how to make this better.

He finally breaks the silence. "Can I ask you a question?"

"What?"

"Why did you leave that night? I never was able to say goodbye to you."

"Because..." Any excuse other than the truth is on the tip of my tongue, but he deserves honesty. "I couldn't say goodbye to you. I saw you save those people and I saw you looking through the crowd for me afterward. I stayed to make sure you were safe, but I was afraid that if I actually said goodbye to you, I'd never get on that plane the next day. And we both needed that distance. I'd already done so much to hurt you."

He nods, but I don't know if he's appeased by the answer or not.

He walks forward, and my heart breaks that he doesn't want to go to the dock. I always saw it as our spot and thought maybe he was leading us there.

"I'm always chasing you," he says. "I feel like I'm always looking like a fool. The guy who can't take the hint that the girl doesn't feel the same. I think it's time we part ways. Learn to be apart from one another again."

My feet stop as my stomach sinks. "What?"

He never looks over at me, not even a fleeting glance. "I can't keep fighting for something that you're so hell-bent on denying. I love my adrenaline rushes, but I'm not stupid about them. I go with guides, and I wasn't going to do that adventure race unless I had my survivalist brother on board. I don't put myself in dangerous—well, okay, I do, but I take all the precautions I can. And I honestly don't think I can change."

"I would never ask you to change."

He nods. "I know, but if I could, I would. For you. And you're right, I would resent you if you told me to never do anything crazy again. So that leaves us here."

I look up to find we're outside his apartment again.

He pulls out his keys. "I'll drive you home and we'll say goodbye."

"You don't want to ever see one another again?" My heart feels as though it's been wrenched from my chest.

"That's not really practical, but we can keep as much distance between us as possible. Just let Tank or Lou know the days you're coming up to the cabin and I'll stay away, even if I'm off."

"Kingston, it doesn't have to be this way."

He stares at me. "It does. For me, it does. It's either all or nothing."

There's a finality in his tone that scares me. He opens the passenger door of his truck, waiting for me to climb in. I do, and he shuts the door right after me, then goes around the back of the truck.

We drive in silence. My heart won't stop lurching. He's really going to just walk away and end us completely. That might have been how it was when I lived thousands of miles away, but now that I'm back in Alaska, it feels wrong. Final.

The drive to my mom's bed-and-breakfast doesn't take long, and he puts his truck into park once he's reached the end of the driveway.

"Can't we figure something out?" I sound like I'm pleading.

His eyes remain fixed forward. "This is the only thing we can do. We've tried everything over the years. Our only hope is to separate as much as we possibly can, like when you were in New York."

My hand blindly finds the door handle and I pry it open. "I just want you to know... I do love you. I've loved you since you shared your textbook with me and didn't say you were sorry when I told you my dad died. And I wish things were different. I do. I wish I weren't so afraid."

He nods and licks his lips, glancing at me. "Goodbye, Stella."

He waits, and when I climb out, he drives off. He doesn't speed or squeal his tires. I watch his taillights until they round the bend, then I collapse to the cold, hard ground, allowing the tears to fall.

I just lost him. And this time it feels like forever.

TWENTY-TWO

Kingston

When I get out of view of Stella's house, I send a quick text to Sedona to make sure she's doing okay. She says she feels great now, so I pull a right to head to the high school. I park in the lot next to Austin's Jeep and stare at the school, a flood of memories rushing through my mind.

Climbing out, I go to the front door and press the buzzer. Fay waves to me through the window, and the door clicks open a minute later.

"Kingston Bailey?" Fay walks around the desk and pulls me into a hug. "You're so tall. Taller than your brothers."

"Yeah."

Fay looks at a younger girl sitting behind the desk. "This is Austin Bailey's younger brother. He used to attend here."

The girl nods and smiles, but Fay rolls her eyes.

"She's new. Did you hear I'm retiring?" she asks.

"No, really?" I lean over the desk and steal a butterscotch candy. Fay moves the dish up and places it on the counter for me. "And what are you and Mr. Murphy going to do with yourselves?"

"Well, he's still going to be working, but I'm trying to get him to go on a Caribbean vacation with me." Her eyes light up.

I cringe because Mr. Murphy is like a lot of people who move to Alaska—he doesn't care for squelching heat. "Good luck with that."

"Thanks." She slides back into her chair. "This is Violet. She's taking my place."

"Welcome," I say.

"She's single and new to town." Fay waggles her eyebrows and nods to the poor girl, whose cheeks are now pink.

"Nice to meet you. I'm Kingston."

"Kingston?" Holly comes out of her office and I welcome the interruption. I definitely don't need more complications in my life right now.

"Hey, Hol, I came by to see Austin. Does he have an off period soon?"

She waves me in. I grab a few more butterscotches before I follow her.

"Thanks Fay," I say and wink.

"Any time."

I knock on the counter. "And nice to meet you, Violet."

"You too."

Holly waits for me to go into her office first and shuts the door behind her. "Everything okay?"

"Yeah, I just need to talk to someone."

"Can I ask what about?"

Holly's great. I couldn't pick a better sister-in-law. She stays out of my business, she doesn't judge my decisions, and she makes my brother happy. But I'm not going to ask for relationship advice from her. She doesn't know the situation well enough. She wasn't here when I was growing up.

So all I say is, "Stella."

"Oh."

See? That one word tells her this is a subject she doesn't want to tackle. It's like someone inviting you on a hike and then you're staring at Mt. Everest when you arrive.

"I'll dial him up really quick," she says. "He has lunch next period, but I think he's helping a student with their science project."

She picks up the phone, and however he answers makes her cheeks flush. Amazing that after one kid and all their years of marriage, he still can pull that reaction out of her.

"I have Kingston here... No. He's fine... He wants to talk to you about Stella... Okay... yeah... Sounds good."

She hangs up, and I slide to the edge of the chair. "I know my way. Same room?"

She holds up her hand to stop me. "He said we can go to him after this period and you guys can talk in his classroom."

"Oh." I glance at the clock above her head. "And when is that?"

She bites her cheek. "A half hour."

I nod. What the hell am I going to do here for a half hour? I point over my shoulder. "I can wait outside."

"Nonsense. You stay here." She looks over my shoulder and back at me. "Would you mind if..." She stands and shuts all the blinds.

"Hey, Holly, I know I can look a little like Austin, but I can't fill his shoes in every way."

She laughs. "No. It's just... sometimes all these people are so nosy."

"Okay. But my brother might beat my ass for just being in here with you when the blinds are shut."

She puts her hand on my shoulder when she passes by. "I need a favor."

My heart rate increases when she pulls her blouse from her skirt. I cover my eyes with my arm. "What the hell are you doing?"

"Uncover your eyes."

I raise my arm and peek out, seeing she's still dressed.

"All the way." I lower my arm and she pulls out a lunch cooler, unzipping it without saying anything. She pulls out a syringe and a vial. "We're trying again for another baby, and we started the shots on Saturday, not even thinking that to keep up with the timing, I'd have to do them at school. We were just so excited to start."

"Okay, but you've done them before, right?" Easton was conceived with the help of fertility treatments.

"It's stupid, but I'm kind of afraid of needles. Austin always does my shots and I told him I could do this, but I'm not sure I can. It's really important to stick to the right timing."

"I'm sure a half hour won't affect it too much, right?" I shift in my seat and look behind me at the closed door.

Her shoulders slump. "It scares me. I just want to do everything right, you know? Do you know what they call a pregnancy for someone my age? A geriatric pregnancy. It's so insulting. I'm not old, but the doctor said it's going to be even harder this time around and you know all the trouble we had the first time. I don't want to mess it up. You're a paramedic. Will you please just give it to me?" Tears fill her eyes.

I saw the heartbreak with both Austin and Holly while they were trying to conceive Easton. "Of course I'll help."

She pulls out antiseptic and a pair of gloves.

"You're so prepared."

She shrugs. I shouldn't be surprised, Easton always has his snacks ready in a neat container, his juice cup and a change of clothes neatly packed in a bag. She's an uber-organized mom.

I sanitize my hands and put on the gloves. While I pull the fertility medicine into the syringe, she raises her blouse. There are a few bruises on her stomach as she turns away. "Right side today."

"Do you want it fast or slow?" God, it feels all kinds of wrong to say that to my sister-in-law.

"Fast." Her free hand grips the desk and she turns her head away.

"Okay, ready?" I aim the syringe and her body tenses. "One."

She groans.

"Two."

Her knuckles turn white on the desk.

"Grandma Dori has a boyfriend."

She turns toward me, but I've already stuck her, injected the shot, and the needle is out before she laughs.

"Thanks so much." She takes it from my hands. "I didn't feel a thing. Dori doesn't really have a boyfriend, right?"

I laugh. "Not that I know of."

"You need to tell Austin about that trick."

"Nah, now you're on to it. Plus, I have to excel over my brothers in some way."

She smiles and packages everything back up. "You know, Kingston, I wasn't here when everything unfolded, so all my information about you and Stella comes secondhand from Austin. But you're a great guy and I think you would bring a lot to any relationship. You remind me so much of

Austin in the way you put others before yourself. From what I know of Stella on the short occasions I've talked with her, she's sweet and caring and smart, but sometimes young love is just that—young love. Being a principal might make me cynical because I see these couples who vow they've met their soul mates, and then a year later they hate one another. There's always something about the one who got away. Sometimes you idolize them in your head."

I interrupt her. "I just told Stella that I thought we shouldn't see one another—at all. I'm going to ask for a transfer and I'm not going up to the cabin at the same time as her."

"Oh. Well..." Holly sits on the edge of her desk. "And that's what you have to talk to Austin about?"

I clench my jaw, wondering what it will be like to live life after giving up the hope that one day, maybe Stella and I can be together. "I just want to reassure him that I'm not going to go crazy."

She nods and sits in her chair. "He loves you. He worries about you."

"He shouldn't."

"Well, he kind of feels like he's your..."

I don't bother to fill in the blank. We both know what word she was going to say. *Father*.

"I'm solid with my decision."

"That's good."

The school buzzer goes off and I rush to my feet. "Thanks, Holly."

"No. Thank you, Kingston."

I nod and head to the door.

"Hey, my advice?" she says.

"Yeah?"

"I shouldn't have said that. It's just my opinion. But you

need to listen to your heart, okay? Don't take other people's advice. You know where you fit. Listen to your gut. It's you and Stella's decision."

"Thanks. It was good advice," I say and walk out the door.

Heading down the hallway, I see couples lingering by lockers. It makes me remember how I waited for Stella to come out of the Lit classroom after fourth period. We'd walk down the hall to our next class. She was so easy to make laugh. I miss the easiness of us.

"Hey." Austin stops me in the middle of the hallway. "I have to run and take care of something. I'll be right back."

"I already did it."

He pulls me to the side of the hall, so we're not trampled on by a bunch of high school students. "What did you do?"

"I gave Holly her shot."

"Oh. Okay, thanks." I can't really tell if he's actually happy I helped or not. "Let's go to my classroom then."

He shuts the door behind him and pulls out an apple, taking a big bite from it.

"I just want you to know that I broke off my friendship with Stella. It's over. I'm going to transfer to another engine, and although I can't stay away from her completely, I'm going to try my hardest."

He rocks back in his chair, his eyes boring into mine. "And this is what you want?"

I lean against one of the student desks in front of his desk, crossing my arms. "No, but it's what needs to happen. She wants someone who plays it safe. I'm not that guy. So there's no shot of us making it. I'm not even myself when I'm around her. I hit Lou last weekend."

He springs up and his chair creaks. "I told you it was stupid to give Lou your blessing to date Stella."

I hold up my hand. "I'm good. Lou and I are good. I apologized to him. They're not even seeing each other anyway, but it opened my eyes. If she can't take all of me, everything about me, then there's no future for us, regardless of how much I love her."

"Are you sure you're my little brother? You sound way too mature."

"Yes, it's me. I can be level-headed *and* an adrenaline junkie. I just wanted to let you know that I'd made a decision. I know you've been worried about me." I head toward the door.

"Can I ask you one question before you rush out of here?"

I circle back around and wait.

"Did you ever think that you might not love her enough if you're not willing to change at all for her? Relationships are give and take. Yes, she should accept that you have this adrenaline junkie side, but you being unwilling to compromise isn't really a sign of a man in love."

I throw my hands in the air. "What do you want from me? You don't want her here because you're worried she's going to crush me, and I'll fall into a depression all over again. Then you say yeah, be friends with her, and now you're telling me I should change my ways so I can be with her? What the fuck?"

He throws his apple core into the trash can and leans on the edge of his desk. "I think you've misconstrued my advice. I love Stella, and I can see why you fell for her. But you seem to want her on your terms. Put yourself in her shoes before you assume that the reason you two aren't working out is all on her. She moved to New York. You weren't banned from crossing the border. There wasn't a line of National Guardsmen refusing you entry into New York state. You didn't follow because you were hurt. Which is fine. Understandable even."

I feel the adrenaline spike in my system. "I honestly can't believe this. You told me not to go!"

"I told you not to be a smoke jumper too, but you didn't listen to me then." His voice raises to match my level. "You were too scared to go after Stella."

I stare at his whiteboard, all the biology lingo written there for his students. "Have you never been scared?" I ask in a quieter voice.

He laughs. "Are you kidding me? I left a career in baseball to come raise you and the rest of our siblings. I then decided again to forego my dream to live here with Holly. And parenthood? I'm shittin' my pants every damn day. But guess what? I did it."

"What if I give up everything for her and she just runs away again?"

This is the first time I've said out loud what I'm really afraid of. It feels scary as hell and yet somehow freeing.

He raises his eyebrows. "That's why it's scary—because of the unknown. But think about it. Do you honestly think if she didn't feel for you the way you do for her, that your relationship would still be so back and forth? Maybe this so-called break the two of you are taking is good. It'll let each of you take a time-out and see what you really want."

I sit for a second and think it over. When I dropped her off, I was prepared to remove her from my daily life. Now I come here and I'm second-guessing my decision. Great.

"But you have to find out how much you love her. How willing are you to bend? And how important to you is her being in your life? Those are the big questions, and I never really understood them until I was older than you."

"I really wish I wouldn't have come to talk to you," I grumble, now more confused than ever.

He laughs. "Love's a bitch. It can make you a little crazy, that's for damn sure."

The school bell rings. "I should go."

"You know where to find me if you need an AA meeting again."

I raise my eyebrows at him.

"You know... Austin advice, AA get it?" He laughs at his own joke. God, he's already turning into a dad with corny jokes.

"Thanks, and good luck with the second kid thing."

He nods. "Be careful and keep your head on straight."

I smirk, opening the door and leaving my big brother with a mass of teenagers filing toward his door. They have to be harder than dealing with me, right?

TWENTY-THREE

Stella

"Stella?" my mom calls from the front door of the house.

I pry myself up off the snow-covered grass and walk toward the door.

She secures her cardigan around her middle and meets me halfway up the driveway, putting her arm around my shoulders. "What happened?"

"Kingston." I wipe a tear. "He... he... ended it."

"The two of you were dating?"

I shake my head. "No, but he's going to remove himself from my life completely."

Her hand grips my shoulder tighter and she opens the door for me to go in first. The worst part about your mom owning a B & B is that guests get to see and hear everything going on in your life. The young couple sitting in the living room, playing checkers, looks up at me.

"This is my daughter, Stella. I'll just be in my art room if you need me," my mom says.

The couple nods, but the woman's lips are tipped down.

My mom guides me into her art room and sits me down on a stool. "I don't understand. How exactly will Kingston remove you from his life? That doesn't sound like something he would say or do at all."

I swipe a tear off my cheek. "You understand why I can't be with him, right?" I need to know that someone understands me in this moment.

"I'm not sure I do. This can't still be about Owen, is it?"

I shake my head. "No. The way Kingston lives his life."

She's still looking at me as though I'm speaking a different language. "I thought you liked Kingston. The whole reason you told him not to follow you to New York was to get some space from him so he and Owen could rebuild their friendship. I know you dodged returning home because seeing him was too hard, but you must have prepared yourself before you returned."

She says that because she would have done that. Prepared herself. Weighed the pros and cons of returning. Know how she was going to handle it, and nothing would change her mind. For some reason, I wasn't blessed with that gene. My mom said she was sick, so I changed my entire life to be here. As usual, I pushed anything negative or uncomfortable out of mind. Kingston was one of those things.

"He jumps out of planes into fires, Mom."

"Admirable. Someone has to do it."

I stand from the stool and glare at her. "And as if that's not bad enough, in his free time, he does other crazy stuff. Like this past weekend, he took a helicopter, landed it on top a mountain, and skied down unexplored terrain."

"He can fly a helicopter?"

"Mom!" I scream and throw my hands in the air.

She gives me that look. The one that suggests I watch my tone with her.

So I sit back down. "He hired a guide. Him and a few others."

"That's not crazy."

"I skied the greens and blues."

"I don't know what that means." My mom was never a skier.

"The easy hills. The safe ones."

She nods. "So he likes a little more thrill than you do. That's not a reason not to be together."

"He's going to kill himself. That's a reason."

She looks off in the distance as though she's thinking and purses her lips. "Is this about your father?"

"Yes. No... I don't know."

"You're afraid you're going to love him and lose him?" She laughs.

I whip my head in her direction. "What's so funny about this?"

She covers her mouth, trying not to laugh again. I pick up a nearby dry paintbrush, running the bristles over my thumb.

"Because I can't believe it took me this long to get it," she says.

"Get what?"

She holds up her hand for me to stop talking. "I've always told you that you can't stop your feelings for someone. This entire time you've been back, you've pushed Kingston away because he's a smoke jumper and likes to do some heart-pounding things?"

"That's what I just said." I'm irritated that she's laughing. Does she not see this as a legit fear?

"So by your logic, I should've never loved your father. Never married him or had you."

"That's different. Dad wasn't jumping out of planes and parachuting down mountains. He didn't want to trek the Alaskan terrain for seven days through ice-covered mountains, raging rapids, and over glaciers."

She smiles and pats my knee. "When you were little, I thought I was so lucky because you were so easy. You liked a clean room. You liked your toys organized in specific bins. Even all your stuffed animals were lined up according to height." She laughs again. "I used to tell your dad that you were way more him than me." She looks around her messy art studio as if to prove her point. The way all the different sizes of paintbrushes are in one bin always annoyed me. Her paints aren't arranged according to color. They're just huddled together in one big group. "Your father agreed. I'm not laughing at you, sweetheart. I'm laughing because if your father was alive, he would've already seen what I didn't. Kingston is a risk and you don't take risks."

"I've never thought of Kingston as a risk. I know how he feels about me. He's never been shy about communicating that, at least after Owen and I started dating."

She huffs. "That boy has always worn his heart on the outside for all to see. It's what I always found sweet about him. But he's a risk to you. You value control and you can't control a man like that. It's a risk to let yourself love someone fully because what if you lose them? A risk because he thrives in areas that are outside of your comfort zone."

I pick up another paintbrush and run it along my palm. My med school peers used to get a kick out of all my highlighting and notecards, the color-coding process I used to help me organize my thoughts, how I had to study my notes in a particular order. Even for a med student, I was neurotic.

"If someone would've told me that your dad was going to die so young, do you think I would've said 'oh, forget him'? Forget the brilliant daughter we'd make?" She pats my knee. "Because that's what you're doing. There's no way of knowing what will ever happen. I can see how Kingston's way of living is scary to someone who lost her father much too young. I always hated that you bore that loss. But he might land on both feet time and time again." She raises her hands. "I'm just your mom, but do you think that it's not the big stuff Kingston does, but more how he lives his life with the small decisions? That he won't fit in that perfect box you've designated for your husband?"

"What? No." I shake my head, but she tilts hers with a "think about it" expression.

"You two will face a lot of challenges. Not just because you value control and he likes a little bit of chaos, but because you'd be an interracial couple."

I give her a 'duh' look. "I know, Mom."

"I know you know, Stella, but it's going to mean that you both need to be stronger than most if you're in it for the long haul. Not everyone will be as accepting of your relationship as you want them to be."

I shake my head at her. "I can deal with all that."

"Then it's the fact that a man like Kingston isn't going to let you sit on the sidelines and let life pass you by. He's going to push you to live life to its fullest. I think that's what you're most afraid of. But another thing I know about you is that you love a challenge. Kingston is the first challenge I've ever seen you run away from." My mom stands, patting my knee one more time. "Think it over, and remember, you can respect Kingston's wishes, but you don't have to agree with them. You can make an argument back." She smiles and leaves the room.

Yeah, she's still the smartest woman I've ever met. I see why my dad snatched her off the market.

My phone dings in my pocket.

Allie: *Okay, I'm in downtown Lake Starlight. Where do I find Grandma Dori?*

You've got to be kidding me.

Me: *Why are you in Lake Starlight?*

Allie: *Last night Lou was razzing me about how great she is, and I want to meet her so I figured I could spot her downtown. I went to Bailey Timber but they wouldn't let me in the offices.*

She's certifiably crazy.

Me: *I'll meet you at Lard Have Mercy. It's a diner at Main and Chestnut. I need your help with something.*

Allie: *Okay but if I help you, you help me, right?*

I laugh, my thumbs poised over the screen.

Me: *Sure, you help me and I'll introduce you to Grandma Dori.*

Allie: *I'll grab a booth!*

I pocket my phone and walk out of my mom's studio. She's busy making tea and putting cookies out for the guests.

"I'll be back. Love you." I kiss her cheek.

"What have you decided?" she asks.

"I'm gonna go get my man."

She puts her arm around me and kisses my temple. "That's my girl. I know it's hard, but your dad once took a chance on a head-in-the-clouds art student who messed up his perfectly precise existence."

I laugh. "And I bet he never had any regrets." I squeeze her hand and walk out of the house, determined to get my man.

ALLIE IS ALREADY in a booth with a huge smile on her face, talking to Karen, who works at the diner. I walk in and Allie waves and points, explaining who I am to Karen.

Karen smiles and opens her arms. "Stella. How are you?"

I nod. "I'm good. Love the pin."

She looks down at the circle photo of her grandson Easton, Holly and Austin's son. "I want to retire and watch him, but I don't want to be his caregiver because then I can't spoil him." She laughs. "You know Holly, everything has to be done a certain way." She pulls out her pad. "Your friend Allie wants a cheeseburger, fries, and a chocolate shake. What are you up for?"

"And a cookie," Allie says, raising her finger.

"I'll just have fries and a Coke."

"Great. I'll be right back."

Karen leaves, and Allie looks out the window toward the gazebo. "It's so cute. I just love it here."

She's so smiley and happy. I'm not sure I ever looked at Lake Starlight like that, but then again, I arrived a year after my dad died. And once I left after college, I had a love-hate relationship with the town because Kingston was here.

"Can we talk?" I ask.

"Of course." She turns back to me, but then her eyes widen, and she leans closer to me over the table. "Oh my God. Did you call her? She's here."

I glance over my shoulder, and sure enough, Grandma Dori is talking to Karen at the end of the counter. Both of them glance my way. I slide down into my booth. I love Grandma Dori, and I was going to introduce Allie, but I want it to be after I fix things with Kingston.

"Stella!"

"She just called you by name." Allie's mouth hangs open.

"Yes, she knows my name. I broke her grandson's heart." I slide farther down.

Grandma Dori steps up to the edge of our table. "Stella, why are you slouching? You know that's terrible for your posture."

I sit up straight. "Hi, Dori," I say in my sweet voice. The one I use when I introduce myself to patients. Not fake, but sweeter than I use with anyone in my personal life.

"I just left Sedona. She told me you were there earlier. Thanks for looking out for her."

Allie rests her chin in her palm, staring up at Grandma Dori. Dori catches her look and scrunches her gray eyebrows at me, wanting to know who this girl is.

"Oh, Dori, this is my friend, Allie."

Dori nods. "Nice to meet you."

"You're the cutest thing. Can I shrink you down and put you in my purse?" Allie says, and Dori's gaze whips to me again as I purse my lips. "Was that too much? I'm sorry. I'm just so excited to meet you."

"Allie likes to read Buzz Wheel," I explain.

Dori nods slowly and looks over to Allie with a calculating look. "That thing can't be trusted." She slides in next to me. "Now, Sedona says things were tense with you and Kingston and that the two of you went on a walk and neither of you came back." She pats my hand.

"Um..."

"Oh, and Stella just asked me to help her with something." Allie leans forward as if she's Grandma Dori's sidekick.

Remind me to "thank" Allie later. There's no point in trying to get out of explaining what's happening with Kingston now. Dori does not take no for an answer.

"Kingston wants to remove me from his life, even as a friend. He's sick of the back and forth, all the games," I say.

"Games?" Dori screeches.

"He punched Lou last weekend," Allie says.

I slide my finger across my throat.

"He what?" Dori asks.

Allie ignores me—because apparently there isn't a lot of reasoning when it comes to her infatuation with Grandma Dori. She spills everything that happened last weekend, including the part about Samantha and Tank having sex nonstop.

Dori turns to me as though she needs me to verbally vouch for Allie's story. I bite my lip and nod.

"And you. Is this what you want?" Dori asks.

I shake my head, ignoring Allie's wide eyes once more. I haven't had the chance to tell her anything yet.

"Well then, tough nuts. Kingston isn't just going to throw in the towel after all this time." She places her hand over mine and squeezes. "Let's figure out how to get you two together."

Allie wiggles in her seat with excitement.

For the next hour, we go through all the possible scenarios, but there's only one I like. Still, my heart clenches with the thought that it might not be enough.

TWENTY-FOUR

Kingston

I drive up to the cabin, alone. It's just me and Lou all weekend. We're the only ones off, according to the spreadsheet Tank made up for all of us. Stella's not coming until Wednesday and Thursday with Allie and Stump. Now that we're all here at different times, some people are bringing others up with them. I might have decided to steer clear of Stella, but every time I think about Stella bringing some guy up here, it's like someone throat-punched me.

Pulling into the driveway, I park in the best spot since I'm here first. Lou had a last-minute errand to run and he was heading to his parents' afterward, so we planned to drive separately. I didn't mind the quiet on the way up. Austin's advice has been on repeat in my head and I'm slowly understanding what he said.

I grab my bag and the case of the beer I brought out of the bed of my truck then walk up the stairs to the cabin. After setting the beer on the porch, I insert my key. My whole plan this weekend is to talk to Tim about the speed riding and coordinate a time with him. We could practice a few times before heading all the way up. In four weeks, the schedule has me, Tank, and Samantha up here. My plan is to leave right after speed riding, so they can break shit in the house with their sexcapades without me having to listen—or worse, witness.

The door opens and I bend down to pick up the case of beer. It almost slips out of my hands when I see a line of rose petals and small battery-operated candles leading to the main living area. I place all my shit down in the foyer. Did I screw up the schedule? Am I messing up someone else's romantic time?

On the hallway door hangs a suit with a note pinned to it.

CHANGE INTO ME.

I TIPTOE around the petals and peek around the corner. Stella's standing in the family room, her teeth biting her bottom lip. She's staring at the floor, her chest rising and falling. This better be for me—otherwise I'll be spending the night in a jail cell.

I go back and take the suit off the door handle, relieved to see it's my own suit from home. Shredding my clothes in record time and putting on my suit, relief washes over me. All the self-talk from last week about getting on with my life fades into background noise. She's finally seen the light, seen what we can be, how good we can be.

My heart rate increases, and my palms are sweaty. After all these years, our time has finally come. I cross the petal path and emerge from the foyer. Stella glances up and straightens her back. She's wearing a light pink dress that falls to her ankles and poofs out at her waist a bit. The top dips all the way down to her belly button, revealing a sliver of her tantalizing dark skin.

My mouth waters the closer I get, hoping I'm the lucky bastard who gets to unzip her out of it tonight.

"Hey," I say like the tool I am.

"Hi."

We stand toe-to-toe, each of us soaking the other in for a moment.

"Kingston Bailey, will you go to homecoming with me?"

She's got to be shittin' me. I'd go to the moon with her.

"Why?"

She takes my hand in both of hers. "I want a redo. I want to start over. I want *you* to take me to homecoming."

"Why?" Damn it, I probably sound like I have a stutter. *Just say yes, dumbass.*

"Because I love you."

I inhale a deep breath and let it out slowly. It's not the first time she's said the words, but it's the first time she's said them like *that*. How long have I waited to hear those words from her mouth?

The urge to take her mouth with mine is strong. Take her in my arms and never let her go. But then my heart weighs in. Is this another moment in time that's going to leave us in limbo after?

"Stella," I say, sighing.

"I know what you said last weekend and I get it, but I've done a lot of thinking and some self-discovery. I'm not going to lie. You scare me. The way I feel for you scares me the most. I don't want to be broken like I was when my dad died."

With a frown, I run a hand through my hair then open my mouth to respond.

"No." She puts her finger to my lips. "I accept it. All of it. Because I'm done denying myself you. You are worth the risk."

My hand gently wraps around her wrist and I lower it to our sides, not letting go. "Are you sure this is what you want?"

She nods. "I just want you. I've loved you since... forever."

"And when I say I want to parachute down a mountain?"

"I'll be biting my nails at the end and loving you pretty hard when you return to me. But..." She takes my head in her hands. "You better come back to me."

I cover her hands with mine. "I'll always come back to you. I always have."

She rushes into me and I wrap my arms around her waist, pulling her flush against me. Damn, I never dreamt it would feel this good.

My heart soars and I grip harder. My hands run along the smooth skin of her bare back. Resting them on the back of her head, I draw back. "I think we need to seal this promise with a kiss?"

"Me too," she says hesitantly.

My hands cradle her cheeks, our faces growing closer. The tip of my nose runs along hers, and we both inhale a breath. My body buzzes with nerves I've never felt except around Stella. How do I make sure a kiss that we've both dreamed about this long will be worth it?

"King," she whispers.

"Uh-huh." My eyes are closed and my nose slides down her cheekbone. My lips rest by her earlobe as she sighs.

"Are you nervous?"

I nod, never letting go of her head. "So fucking nervous."

She smells like she always does, but it's much more potent when I'm this close to her.

"You're so beautiful." I hook my finger under the strap of her dress resting on her shoulder, delaying the kiss.

"Thank you," she says softly.

My lips drag down her jawline until they hover over her lips. "I'm going to kiss you now."

She giggles. "Okay."

"This is what you want, right?" I clarify once more.

"King?"

"Yeah."

"Kiss me."

I bend my head until my lips land on her full, soft ones, the lightness of our touch barely registering as a kiss. My heart pounds and I press my lips to hers again, this time not holding back, waiting for her to get used to me. Our mouths collide and it's like fireworks are shooting off around us. The chemistry between us is hot and all-encompassing. My tongue slides along the seam of her lips, invading her mouth, meeting her tongue. Shivers rush up my limbs and I take charge of the kiss, setting the pace, unable to get deep enough.

After a couple minutes, she pulls back and touches her lips. My heart drops like a boulder in the deep of the ocean. She regrets it. She didn't feel what I did. Fuck. I never thought once we were actually together, she wouldn't feel our connection.

"I know I asked you to homecoming and I have all this music loaded on my phone so we can dance and set the mood, but I'm not sure I can wait. Want to strip out of these clothes, get into our bathing suits, and slide into the hot tub?"

Yeah, she's perfect for me.

"Why bother with the bathing suits?" I shrug off my jacket and kick off my shoes, leaning forward to kiss her one more time. Now that my lips have been on hers, I'm not sure I'll ever be able to not kiss her when we're this close.

"Can we slow it down?" she asks quietly.

My hands stop. Shit. *You're gonna blow this, Bailey.* I step closer, her breasts pushing against my chest. "Sorry. We can go as slow as you want."

Her forehead falls to my chest and her hands rest on my waist. "I just need to breathe for a moment. I was worried... I was scared you wouldn't..."

I run my finger under her chin and raise her head to look at me. "Let's start with a clean slate. We're just two people who came up to a cabin and want to get in the hot tub."

She giggles and nods. "Okay. I'm going to go change."

I step to the side for her to get by, and she walks through the rose petals. "Stella?"

She turns to face me at the top of the stairs.

"You'll wear that dress for me again sometime when I can strip it off you?"

She smiles and nods. "Promise."

I watch her disappear down the stairs before I turn off all the candles and grab my bag, not bothering to go to my room. I change in the foyer—then realize I need to message Lou before he gets here.

Grabbing my phone from the pocket of my discarded jeans, I pull up Lou's contact.

Me: *Hey man, sorry to do this but do you mind not coming to the cabin tonight?*

Lou: *What the fuck? Why not?*

Shit, I know he's paid his share and it's an asshole thing to ask of him, but it'll be all kinds of awkward if the three of us are here. I've waited so long to have this with Stella—I want tonight to be perfect.

Me: *Stella's here and things are developing. I'll totally pay you the money back for this weekend. I'll even take your shifts or whatever.*

Lou: *You're a dumb ass.*

Lou: *I wasn't coming up anyway. It was all arranged.*

Lou: *Stella's one step ahead of you.*

Lou: *You got played. :P*

I stare at the phone. She's already made sure we're up here all alone. Just as I'm about to message Lou back, she comes up the stairs in a plush white terrycloth robe, her locs piled up on top of her head in a bun.

"If you're naked under there, I might just lose my willpower."

She laughs and slides down one side for me to see the white strap of a bathing suit. Well, a guy can dream.

I break the distance, take her hand, and plant a quick kiss on her lips. I guide her to the sliding door.

"It seems like a waste." She looks down at the unlit candles.

"No. It was romantic. I swooned."

She playfully hits me on the back with her other hand and I chuckle, opening the patio door, allowing her to go out first. The water is bubbling, steam rising into the cold air, and the color-tinted lightbulbs change color underneath the water.

I step in first, pretending not to be freezing my ass off. The warm water a welcome relief to my chilled skin. I lean back in one of the curved seats and her hands shake as they reach for the tie of the robe.

"Stella?" I ask, inching across the water. "Are you nervous?"

"It's just. You've never seen me and..."

I grab one of the ties and pull her forward. "I promise you, I'm going to love whatever is underneath this." I tug on the tie.

"What if I have three boobs?" She raises her eyebrows.

"Do you honestly think I would have a problem if you had three boobs? Talk about motor boating."

She smiles but doesn't laugh. I slide my hand under her robe, feeling the silkiness of her swimsuit, and rest it on her hip.

"Relax. It's me." She says nothing about my hand, so I chance pulling the tie of her robe again.

She stares at me as the robe slides open. I'm breathless at the sight of her white one-piece swimsuit that shows off her amazing curves and contrasts beautifully with her ebony skin. Her nipples poke through the fabric, teasing me.

She slides the robe off her shoulders and steps up onto the stairs to get in. "It's freezing."

"Get in here with me."

As soon as she's in the water, I wrap my arms around her, and our lips lock in a kiss that would've warmed me up without hot water around us. My hands don't stray too far, not wanting to push her past her limits. When I lean back, she straddles my lap and I glance down to see her amazing tits right there for the taking. I desperately want to lean in and run my tongue along her cleavage.

"God, Stella, I'm so fucking hard." My voice sounds as rough as sandpaper.

"I can tell." She grinds against me.

Stella's never been one to not communicate when she doesn't want something, so I take my chances. My hands fall to her ass, pulling her closer. She moans and wraps her arms around my head, her lips finding mine.

Oh, tonight is going to be a good night. The best night ever, in fact.

TWENTY-FIVE

Stella

Never have I felt this good. I don't have a ton of sexual experience, but enough to know this is different. This is earth-shattering, good old-fashioned making out. Kingston's lips never stray too far from mine. His tongue explores my mouth, his hands run along every surface of my body.

He was so tentative at first that I wondered how we'd get this started. There's been so much anticipation. So many years of starving my body of his. I can hardly believe we're here, living out the fantasies we've both imagined alone in our beds late at night.

"Jesus, you're so soft and delicious." He slides down one strap of my bathing suit, kissing my exposed flesh, then positioning it back in place.

His hands have yet to venture to my breasts or between my legs. The ache between my thighs grows, wanting and needing him to quench it. My hips roll along his hard length, spurring my need for an orgasm.

I can't get close enough. It's like I'm trying to burrow myself into his flesh. I'd be embarrassed if it didn't feel so damn good or he wasn't doing the same. Tender touches, noses and cheeks running the lengths of our faces, wet tongues, and lips caressing skin.

I want to pull down his board shorts and sink down on him. Tear off my swimsuit so his hands are on my tits as I ride him without any worries. But my brain won't turn off.

That annoying seed of doubt is there. Am I fulfilling what he dreamed it'd be all these years? Does he like what he sees? What he feels?

Then I sit back, and our eyes catch under the moonlight. The colored lights of the hot tub add to the effect on his gorgeous face. And it's there, his eyes so full of want and lust. That seed of doubt dies.

I crash my lips to his and he meets me full force, his strong hands splayed across my back as if he's afraid I'll try to pull away. He's crazy. I'm going to become a stalker. Kingston Bailey's stalker. How did I ever run away from this man when it feels so right for us to be here together?

"Kingston," I say, holding his head to my collarbone as he casts a line of open-mouth kisses across my flesh.

"Uh-huh," he mumbles.

"Touch me."

He draws back and my skin aches for him to treat it like the treasure he has been. "I don't want to rush you."

"I'm not a virgin."

He chuckles. "I know, but I guess a small part of me wants to savor you. I've waited so long." He runs his knuckles over my breast. My greedy pebbled nipple demands more of his attention. "I want to know exactly what gets you hot and aching. But if you want me to grab your tits..." His hand slides out from the water and cups my breast over my swimsuit, his thumb rolling over my nipple. "I have no complaints. I'm happy to oblige."

I laugh, but his other hand cups my other breast and my back arches on its own accord as a strangled moan falls from my lips. He's good with his hands all right.

"Just so you know, you won't be wearing this swimsuit when anyone else is here. This is a Kingston special."

I straighten my back and cock an eyebrow. "Are you already telling me what to do?"

"Don't worry, I'll replace it with a new one. You're not opposed to skirt swimsuits, are you?"

I shake my head, but he swallows my laughter with a kiss.

As though the talking took too much time away, we devour one another again. His lips glide along my jaw, neck, and collarbone. His heavy breaths tickle my ear. My grinding on his length speeds up, and his finger hooks the strap of my swimsuit, tugging it down so my breast pops out. He arches me farther back as he takes my breast into his wet mouth. His tongue swirls around my nipple, and when he blows out a steady stream of air, my nipple could cut glass.

"Let's get out of here," I whisper. The needy tension is too much to bear.

His mouth pops off my breast and he looks me in the eye. "Stay in my bed tonight?"

He poses it like a question, and it's easy to see he's still unsure about where this new us will lead.

"Yes," I answer.

Again he pulls my chest against his, but now it's my bare breasts to his chest and the heat forming between them is deliciously hot and the ache between my thighs grows to epic proportions. His lips, his mouth, his hands, his hard length are perfection and I'm not sure I'll ever not crave their attention now that I know how they feel.

I slide off his lap because I want to see him, feel the weight of him over me, nestle his length between my thighs as he thrusts into me. I want skin-to-skin contact, and the ability to explore without the constriction of water and the cold air above.

I only make it halfway across the hot tub when he comes up behind me and pins me to the side. His big, rough hands cover my breasts, squeezing and pinching and pushing them together. "Tell me I get to have you tonight?"

My hands reach around and mold to his ass, pushing him into my own. His hard dick pokes out of his board shorts and settles between my ass cheeks. "I'm not a tease."

"Yeah, but I won't be upset if you wanna take it slow. I just have to know now." His tongue licks up the side of my neck and I shiver.

I swivel around and his arms lay over the side of the hot tub. My body floats to the surface, wrapping my legs around his waist. "I'm yours tonight and always."

"Music to my fucking ears." He kisses me again. This time there's no frantic need. It's long and lingering and sublime.

Turning quickly, I climb out. "Holy shit, it's freezing." I grab my robe and bolt into the house.

Kingston's wet footsteps follow right behind me. He reaches for me, but I run toward the stairs, my feet sliding on the hardwood. Right at the turn, he's there with me, and I giggle, not sure why I'm playing a game of cat and mouse with him. He almost has me until three stairs from the bottom. One foot flies out from under me and my ass hits each stair with a thump until I land on the bottom.

"Oh shit, are you okay?" Kingston rushes down the rest

of the stairs while I get back on my feet. He takes me in his arms and rests his hand on my ass. "Want me to make it all better?"

I laugh and shove him. "If you had put daddy in that sentence, you would've doused my imminent orgasm with a firehose." I rub my ass because it hurts.

He swoops me up bride style and walks me to his room. "Yeah, no worries, that isn't a turn-on for me."

"Good. We have one thing in common."

"But I do have a firehose I want to show you."

I can't help but laugh. "Oh my God, that's so cheesy."

"Save calling me God for a little bit, okay?"

I swat him in the chest, and he lowers me so my feet are on the floor. His hungry gaze runs down my body, causing heat to rush through my veins. "You're so beautiful, Stella."

"Thank you."

He steps closer, his finger sliding under the hem of my swimsuit by my ass. "Can I take this off?"

I nod and bite my lip.

His thumb reaches up and he frees my lip from being pinned down by my teeth. "There's no need to be nervous. This goes as long or as short as you want. If you don't like something I do, you tell me. Got it?"

I nod and smile instead of biting my lip.

He pulls down the strap of my swimsuit and drags it down my arm until I slide my arm out from under it. Doing the same on the other side, he leaves me topless, but he doesn't stop there, tugging the wet fabric off my body until I'm stepping out of it and his face is in front of me at waist level.

His finger runs through my folds and I moan. When he stands to his full height, his fingers continue to play with my clit, his free hand splayed on the back of my head to kiss me.

He applies more pressure between my legs, and if he isn't careful, I'm going to come.

I strip my lips off his, wanting to see him. Back stepping to the edge of the bed, I let my ass fall down and I hook my fingers into the sides of his board shorts. His hand caresses my cheek, watching for my reaction as I pull the shorts down over his hard length.

He steps out of his wet suit and it remains a heap on the floor. I run my palm over his length, my thumb over the tip. His head falls back, but his hand never stops cradling my cheek, his thumb running over my lip. Wrapping my hand around his thickness, I pump, and he groans.

"Stella, I really need to be inside you." His voice holds a quality I've never heard before.

I slide up on the bed and he crawls toward me, stopping between my legs. He nudges my legs apart with his shoulders and his mouth hovers over me. His finger runs through my folds and he teases me with his finger at my opening.

"I thought you had to be inside me?" I say in a breathy voice.

He laughs and his eyes stay on me while his tongue licks me up the center. "I have to get you ready."

"I'm ready," I say.

He pushes one finger inside me, then another before sliding them out and into his mouth. He sucks them for a moment then slowly pulls them out.

"Yep, I'd say you're ready." Pushing up on his forearms, he crawls the rest of the way up. His weight over me feels delicious. "Shit, my condoms are upstairs in my wallet. I'll be right back." He shifts to get off me.

"King?"

"Yeah?"

"Are you clean? Like, have you been tested?"

He tilts his head.

"I have an IUD and I'm clean. I haven't been with anyone for…"

He smiles, waiting for the answer.

"Let's just say I'm clean."

He chuckles. "I am too. Just got tested last month." He crawls back on top of me, situating himself between my thighs. "And I haven't been with anyone for a while either."

I smile and trust that he isn't just saying that to appease me.

"Now that that's decided." He kisses me and the tip of his dick pierces my opening, teasing me, driving me crazy.

Inch by inch, he slowly enters me. Once he's fully inside, I relish the moment of us being connected.

"You good?" he asks.

I nod, and he cradles my head between his forearms on the bed. He starts with small circles, kissing me once then burying his head in the crook of my neck.

"Damn, you feel amazing," he whispers, and goose bumps spread where his breath hits my neck.

"So do you." My fingers dig into his shoulder blades and my head sinks into his pillow as he thrusts into me.

Then he's kissing my lips, my jaw, my ear, my cheek, whispering small tokens of how much he loves me, how beautiful I am. My thighs clench harder, my legs running up his thighs, my heels resting on his calves. Now I understand the difference between making love and just having sex. The tenderness that comes when you love someone is something special. Wanting the moment to never end, even when your orgasm hangs by a thread as thin as a spider's web. This is an expression of love. It's not about the end result. It's about what you're promising that person with your body.

"I'll never hurt you," Kingston says as though he can read my thoughts. "I promise." He rises up and stares at me, locking my gaze with his. "Tell me this isn't a dream."

I put my hands on his face and don't look away. "It's not a dream. I love you with every piece of me."

He kisses me and increases his speed. Our kisses become a frantic mess of lips, tongue, and teeth. My impending orgasm can't be held back any longer.

"Oh God, harder," I pant.

I clench in an effort to delay the gratification, but he doesn't relent, and my body tightens before I skyrocket into the air, free-falling back down to Earth.

Kingston doesn't stop, drilling in and out of me, his lips still on any of my skin he can reach. "Jesus, I don't wanna come."

But he pumps into me, pausing for a second, then pumps again. My name falls from his lips and he cranes his head back as he comes. Then he leans in to kiss me. His kiss slows, his tongue lazy compared to minutes before. I decide I love the post-orgasm look in his hooded eyes.

"I'll be right back," he says.

After we clean up, I grab the satin pillow I brought with me. When I return to the room, Kingston pulls the covers down. I slide in under them, my fingers playing with the small patch of hair on his chest. There's no denying it any longer—this is where I've always belonged, risky or not.

TWENTY-SIX

Kingston

My eyes open and I jolt up from the bed. My head flops to the right and I breathe easy. She's here. Last night wasn't a dream.

I snicker, admiring her sprawled out on her stomach, both arms under her pillow. It's ridiculous how happy I am that suddenly the years of waiting have proved worth it. I have her with me—and it's only been one night.

I run my finger down her spine and she murmurs something, swatting at me and rolling to her side. I chuckle, spooning her from behind, my hand sliding between her breasts. She sighs and rocks back.

"I'm going to make you breakfast," I whisper.

She hooks her leg back over mine and locks me to her. "Not yet. And I'm not a breakfast person anyway."

"You need your energy if we're going to keep last night as the gold standard of our relationship."

Twice in bed. Once on the kitchen counter when we thought we were hungry but had a hard time keeping our hands to ourselves. Deciding on a shower, I took her against the shower wall. Talk about easy cleanup. In all my years of being sexually active, I've never had shower sex. Although I don't find it as great as having an entire bed to roll around in, Stella seemed impressed that I could hold her up the entire time, which earned me a blow job two hours later when she woke me.

My cock slides between her ass cheeks, happy to stay there all day. I kiss her shoulder, my fingers running down the valley of her breasts, inching closer to between her legs. "Are you sore?"

She moans. "Not enough that I'm going to stop you."

I smile against her dark skin, my hand sliding her hair out of the way, and cast kisses to the back of her neck. She sighs like she did last night when I used an ice cube on her in the kitchen. My fingers circle her clit slowly, lazily, leisurely, hoping to drive her crazy. I've tested how she likes to be played with and slower seems to be better. When I concentrate on her clit, she usually comes quickly, coating my fingers.

She rocks back into me and I straighten out my cock so it slides between her legs, the slick wetness there. I lower my body, my lips casting small kisses down her back, ready to flip her so I can nestle between her legs, but she turns around, pinning me to my back and straddling me.

"Have I mentioned I'm kind of a control freak?" She smirks, inching up and positioning my cock so she can sink down on me. She places my hand between her legs. "Feel free to continue though."

My thumb circles her clit and she leans back, her hands on my kneecaps with her tits on full display, making my mouth salivate.

"I like this side of you."

She pumps up and down on me, unapologetically stealing her pleasure. I'm not complaining—the visual alone has me thinking of fire safety and my routine when I enter a burning building, so I don't come before she gets off. Her tits are so tempting, bouncing and jostling above me, the nipples peaked. I grab one, pinching her nipple between my finger and thumb.

She bolts up and smiles. "Do it again." I do and she groans, rocking her hips. "I'm so close, don't stop with my clit."

I increase the speed just a little and her walls constrict around my dick. I don't lighten up and my hand falls from her breast to her hip, gripping it to help her get high up on my cock so she can feel my tip pound into her sweet spot.

She falls forward, her eyes hooded with lust as her hands splay on my chest, pumping up and down, grinding her clit on my pelvic bone. I watch her come and it's the most erotic thing I've ever witnessed. Porn has nothing on Stella Harrison.

I suck her nipple into my wet mouth, and she takes my head, pushing it into her. Tensing, she clenches my cock so hard from the inside that I almost come right there. She falls on me and I roll us so she can lie on her side. Holding her leg up, I slide back into her from behind, pounding in and out of her.

"I'm never gonna have enough of you," she says, panting.

"Good, because you're stuck with me forever," I say, losing control and coming inside her. My dick softens a bit and I roll onto my back, catching my breath. "Man, I think you used and abused me there."

She giggles, getting up to go to the bathroom. "Men

might wake up with morning wood, but that doesn't mean women don't wake up aroused too."

"I'm not complaining. Use me any time you want."

I hear her laughing down the hall on the way to the bathroom. For the first time in the light of day, I look around at our clothes strewn all over the place, the sheets more off the bed than on. What a perfect night last night was.

Sliding out of the bed, I grab my sweatpants and head to the bathroom with her. After cleaning myself off, I put my sweatpants back on, kissing her cheek as she brushes her teeth. "Come up for breakfast."

"Just coffee please."

I shake my head and go upstairs, spotting the beer I left by the front door. I completely forgot about it, so I grab the case and put it in the fridge. Shit, I never got food. Lou said he'd bring some, so I expect to find an empty fridge, but when I open it, it's got all the essentials. There are small notes on things. "You better be naked when preparing these tomorrow morning" is written on a Post-it note on the eggs.

I pull off the note on the whipped cream and read, "Could be used for food or body—your choice."

I find another blue Post-it note on the chocolate syrup. "There's ice cream in the freezer, but I get it if you'd rather lick it off Kingston."

I shake my head, tearing all of Allie's little notes off the items. Especially the one that suggests we'd like to take milk and chocolate sauce and make chocolate milk with our mouths. She's such an oddball.

Stella walks up wearing her robe. I have to say, I half expected her to be dressed for the day. Stella isn't one for lazy days. I didn't know if she'd be cool with us spending the day lounging around in bed.

My hands grip her hips and I hoist her up on the

counter, parting her legs and letting my fingers inch up her bare thigh enough to check if she's wearing panties. But there's nothing but her neatly trimmed hair. "Hmm... I like this."

She wiggles on the countertop. "I thought you might." She pulls one side of her robe to the side to show off her tit. Damn, I could take her again right now.

"You better watch out or we might never leave here."

She captures my lips, sliding her tongue into my mouth. It feels so fucking good to be able to be with her in this way, and I take the opportunity to deepen the kiss until I leave her breathless.

She pulls back and picks up the Post-it notes off the counter. "What are these?"

"Allie's idea of a joke."

She reads them, laughing at each one more than the last. "She's been a blessing for me since I returned." She crosses her legs but positions the robe so she's not flashing me. There's the Stella I know and love.

"You two did get close rather quickly." I dump the coffee grinds into the filter, fill the machine with water, and start it. "I've always liked her."

"Yeah, what do you think about her and Lou?"

Truth is, I had every intention of talking to Lou about Allie this weekend before I got ambushed with my glorious surprise. "I think they'd be good together, but I worry about Lou hurting Allie."

Her eyebrows scrunch. "Why? Lou was a great guy when I..."

"Go ahead, I'm not going to get mad." I smile so she knows it's okay. I'm secure now in the fact that I'm the one she wants. I always thought she felt that way, which was why it was so frustrating when she wouldn't let us be together.

"Well, he respected me when I told him about my past with you. He didn't push anything."

"He did still try to date you," I remind her.

She hems and haws but eventually nods. "But I think he knew deep down it would never work. He knew I was hung up on you."

"Is that so?" I abandon the eggs and pancake mix to put my hands on her again. How will I ever get shit done if I can't stop touching her? "Want to play a question and answer game?" I kiss the tip of her nose.

"Depends what kind of questions they are. I don't want to talk about the past."

I shake my head. "Neither do I, but there's a lot I don't know about grown Stella. The fact that I had to find out through Lou that you don't like breakfast pissed me off."

She laughs, her head falling back. "The only reason he knows that is because he asked me for a breakfast date, and I told him I don't eat it."

"Well, that makes me want to maul you. I feared it was something else."

"I never slept with him," she says, her voice serious. "I never slept with Owen either."

My eyes widen and I tilt my head. She and Owen dated for a while and he always made it sound like they did. "You didn't?"

She shakes her head. "I went to college a virgin."

"Oh."

She bites her bottom lip.

"Well damn, I'm not sure you should've told me that." I squeeze her hips.

"Why?"

"Because I feel like a fucking X-Man or a superhero who just got the opportunity so many before haven't." Fuck, that came out wrong. "I mean—"

"Was this a competition to see who could win me?" Her voice is low and unsure. She uncrosses her legs, letting them drop down over the edge of the counter as if she's ready to bolt.

"No... yes. It was, but I didn't want a damn trophy. You're not the trophy." I put my arms around her and bring her to the edge of the counter. Thankfully, she lets me. "You're like the treasure chest at the end of a long, torturous journey. The one thing I wanted for so long and now I finally have it."

"Maybe you'll get sick of me."

I put my finger under her chin and raise her face to meet my eyes. "Never. If anything, I worry I'm going to suffocate you."

"Well, great. We're not even together a day and we both have concerns." I chuckle and lean in to place a chaste kiss on her lips. "I'll prove to you that you're not just some prize to win. To me, you're like that stuffed animal kids don't ever part with. The one they keep forever even after it's been sewn back together a million times and one eye is missing."

I lean forward to kiss her, but she puts her hand in front of my face. "Did you just compare me to a ratty old stuffed animal?"

"In a good way though." I chuckle.

"Not really."

I shrug. "You see what I was getting at."

"No." She shakes her head and is silent for a beat. "Kingston, have you considered what it might mean that we're an interracial couple?"

I run my thumb across her cheek and frown. "I don't care if some people have a problem with it."

"Some people might have enough of a problem with it to be vocal about it. Maybe not in Lake Starlight where everyone knows us, but certainly elsewhere. Are you ready for that?"

"I'm ready for anything as long as it means I'm with you."

She places her hand on my chest. "I'm serious. It won't be easy for us."

I hold her gaze. "I know. But we will be stronger for it. We can work through anything that comes our way. All we have to do is be honest with one another and push back against the haters."

"You sure you're up for it?" she asks.

"Stella, I told you. I'm in. One hundred percent." Smiling, I pull open the tie of her robe, exposing her. "I think I have to cherish your body to prove my point."

"Do you now?" She doesn't attempt to cover up.

My thumb slides down her center and I'm about to feast on her breasts when we hear the front door open.

"Whoa, babe, wait until you see this."

Denver. I told him and Cleo they could come up for a night. Shit. I completely forgot.

My forehead falls to her flat stomach, but she bolts up, pushing me to the other side of the kitchen. My back hits a knob and I go down to the floor in a heap while she ties her robe around herself and jumps down from the counter.

"I think we're interrupting something," Cleo says.

"Why?" Denver asks.

"Oh, I don't know, but unless you did these rose petals and candles for me, this is for someone else."

"Yeah, I did it and the fuckers didn't turn the candles on. Here, let me pick you up."

I shake my head at Denver.

"You're such a liar." Cleo walks into the main room and finds us, her eyes widening at my bare chest and Stella in a robe. "Oh crap. We'll go."

Denver joins Cleo, putting his arm around her waist. "Go? I'm not going anywhere." He grins and looks from Stella to me and back. "Well, it's about fucking time." He beelines it over to Stella, picking her up and hugging her. "Welcome to the family. Finally."

There goes my fuck fest.

TWENTY-SEVEN

Stella

"So what's the word?" Allie bites a carrot stick, leaning back in her chair at the nurses' station.

I put on my badge and look at the board, unable to strip the smile off my face for the past two days since Kingston and I got together. "What do you mean?"

"Don't you dare hold out on me!" She takes another bite, her eyes following me.

I laugh and sit on a stool. "All's good. We're an official couple."

"*Yay*!" She jumps up and pulls out her phone. Her thumbs rest on the screen and she hammers out a message to someone.

"Who are you messaging?" I ask.

"Dori. She told me to let her know if our plan worked." She sets her phone back on the desk when she's done.

"You have her cell phone number?"

"Yep. She likes me. Told me it's a shame she doesn't

have any more single grandsons otherwise she'd fix me up with them."

I nod. I took their advice on sneaking up to the cabin to surprise Kingston, but they don't know about the sappy candles, rose petals, and asking him to homecoming. Sedona helped me snag his suit. Allie thought I should be naked in the hot tub when he got there. Imagine looking at Grandma Dori after that suggestion. All kinds of wrong.

"Looks like you got what you wanted."

Her phone buzzes and her lips turn down after reading. "She said she already knew. How did she already know?"

"Maybe because Denver and Cleo ended up coming? But they stayed up there an extra day when we left. And Kingston dropped me off at my apartment only hours ago so he could get on shift, so I don't think it'd be him. I don't think Sedona would say anything." I shrug. "I don't really know."

Her phone buzzes again and she picks it up, that smile I'm so used to shining once again. "She just sent me a high five emoji." Her thumbs rush out a text and she places it down, exchanging her phone for a carrot stick.

"I'm concerned that your best friend is in her seventies."

Ralph approaches the nurses' station, a med student on his heels. "Dr. Harrison, you have a nice two days off?"

"I did, and now you can have a nice couple days off. Thanks for covering for me, Ralph."

"That's what a good colleague does. Let's go over the board." He pulls out his special blue marker.

I roll my eyes behind his back at Allie. She giggles quietly and picks up her phone to hammer out another text.

We go over all the patients before Ralph leaves me to take over. I head out to do my own rounds and assess the patients after he goes into the break room to get ready to leave for the night.

Five hours later, Allie's waiting for me outside of exam room five.

I sanitize my hands. "What's up?"

"There's a Sedona Bailey here asking to see you."

I tilt my head. "Sedona? She came all the way here?"

"She did. I can't believe how much she reminds me of Kingston."

"Which room?" I head down the hall, following Allie blindly.

"She's in eleven."

We cut through the nurses' station as Phoenix barrels into the emergency room, Cara from admitting trying to stop her.

"It's okay, Cara."

Allie looks back at me. "That was her, but she was pregnant." She points at Phoenix's flat stomach.

"Oh, Stella, thank goodness. Sedona called me. She was up here shopping for something for the baby. I swear I'm going to kick her ass for doing all this shit on her own." Phoenix barrels up to me. "I mean, she's pregnant and her asshat of an ex-boyfriend is nowhere to be found. The rich fucker could at least pony up some money to buy his kid a crib."

Allie's eyes widen at me, so I say, "Allie, this is Phoenix, Sedona's twin sister."

"I thought the fact I haven't had a proper orgasm in six months was starting to affect my vision." Allie blinks and walks toward room eleven.

"Now I know you're not Buzz Wheel's most avid fan," I tease her.

"It never said they were twins," Allie whines.

I shake my head at her and turn back to Phoenix. "She's in eleven, and Phoenix?" I put my hand on her arm. "If Sedona is in labor, let's hold off on bringing all this up to her, okay?"

Phoenix walks into eleven before Allie or me, and I sanitize my hands. "Why are you in Anchorage on your own?"

Sedona is on the bed, rubbing her stomach. "I was picking up the crib."

"I told you I'd buy you the crib."

Allie leans into me. "It's weird watching them fight, no?"

I laugh. "Hey, Sedona, how are you feeling? What brings you here?"

"My water broke. I just came directly here instead of calling my doctor."

I sit on the stool and wheel across the room, then I put her legs in the stirrups to examine her. "Any contractions?"

"Yes, but I haven't had one in a while."

"Please tell me asshat isn't going to show up here," Phoenix says, holding her sister's hand.

I shoot her a look. "I'm going to call labor and delivery. Your little girl is on her way." I smile, taking off my gloves. "We'll get you moved up to that floor."

Sedona nods, looking uncertain. This is her first child and she's doing it on her own. She turns toward her twin. "You can't be like that when she comes. I won't taint my daughter by allowing people to say bad things about her father."

I'll let them fight it out.

I head to the nurses' station, Allie following me. "Call up to labor and delivery and see if there are any beds."

She picks up the phone. I'm writing on the board when Kingston's voice comes over the radio in the nurses' station. Even though he's telling us how many minutes they're out and the patient's condition, so we know how best to be prepared, a rush of excitement that I'll get to see him runs through me. Allie answers while she's on hold with labor and delivery.

"She has a while, so we can keep her here for a little bit if they need time," I tell Allie.

I walk over to the ambulance drop-off just as it's pulling up. Kingston's smile is wide and welcoming when he sees me.

"Another flu case," Lou says, stepping out of the back of the ambulance.

They wheel in the patient while Lou tells me all the stats of the patient. Allie comes out and helps me get the elderly patient situated, hooking her up to oxygen and doing vitals. Once we know she's not in immediate danger, I walk out of the room, ordering blood work.

"Hey, you." Kingston looks side to side down the hall and grabs me by the edge of my lab coat, tugging me toward him.

"You know I can't do anything right now." I slide my hand into his and lead him around the corner, sneaking into the break room that's blessedly empty right now.

"And here is safe?" he says, caging me to the wall.

"Safer."

His large hand slides under my jacket and molds to my hip. "I missed you." He bends down and kisses me. "I'm not sure I can get through my shift."

"Crossing your fingers that you keep getting calls that send you here?"

"I might just tell Captain it's better for me to stay here."

He kisses me again, this time sliding his tongue into my mouth.

I moan, my back falling to the wall, my hands fiddling with the hair on the back of his head. His hand inches up my torso, over my ribs, and I anticipate his next move. But just as he's making his way to my breast, the break room door opens.

"Hey, I'm all for the sneaky sneak and I totally would've allowed you two to do whatever, but Sedona is screaming, and labor and delivery is full at the moment. Dr. Foster is on his way down, but I figured you might want to help her in the meantime. Hey, Kingston. You're welcome." Allie leaves.

I push off the wall, but Kingston locks me once more, his large thigh sliding between my legs. "My sister's here?"

"She's having the baby."

He nods. Not alarmed I guess since first-time moms tend to labor longer. "One more kiss?"

I glance toward the door and smack my lips to his. Our mouths tangle and our hands run along one another's body as though we forgot what we felt like in the hours we've been apart.

The door opens again. "Lovebirds, get the fuck out here." Lou shuts the door, laughing.

"I better go check on your sister. Phoenix is here too."

We walk out of the nurses' station to find Phoenix doing some kind of handshake with Lou. She points at us and her mouth slowly opens. "Does Grandma Dori know?"

"Give it a rest," Kingston says, his hand sliding over my ass when he passes.

"She does." Allie beams.

Phoenix looks at her then me. "Who's this?"

"Allie is Dori's new best friend."

Phoenix puts it all together and she sighs. "She recruited you to get those two together, didn't she?"

Allie smiles wide, nodding. "I want to be her when I grow up."

Phoenix's dark eyebrows shoot up. "Oookkkaayyy."

"Did you call the family, Phoenix?" Kingston asks, looking all authoritative in his uniform. His ass is magnificent.

This is when I wish I could openly touch him. But he's an EMT and I'm the ER doctor—hardly ethical if I'm groping him during work hours. At least in front of others.

"Not yet. I wanted to make sure."

We all file into the hospital room. Dr. Foster is already there, head peering out from under the sheet.

"Whoa." Kingston covers his eyes with his arm and backs up, pushing the rest of us to back up with him.

"You've seen plenty of pussies, King, don't be a moron." Phoenix slides by him and disappears into the room.

"Not my sister's." He cringes and looks at me. "Not my sister's."

I laugh and pat his shoulder. "I know. I know. You stay out here, and I'll fill you in."

Fifteen minutes later, Dr. Foster says Sedona is in active labor and since there's no room up on the floor just yet, he'll deliver her in the ER.

Dori's voice sounds from down the adjacent hall, veering closer. "Thank you, Allie. My ungrateful grandchildren can't even call me." She rounds the corner. As she approaches, Kingston and I make the same sound—one of disbelief.

"Do you think she looked in the mirror?" Kingston whispers.

She points at us halfway down the hallway. "You two

have finally come to your senses, but now I have to deal with Sedona. I'll talk to you later." She ducks into room eleven as Kingston and I share a look of shock.

"What the hell happened to your hair?" Phoenix asks.

"I was just at Clip and Dish. What's wrong?"

"If you don't want people to make jokes to you about Dory the fish, you need to tell them to tone down the blue in your hair. They're gonna start calling you Smurfette."

Leave it to Phoenix to speak her mind.

"Well, Smurfette was hot, so I'm not sure that's an insult. Sedona dear, how are you?"

Kingston's hand slyly slides behind me and he leans in close. "I'd do about anything to be buried inside you right now."

"How about I meet you at your apartment after your shift? Sedona should be here with the baby."

He pulls his keys from his pocket and takes off his house key. "Be naked in my bed."

I take the key and put it inside the pocket of my white lab coat. "See you then."

"Hey, King, we got a call," Lou says.

"Shit, can you call me if she has the baby? I wish I could stay but..."

I look up and down the hall before kissing him once. "Go, I'll let you know. She's in good hands."

"Well, I know that. Your hands are fucking amazing."

"I meant Dr. Foster." I chuckle and push him down the hall.

Kingston puts his hands on his chest as if he has breasts. I shake my head until he blows me a kiss and turns to Lou, the two of them walking out the sliding doors.

God, I love that man.

TWENTY-EIGHT

Kingston

It's been two weeks since Stella and I got together. The fact that she's lying in my bed right now, sprawled out like an octopus, lightly snoring, still makes my heart pitter-patter like a lovesick fool's.

A nap was essential after both of us had to work horribly long shifts this past week. That wasn't the first thing on our agenda though, which is why we're both naked.

The small cry in the other room causes Stella to stir. So I pull on a pair of sweatpants and tiptoe out of my room. Sedona named my new niece Palmer Doris Bailey and if she wasn't already Grandma Dori's favorite, she is now. Now it's just a running joke between all us Baileys that Sedona is a kiss-up.

I swoop my niece out of her bassinet next to Sedona, who's also asleep in her bed. Palmer looks at me with her big blue eyes like her father's.

"Hungry, wet, or just needy?" I ask softly, going into the kitchen to grab the breast milk that Sedona's been pumping.

Another reason Stella and I are exhausted is because we've been helping Sedona as much as we can when we're not working. I put the bottle in the warmer and carry Palmer to the changing table.

"You're going to make me a pro by the time it's my turn," I whisper, and she smiles, letting out a puff of gas as soon as I undo her diaper. "Was that just for Uncle Kingston? You really are a Bailey if that's the case." I tickle her stomach and her mouth opens in a yawn.

After changing her diaper and grabbing the bottle, I head to the couch and cradle her with my arm. She takes to the bottle, sucking away, and I flick on the television.

My bedroom door creeps open and Stella walks out wearing my T-shirt. She leans against the doorframe, watching me.

"That should be illegal." She points and comes to sit down next to me. "Good afternoon, Palmer." Her fingers run up my niece's torso before touching her nose.

"She eats like Allie," I say and pucker my lips to Stella.

She kisses me way too quickly for my liking. "She's a growing baby. How is Sedona?"

"Sleeping."

Stella grabs the remote and stops the channel on soccer. Jamison's old team is playing. His picture is plastered on the screen, even though he's no longer on contract with them. The commentators are talking about him and his failed future.

I shake my head and look at Palmer, silently promising I'll be his fill-in since he's not deserving of her right now. Not to see her sweet mouth open in a yawn or the small smiles that might just be gas but can still turn your mood from sour to great. "Change the channel."

Stella's lips dip, but she turns it to a daytime talk show.

"I've been meaning to thank you," I say to Stella, removing the bottle and propping Palmer up to burp her.

Stella watches me with fascination. "For what?"

"For spending so much time in Lake Starlight. For agreeing to spend some nights here so I can help Sedona. Everyone else has their own lives and I know they're doing what they can to make room for Sedona and Palmer, but I also know Sedona doesn't want to ask for help."

Stella's hand runs along my back then up to the back of my head. "You don't have to thank me. I'm happy to help her. I can't imagine what she's going through. And watching you with a baby is not a horrible thing."

Palmer lets out a huge burp and we both laugh.

I reposition her in my arm and feed her the rest of the bottle. "You like me with a baby?"

Stella sighs. "King, I saw the Instagram post-Sedona put up of you holding Palmer and how many women commented. You know as well as I do that you with her makes ovaries explode all over the world."

I shrug it off. "I only care about making one woman's ovaries explode." I lean forward and kiss her.

"Don't worry, they explode on a regular basis. Just happened two hours ago." She snuggles into me.

"So you want to have kids?" I ask. I know she's said she does, but the question feels like it holds more weight now that we're together. We've never talked about what we want our future to look like.

"Yes, I want kids. Not a lot though. Not nine." She widens her eyes.

I laugh. "Eight?"

"More like two?" She shrugs.

"Twins run in the family, so two pregnancies could equal three, or even four, babies."

"I could handle that."

I smile. "What's your end game when you're done with your residency?"

She shrugs and puts her head on my shoulder. "I was thinking of maybe having a family practice?"

"Really?"

She nods against my shoulder. "Being your family's on-call doctor—" She chuckles. "I think family practice might be where I want to concentrate. I'd get to see a lot of different types of cases and patients—from young to old. I think that might be where I fit."

"And where would you have this family practice?"

She slaps me on the chest. "Ask the real question you want to ask."

I chuckle and it startles Palmer. The bottle pops out of her mouth. Stella takes the empty bottle from my hand and sets it on the table. I burp Palmer, and once again, she lets out a burp like a college kid who just did a keg stand.

"Are you staying in Alaska?" I ask.

She doesn't answer right away, and I wait with bated breath. I'll follow her wherever she goes this time and she needs to know that. "Yeah. I think I'd open a practice in Lake Starlight."

Her full lips part and perfect white teeth shine as she smiles at me. My fingers thread through the back of her hair, pulling her mouth to mine.

"I fucking love you," I say.

"I love you too, and you don't need to say fucking for emphasis."

"Yeah, I do. I'm using it to reflect the magnitude of my love."

She nods, giggles, and backs away. "What about you? Are smoke jumping and firefighting your true calling?"

"I can't say I've thought about smoke jumping as a long-term career. I love it, but as I get older, I might not be able to keep doing it. Plus when I have a family, I'm not sure I want to be away as much as the job requires. I guess I'll have to go to full-time firefighter at some point."

"And always Anchorage FD?"

"I think so. Lake Starlight is way too slow."

She nods and turns her attention to Palmer. "I need a baby fix."

She takes Palmer from my arms and sits cross-legged on the couch rocking the baby. I don't say so, but watching her with Palmer these past two weeks has slayed me. The fact that Stella's given up all her freedom to help with Palmer has only made me love her more. And watching the way Stella makes faces at her, always pretends to be sad when she's sad, or happy when she's happy... for the first time in ever, I've given thought to what kind of father I'll be. I haven't figured it out yet, but I know one thing for sure—I want Stella to be the mother of my children.

Unfortunately, I also registered the lack of enthusiasm on her face when I said I wouldn't transfer to Lake Starlight. It's the first blip of dissatisfaction I've seen from her in the past two weeks. Then again, we haven't talked about me doing anything dangerous in that time. The Alaska Expedition Race isn't happening because Samantha and Tank got their own group and I wasn't doing it without Denver. But in two weeks, I'm doing the speed riding excursion with Tim and Tank. Samantha is a little salty she can't join in, but she said she'll train for next year. It will be the first time since we've been together that I'm doing something Stella deems too risky, and I can't deny I'm worried everything we've built is gonna go straight to hell.

Sedona comes out of her bedroom. "You guys. You can't keep taking care of her. I have to do this myself." She sits in a chair, yawning and pulling her knees to her chest.

"Who says that?" Stella asks. "Who says you have to do this all yourself? Everyone says it takes a village to raise a baby. We're your village right now, so just sleep." I raise my eyebrows at Stella, so she says, "What?"

"There's that bossy side of you I love so much."

"Ew… is that foreplay, King? Gross. I'm never having sex again." Sedona lays her head on the back cushion.

I grab the remote from Stella and flick through the channels, crossing over a different sports channel. There's Jamison's face front and center once again. The report says that he's been in an accident in his hometown in Scotland. I look at Sedona and see that she's sitting up straighter in her chair.

"She has his eyes," Sedona says, not even paying attention to the report that says he was intoxicated while driving. "And his nose." She looks at us. "Do you know how hard it is to look at her and see him? Why couldn't she have gotten all the Bailey genes?"

Sedona breaks down and Stella hands me Palmer, making room for herself on the chair to hold Sedona. "Her mouth is all you. Plus she's going to change so much as she grows. You'll see more you than him."

I have no idea if Stella is telling the truth or not, but it appeases Sedona because she stands, wiping the tears from her face, and walks over to take Palmer from me.

"You two go out to dinner or something. You weren't the idiots who didn't use protection and got pregnant." She shuts her bedroom door without another word.

I hate seeing her like this. Sedona has always been a person who looks at the positive side of things and lately she's seemed really down.

Stella crawls into my lap. "I hate that she's so upset. This should be a happy time for her."

I cock an eyebrow. "People say that the first two weeks of having a baby is a happy time? Really?"

She laughs. "I guess not, but he should be here to help her."

I nod. He better watch out if he ever shows his ass in this town again. "Let's go to dinner tonight. I'll get us into Terra and Mare."

"You mean a real date where we shower, and dress and you get lucky after instead of the reverse order?" She chuckles.

"I don't want my ego to seem too big here, but I don't think you've had any complaints that we've been doing it backward?"

Her head falls to my shoulder. "Sadly, you are correct."

"Come on. I'll call Rome."

She gets off my lap and I pick her up, carrying her into my room. When I drop her on the bed, she lies there, my T-shirt inching up, showing off her silk panties.

I climb up the mattress, my knuckles sliding along the outside of her panties. "Why, Dr. Harrison, you're soaked."

"You want to role play?" she asks.

I laugh while my hands dive under the waistband of her panties and pull the flimsy fabric off her. My stomach falls to the mattress and I let her legs rest on my shoulders.

"I just want to taste you." I stare up at her through the opening of her legs, sliding my tongue along her slit.

"Well by all means, if you want an appetizer before dinner."

"And I'll have dessert later."

I bury my head into her core. A few minutes later, she's quietly coming with her fists clenching the comforter, her heels digging into the small of my back. I'd say it's a good start to the night.

TWENTY-NINE

Stella

Kingston and I walk out of Terra and Mare after dinner, the cold wind hitting us square in the face.

I put on my gloves and hat. "It's so cold."

He wraps his arm around my waist, pulling me closer. "I'll get you home and warm you up."

The problem is Sedona is at home. I love the girl and I love that we can help her with Palmer, but I wouldn't mind just one night with Kingston where we can mess around anywhere we want, and we don't have to worry about being discreet. Not to mention every time I have an orgasm, I'm riddled with guilt because there's an exhausted single mom in the next room.

"The two glasses of wine warmed me up. Let's go for a walk," I say.

His hand slides into mine and he leads me down the sidewalk. We pass the bakery and the children's store. I find myself window shopping for Palmer. Then we pass Smokin' Guns with no sign of Liam inside, but rather a burly guy tattooing some girl who seems to have a group of friends waiting for her in the waiting room.

"Lucky's!" I say, tugging him forward. "I've never been inside. I wasn't old enough and there hasn't been a reason since I've been back. Let's go."

"To a bar?" Kingston asks. "Really?"

"One drink." I hold up my finger to him. "Come on."

"My family has already been a bunch of cock-blockers for us. Why not go into the town bar? We'll probably find Grandma Dori and Ethel to spend our night out with." Kingston rolls his eyes.

I nudge him playfully with my elbow. "Are you complaining about how much you're getting laid?"

He laughs and shakes his head. "Not even a little."

"That's what I thought."

I open the bar's door and we walk inside. I've never been in Lucky's before, but I'd bet good money it's never been this quiet. All eyes are on us—and it isn't until I scan the room that I see a familiar set of eyes staring at us from the pool table. Kingston's body comes flush to my back, his hands possessively on my hips, and I'm positive if I looked up, I'd know where he's looking. Right at Owen in the back corner of the room.

I just couldn't leave well enough alone.

Disregarding all the watching eyes and focusing on the bar, I make my way over and sit on an open stool before ordering a chardonnay for myself and a beer for Kingston. He places a twenty on the bar top.

We're just getting our drinks when the noise level goes back up, except I'm fairly sure they're probably all talking about Kingston and me. I'm not immune to the sting of the gossip in this town. We're together, so eventually we have to own that and to hell with what people might think.

I sip my wine and, from the corner of my eye, catch Owen walking over to us. "He's coming."

"Great," Kingston murmurs. He downs a hefty amount of his beer, like the sooner he finishes, the sooner we can leave. Which at this point seems like a good idea.

"Well, I guess that wedding wasn't just a fluke, huh? You guys are... together now?"

I open my mouth, but Kingston beats me to it. "We are. It's been years, Owen, and I'm not going—"

"Congratulations." Owen pats Kingston on the back so hard, he almost chokes.

Kingston shifts to stand, but I put my hand on his thigh and he eases back down.

"Thanks," I say.

"I always knew you two were meant to be together."

I inwardly roll my eyes.

"Have a great night. I guess I'll be seeing you around sometime." Owen walks two steps away then turns around. "Hey, Stella, give me a call. I'd love to catch up sometime." He winks just like Kingston does when he's acting arrogant.

I say nothing.

Kingston downs his beer then places the glass on the bar top. "Can we go now?"

I sip my wine, but he steals my glass out of my hand, finishes it, and sets it down with a clank.

He gets to his feet and holds out his hand. "I'll buy you a bottle from Liquory Split."

Without argument, I leave with him, feeling Owen's eyes on us the entire time.

We walk back to Kingston's apartment in silence, and when we arrive, he says he wants to work out and do I mind staying while he goes for a run? I smile and nod, pretending it's all normal behavior, but I know that Owen has spooked a reaction out of Kingston. I'm just not sure if it'll be short-lived and he'll shake it off or whether it's something we need to deal with.

I change into my pajamas, take off my makeup, and sit on the couch. Sedona and Palmer must be sleeping in her room. I pull out my phone with the intention of scrolling through social media, but a text message pops up.

Allie: *You're kidding me, right? I missed it. The moment everyone was waiting for.*

Me: *What are you talking about?*

Allie: *It's on Buzz Wheel. You guys saw Owen?*

I disregard her string of texts asking for more information and pull up the Buzz Wheel blog. There you have it. Owen standing between Kingston and me at the bar. You can't really see any of us in detail. It's blurry, but if you knew us, you could tell it's us. How does this thing get information so quickly? With mild trepidation, I read on.

The moment everyone was waiting for...

It happened tonight in Lucky's Tavern. It's rumored that after a dinner date at Terra and Mare, Stella Harrison dragged Kingston Bailey into Lucky's. The minute the two stepped in, warning bells shot off to all the patrons. The usually loud bar was more like church on Sunday. All eyes followed the couple to the bar, and the bartender reported that Kingston ordered a beer and Stella a wine. Apparently, Kingston finished both after Owen approached them.

Owen told Stella to call him to catch up, which had Kingston rising from his bar stool, but Stella managed to keep him at bay. If she hadn't, I think we can all agree that Sheriff Miller would've been called down to break up another fight over Stella. It's been eight years, but I'm sure no one forgets the disastrous outcome of the first one. Let's hope history does not repeat itself for these three.

The good news is that it appears that Kingston has finally won the heart of the girl he always loved. Can I get a hallelujah!

In other news, it's spreading like TikTok dance videos around Lake Starlight High School that Holly and Austin Bailey are trying for baby number two. Let's keep them in our thoughts, Lake Starlighters.

Xo,
　　Buzz Wheel

I FLIP BACK to the string with Allie.

Me: *Well that's great. Just when I thought Kingston and I were in smooth waters.*

Allie: *I'm about to go to Lucky's, hop on this Owen's back, and gouge his eyes out. Taunting Kingston like that? What an asshole.*

Me: *It's a long history, but I'm going to forget what I just read and chill for the night.*

Allie: *Okay, we can talk later. How is Terra and Mare? I think I might want to check it out.*

Me: *Why don't you just move here? LOL*

Allie: *Because I don't want to be part of the gossip. I just want to be the outsider looking in. Oh and to be Grandma Dori's Thelma. :P*

I laugh and click off my phone, praying and hoping Kingston doesn't run by Lucky's Tavern.

THIRTY

Kingston

I allow a week to go by to cool my anger before I seek out Owen. He's in the dock bar with his fisherman buddies when I find him. Approaching him here when he's with his buddies might be a bad decision. I hope I'm not subconsciously doing this as a reason to beat his ass—allowing his friends to swarm me just so I can claim I had to stand up for myself.

As I wind my way through the tables, he spots me before any of his friends. A long stare over the top of his beer glass, perusing me as if I might have a weapon on me or something. What is he thinking? We were friends—*are,* I suppose, just not how it used to be—and I want to make it clear about Stella and me.

"Can we talk?" I ask.

He finishes his beer, his eyes never leaving mine. A few buddies turn, but I don't know any of them and I'm sure they don't know me. But I'm still cautious, because if they're true friends, when he throws a punch, they'll be there to back him up.

We made amends years ago after we rolled down a set of stairs and I threw away my shot to be with Stella. I have to think we can do the same now.

He sets his mug on the table, throws money on the bar, and leads the way outside.

"Are you here to issue a warning? Stay away from your girl or else? I thought you were more original than that," he says.

I shake my head, burying my hands in my pockets of my jacket because it's fucking freezing out. "I want to apologize. It was wrong for you to find out about Stella and me like that."

"You're apologizing. And what? You want me to apologize again to you for what went down in high school?"

"Hell no. That's ancient history and we put it behind us while she was in New York. But I also understand how hard it is to watch her with someone else. And I should've warned you when we started seeing one another. I shouldn't have let you be blindsided."

He leans on the railing and I keep my distance. The words sound good, but Owen is temperamental. It takes very little to set him off, and I want to be able to react if need be.

"You think I care about some girl I nailed in high school? Give me a break, Bailey."

I say nothing to refute his words about nailing Stella. I trust that she told me the truth. I'll let Owen have that one if it makes him feel better.

"I think Stella has been different things to us," I say. "To you, she was something you had that I wanted. To me, she was more."

He looks out at the lake. "You know what your problem is, Bailey? You're too fucking sentimental. You think she's going to stick around? She's a doctor, for fuck's sake. You're a smoke jumper. Hell, I probably make more money than you."

I don't take the bait he's slinging. I just want this over with to clear my own conscience because of how back-stabbed I felt in high school when he asked her to homecoming. Clearing the air with him felt like the right thing to do.

"I guess I'll find out. I just wanted to apologize, so I'll go now." I turn to leave.

"Bailey," he says. I look over my shoulder and his hands are shoved in his pockets. "I hope she's everything you think she is."

I circle back around. "What does that mean?"

He laughs. "Jesus, stop protecting her. I just meant you put her on this shelf so high up… maybe she won't live up to what you've idolized her to be."

She already has.

She's everything I want.

Everything I need.

"That's not something you have to worry about."

"I didn't mean it in an asshole way. I really do hope it works out for the two of you. But you're wrong—she wasn't just some trophy to steal away from you."

He's piqued my interest. I break the distance, wanting him to expand. "Really?"

"At first, she might've been, but do you think I would have dated her that long just to stick it to you? My intention was only to take her to homecoming, but before I knew it, I liked her. But it was a hard pill to swallow that she was into you. Every time I was with her, she'd ask about you, tell me to fix what went wrong with us. Then the night of the fight, well..."

He apologized to me months later, when the town was sparse because most of our graduating class had gone to college.

"It's all good," I say.

He eyes my shoulder. "Still, I felt horrible about your shoulder and ruining your scholarship. I mean, we grew up wanting to play ball and you lost your opportunity because even after Stella and I broke up, I couldn't stand to let you have her. If the two of you would've started dating, that would've proven my theory correct." He shakes his head.

"What theory?" My forehead wrinkles.

He looks up. "That when she was with me, she really wanted you."

I'm not sure what Stella's feelings ever were for Owen. She's not the type to get involved with someone she doesn't like. Maybe a small part of her loved both of us in different ways.

"But I'm happy you two figured it out. I should've never stood in the way."

I nod and fiddle with my keys in my pocket. "I should've stood back and given you a fair chance."

He chuckles and shakes his head. I laugh too.

"You've loved that girl since the first day she walked into our class. She picked you from day one. It was a sign."

"You going all sentimental on me?"

"Hell no. But you and Stella, there's something there I can't explain because I'm obviously the better guy." He clasps me on the shoulder. "Now stop standing around here before you go back to your girl smelling like fish and she thinks you're fucking around on her."

"We cool?" I ask.

He nods. "We're cool." He grabs the door handle to go back into the bar and I step off the porch. "And Bailey?"

I turn back around. "Yeah?"

"You give me that sympathy look one more time when I run into the two of you and I'm gonna punch it off your face."

"Noted," I say and chuckle.

He opens the door, loud voices pouring out before the door shuts and it's quiet again.

Finally some closure. That was a long time coming.

THIRTY-ONE

Stella

Today is the day. The day I have to stand by quietly and watch Kingston fly to the top of a mountain in a helicopter and parachute down on his skis. We drive up to the guide place, where some Tim guy Kingston keeps talking about is. He's going with Kingston and Tank. Everyone is here with us—Allie, Stump, Lou, and Samantha.

I sit on a park bench outside the tour place where Kingston is laughing with Tank and the guy who looks way too much like his dad—and ironically, bears his dad's name. I'm really trying to appear all smiles and carefree, but the closer it gets, the more I want to drag him by his arm to safety. Panic and anxiety are like rubber bands around my chest and I feel like a watermelon almost ready to burst under the pressure.

A golf cart rolls down the shoveled brick pathway, someone waving their arm out the side. It stops a few yards away from the small building. I raise my eyebrows when

Dori steps out after leaving a smear of red lipstick on the teenage driver's cheek. Ethel's with her. Both of them might be wearing boots, but not snow boots.

"Dori, what are you doing here?"

"I wanted to see Kingston. Allie told me what was happening today."

I blow out a breath and glare at Allie over my shoulder. She shrugs as if she has no control and bites into a big salted soft pretzel. Lou bends over to get some and she circles away from him, mumbling to get his own.

"Oh, Dori, it's going to be up and down. It's not going to take that long. You came all this way."

She peers around. "Where is he?"

I point at the guide tours shop and she beelines in that direction. I go with her, holding her arm to make sure she doesn't fall. Once we're on dry ground again, she takes no time to walk inside and reach Kingston.

Dori comes to an abrupt stop when she sees Tim. "Now I know I only had one baby, and unfortunately he's passed. Who are you?"

Kingston glances at me over her head, which is still as blue as when Sedona delivered.

"I'm Tim."

"What?" She seems taken aback by his name but recovers quickly. "What kind of game are you playing? Trying to talk my grandson into doing this thing by pretending to be some resurrection of his father?" She waves her finger in front of the poor man's face, inching closer and closer.

Tim steps farther and farther back.

But the light changes or something, because Dori's expression eases and she says, "Oh, you don't look like him.

The dark hair and those eyes might have thrown me for a second, but you're not my son."

"No, ma'am I'm not."

Kingston blows out a breath and shoots Tim an apologetic look.

"Now I'm leaving you in charge." She pinches Kingston's cheeks. "This is my grandson, and if he doesn't return to all of us in one piece, you'll have us to answer to."

Tim nods. "I've listed all the risks to both Kingston and Corey."

It still takes me a second to realize Corey is Tank.

"I don't care." She shakes her finger at him again.

Kingston puts his hand over hers, lowering it to her side. "Thanks for the concern, Grandma, but we're all set and we're going to head up now." He kisses his grandma's cheek. "You should go to the lodge and get a hot chocolate. I'll come once we're done."

"Silly, I'm going to hang with Stella." She slides her arm through mine.

Kingston mouths sorry to me. "Well, I'm going to steal her away before I leave."

"That's okay, I want to talk to Tim some more. And what happened to Ethel?" She looks behind her, but there's no Ethel.

Dori walks toward Tim and Kingston puts his arm around my waist, pulling me to the other side of the small shop where there are no prying eyes.

"You good?" he asks.

"Yeah," I lie.

"It's okay to say you're not." He looks down. "I wish you would've opted to ski today to get your mind off it. We're doing a few black diamonds before Tim takes us up in the helicopter."

I nod, my stomach ready to throw up the coffee I drank this morning. "I'm going to shop. I'll keep Dori busy. But the minute your feet are on the ground again, I want word, okay?"

He inches closer to me, one arm resting above my head. "Okay, boss." He kisses my nose.

I grab his jacket and pull him toward me. "Now really kiss me this time."

"Yes, ma'am." He gives me a kiss that makes my knees weak and ruins me for anyone else.

"Kingston!" Tim hollers.

Kingston kisses me one more time. "I'll be back before you know it."

I smile although I know it doesn't reach my eyes. I remind myself of my mom's words—I'd rather have him like this than not at all.

He winks, the cocky side of him that scares me making an appearance, and he disappears out the door.

I close my eyes, inhale a breath, and follow him out, watching the three men putting on their skis. Kingston waves to us and skis over to the chair lift. I look at my watch. I have four hours to kill. Great.

Allie throws away her wrapper. "Come on, let's do some shopping to get your mind off it. Don't worry, he'll be back in no time."

"Yes, dear, we saw a cute knitting shop Ethel wants to go to," Dori says.

I nod, following them but glancing back to where he was. Where I last saw him alive.

THIRTY-TWO

Kingston

After a couple runs down the double black diamond, Tim okays us to go up in the helicopter.

On the way up, he leans forward although we're all equipped with microphones in our ear so that we can communicate up there. "Listen, I'm going to give you instruction through the radio. If I tell you to do something, you do it. Understand?"

We both nod.

"Everyone thinks this is easy, and you guys are more educated than my normal clients, but that doesn't mean things can't go wrong. Even with the most skilled skiers, all you need is to become distracted for one second and disaster strikes."

"Thanks, Dad." Tank elbows me, laughing.

I see the anger brewing in Tim's eyes at Tank's lack of care. I feel like there's something Tim's not telling us.

The helicopter drops us at the top and we all climb out.

Tim double-checks our gear and we wait for him to get his own equipment ready before we ski off the mountain. Another group is going down without parachutes next to us, all watching us with vast interest.

Tank makes a growling sound like he does right before he jumps from the plane when we're smoke jumping. I'm not going to judge what gets one man's adrenaline going. For me though, I keep my excitement inside.

Once Tim gives us the okay, we ski. I feel the lift of the parachute until my skis only lightly touch the snow. I'm not prepared for the butterflies, or the way I have to go one way or another. Tim's in my ear, giving more direction to Tank than myself, but I've never felt this out of control. Like the wind could take my sails and I could face-plant into the side of a mountain.

My skis fly off the ground and I'm airborne for a few minutes. The views of the mountains and the snow are majestic, but all that's on my mind is Stella and the way she's nibbled her bottom lip ever since I picked her up yesterday. She's putting up a good front, but hopefully when I return safely today, she'll understand it's okay to be worried, but I'll always come back to her.

"King, you need to go left. *Left!*" Tim screams in my ear, so I adjust. "There you go."

He rattles off more instructions to Tank. Seeing the bottom, I pull my cords and slide to a stop at the base of the helicopter run.

Tank follows with Tim coming up behind us.

"Way to go, boys! You did great. Want to go again?" Tim's much more relaxed now that we have our first run under our belt.

"Hell yeah!" Tank screams, and I nod enthusiastically.

The adrenaline hits me, and I understand why Samantha and Tank want to get it on so much after the rush. I'm on a high after flying in the air over terrain that's not always reached. Next, I want to fly somewhere no one can reach unless you're speed riding.

We're in the helicopter when I pose the question to Tim. "How do we get a ride up somewhere only speed riders go?"

Tim's face falls and he shakes his head. "You're not ready."

I knew it.

He must see the look on our faces because he holds up his hands. "Just give me a few more times and I promise I'll get you up there. You guys are quick learners, but you're not there yet."

"We're professionals," Tank says.

I kind of agree. We have parachuting down to an art. We deal with wind conditions and weather all the time. Sure, we're not often being dropped in the mountains, but I could handle it.

We reach the summit and go through the motions of checking all our equipment again. There are no other skiers this time and I realize that this place doesn't look familiar from when we went helicopter skiing.

"We don't bring a lot of clients up here, so consider this my treat. You guys still need to give it some time before going out to uncharted territory," Tim adds.

Tank slaps Tim on the shoulder. "Let's do this."

He skis off before Tim gives the okay and Tim shakes his head.

"You go," he tells me.

My skis dip and I'm only skiing on snow for a minute before I feel the lift of my parachute. Shit. This is more intense and feels more uncontrolled than the last run. Tim's screaming in our ear a lot more. Tank is pretty much disregarding him, and I take flight after coming off an edge, a white cloud obscuring my view. My heart rate picks up, but thankfully, I come through to clear skies.

"You cannot do that, Kingston. You have to think on your feet. Go right," Tim says in my ear.

I move to go right, but a wind shear tucks under me and I circle around in the sky before falling down on the snow. My skis pop off and I face-plant into a pile of snow.

Tim lowers himself and meets me, staring behind him. "Get your skis, Kingston."

I follow his gaze and see what he's seeing. Small chunks of snow breaking apart. I must have stirred something when I fell. I scramble in the snow for my skis, clicking my boots into them as Tim positions my chute.

"Go. Go. Go!" he screams.

"I'm going," Tank says, oblivious to what's happening behind him.

I slide my skis, pushing off my left leg to gain momentum. I ski down but keep looking over my shoulder.

"Eyes ahead, Kingston. Go. Don't look back."

The panic in Tim's voice is clear and scares me in a way I've never felt before. Like there might be no getting out of this one. Dread feels like a ball and chain strapped to my ankle, keeping me tethered to this mountain.

I try to lift, but the wind has died down and all Tim keeps saying is, "Left. Left."

I follow his instructions, finally finding a cross wind that lifts me into the air. I look down to see the cascade of falling snow tumbling down the mountain under my skis.

Shit, I'm not flying any faster than this avalanche.

"Just concentrate on getting to the bottom. We're in good shape," Tim says in my ear.

I think he's lying as a puff of white surrounds me, and now a haze is blocking the visual of my surroundings. Fear grips my heart and all I see is Stella. The despair on her face when they tell her I'm buried in a pile of snow, most likely dead. A headline in Buzz Wheel, "Kingston had it all and threw it away for a thrill ride down a mountain." Her finding another guy and his kid growing in her belly.

"Stay straight, Kingston." Tim says in my ear.

But I'm too busy thinking about Stella living a life without me. My gut twists and I choke on my own vomit, staring at the snow growing faster and denser under my skis.

I come out into a clearing and breathe fresh air. Tank is up ahead completely unfazed by what's happening right behind him.

"We're going to land, but the helicopter had to leave, so we'll see what the conditions are like," Tim says, and I nod. "Say something, Kingston."

"Got it," I say, but I can't stop examining the impending avalanche.

Then it all stops. I look behind me, seeing a classic V shape, but it's not chasing us any longer. We land five minutes later.

Tim's not playing games. "We're not taking any chances. There's a van coming to get us to take us back to the lodge." He doesn't even let us pack our parachutes away properly.

"What happened? That was fucking awesome," an oblivious Tank says.

I do what Tim says. We're in the van ten minutes later, still no sign of the avalanche getting worse. Tim and I sit in the back of the van while Tank sits up front with the driver, telling him what an awesome thing we did and how he's going to nail his girlfriend in every position he can imagine when he gets back to the cabin. I figured they were just fooling around but I guess there's more there because Tank told me they're official.

Tim knocks his knee to mine. "You can breathe."

I run my hand through my hair. "I've never been so scared. With everything I've ever done, I've never felt out of control like that." I clench my hands.

"Sometimes small avalanches like that happen, but those aren't the ones we hear about on the news. I'll alert the authorities and they'll handle it to make sure skiing is safe again. It was a loose snow avalanche, not a slab, so we were lucky. But the threat is there any time you ski." He runs a hand down his face and blows out a long breath. "You want to know why I agreed to take you two out?"

"I have wondered," I say.

He nods and doesn't say anything for a few seconds. "I took you guys speed riding because once I denied a group of kids. Said they weren't ready. They ended up hiring a helicopter themselves because their parents paid for it. They had some stupid guide who didn't know his ass from his asshole and two of those kids died when they flew into the side of a mountain." He pats my knee. "You were smart and listened to me." He nods toward Tank. "Talk some sense into your friend though. I know when you're young you feel like you're invincible, but no one is."

That's something I should've already known with my parents dying so young and leaving nine kids behind. We have so many unanswered questions regarding their death and how they ran into the tree when they were snow-mobiling.

"You're smart. You should definitely try this again," Tim adds.

"Yeah, maybe." But it's not an adrenaline rush I want right now. I want Stella in my arms.

We sit back in the van and I blow out a breath, closing my eyes. I've never appreciated my life more than right now. Suddenly, Austin's advice makes all the sense in the world. Who knew he was so smart?

THIRTY-THREE

Stella

Shopping was a bust. We sit on the park bench again because I won't relax until Kingston comes back. Looking at soaps and lotions and handmade crafts isn't going to distract my brain from the fact he's up there risking his life for a thrill. A couple of kids walk past us on the bench.

"I heard they were speed riding and there was an avalanche. That's why the helicopter came back."

Before I know it, I'm calling out to the kids. "Excuse me!"

One of them turns around. "Yeah?"

"What were you saying about an avalanche?"

"Don't worry, it's not going to come here. It was the other side of the mountain." He turns and continues to walk to catch up to his friend.

Allie drops her gummy worms in my lap, stalking toward them. "Hey, kid!"

Both of them turn around and look her up and down. "Yeah?"

"We have friends who are speed riding. What kind of avalanche and are they okay?" Allie asks.

I hold my breath, waiting for the answer, tears pricking my eyes.

"Not sure. All I heard was the helicopter had to get off the mountain and they were hitching a ride in a van. That's if they're not buried six feet under. Maybe they're ice pops by now."

My mouth opens.

Allie huffs.

"Little boy, let me tell you something." Ethel follows them.

Dori sits down next to me. "Sometimes I just don't have the energy but watch this. Ethel learned everything from me."

Ethel pokes the kid in the chest. "One of those men up there is her grandson, the other one's boyfriend. And that one." She points at Samantha. "Well, from what I understand, they only have nookie. Not sure what you call that." She scowls at Samantha.

Samantha tucks over by us, snatching one of Allie's gummy worms. "Actually we're official now," she says.

"Well thank God for small favors," Dori says.

"Don't speak so lightly of people's lives," Ethel says to the boys. "It's disrespectful. You two been smoking that whacky weed?"

One kid raises his eyebrows like, 'what the hell is wrong with this woman.'

"And before you open your mouth, I'll remind you, I'm someone's grandmother. So speak to me with the respect you do your own grandparents."

"Sorry, ma'am," the one who hasn't spoken yet says, weaving around Ethel. "I'm very sorry. If we knew more, we'd tell you."

"Whatever," the other one says to the quieter kid. "You're such a pussy."

"Grandmas are badass. Mine hit me with her cane once when I back talked her. You don't want to fuck with them."

The boys walk away and Ethel shuffles back to us.

Allie claps for her. "Now I'm not sure whose sidekick I want to be," Allie says.

Lou disappears inside the shop. I watch him talk to the guy at the counter, trying to decipher body language.

"What if?" I ask.

"Kingston's a smart boy. He won't let anything happen to himself," Dori says. But she doesn't know. And she doesn't sound that confident in her words either. "By the way, does Kingston know that I'm the reason you two are together?"

"You and me," Allie adds.

A van pulls up in front of the building, and my eyes scour the tinted windows. First the driver gets out, not bothering to acknowledge us. He rounds the back and opens the doors in the rear. Tank walks up and grabs Samantha, walking her away from everyone. I roll my eyes.

Standing, I nibble my lip. Allie's chomping on her gummy worms and it's all I can hear. Finally, Kingston comes into view, shaking Tim's hand near the back of the van. Relief washes through me. I run over and jump into his arms, wrapping my legs around his waist.

"Are you the avalanche people?" I hug him tightly.

"Yeah, but I'm okay. Not even a scratch."

I'm not sure how much my heart can take of these stunts, but maybe if I would've waited at home and not heard the rumors, it would have been better. He would've just returned to me safely and I never would've been the wiser. I cast kisses all over his face. His forehead, his nose, his cheeks, his lips, his jaw.

"Hey," he says, drawing back. "I was wrong."

"What?"

"Being up there and watching that avalanche chasing me down, all I thought about was not returning to you. Not being with you. I don't need to chase some high that risks my future with you. I want the risks of marrying you, having a family. The adrenaline of getting you to the hospital when you're nine months pregnant and the sweet reward of our baby being born. Or trying to choose the perfect anniversary gift and waiting while you open it to see if I did good. I want the challenges of raising our kids and the wild ride of parenthood we'll face together. Because all I could think up there was that what I was really risking was you. And I don't want to be the guy in a story you tell one day to your kids that you had with some other asshole."

"What guy?"

He shakes his head. "No one. Nobody. Just know you are always first, and I'll never put our life together in jeopardy." He kisses me. "And now I'll have to hear Austin say I told you so."

I laugh. "What are you talking about?"

"Just that I love you more than all that shit. So much fucking more."

His lips press to mine, and he dips me for dramatic flair. Our friends clap behind us.

"Just remember I got the two of you together," Dori says.

My lips vibrate with laughter against his before he asks, "What is she talking about?"

"She's old. Let her have the credit."

He pulls me upright. "I love you."

"Always and forever."

EPILOGUE

Kingston

Eighteen months later...

"I'm not sure I can actually do this again," Stella says while I zip up her wetsuit. I'm going to be sporting a fucking hard-on while we surf the bore tide in Turnagain Arm. This is year two for us and I've been anticipating today for three months.

The bore tide only arrives April to October, and the long, slow-going wave can be ridden for over thirty minutes and as long as a mile if you do it right. Last year we only got ten minutes—which was still fucking awesome—and Stella fell in love. With some help from a friend who is a guide, we're hoping to catch it early today.

"You totally have this. Come on." I zip up my wetsuit.

We venture through the throngs of weeds to get closer to the water, our boards snug under our arms. We put our boards in and Stella kneels while I stand. With our paddles in hand, we get out, waiting to hear the rush of the water and the slow waves coming to announce the bore tide's approach.

I lie back on my board, exhausted from my shift last night. Stella's doing her family practice residency now, so she's working regular hours. I'm still all over the board.

"Are you going to miss smoke jumping this year?" she asks.

I knew she would. Stella worries too much that she's not enough excitement for me to quit doing crazy shit.

"No. I told you, I made my peace. I'll miss the guys, but it was time to move on." I'm good with my decision. I'm getting older. Plus, I didn't quit because of the danger aspect as much as it was being away from Stella all the time. One time it was a whole month. Yeah, sorry, I tap out.

"Okay."

I run my hands through the water to reach her. "I'm not spending my life away from you. We already wasted enough time apart. So stop worrying."

She nods and I lean in and kiss her lips.

Now I have to figure out if I want to stay in Anchorage or transfer to the Lake Starlight fire department. And without smoke jumping, I have to find a side gig. Lou offered me an in on his contracting business, but I'm not really interested. Denver asked if I wanted to do some things for him, but I'm not sure yet. Lucky for me I have some savings to help me along while I figure it out.

The rush of the water echoes through the air and Stella looks as if she might throw up.

"Relax, baby. I'll dive in and save you if need be, but you're badass, remember that."

She smiles and I kiss her one more time.

"I'm excited and nervous," she says. She hasn't fully warmed up to the feeling of doing something out of her comfort zone, but she's got an A-plus for trying.

The wave approaches. We paddle and paddle until it takes us and another guy—who's standing and looking like a pro surfer, his paddle barely used. I laugh because that was me years ago, solo or with some buddies, but now I get to share this with Stella. She's probably searched out every online tip she could find.

We ride the wave for twenty minutes before we lose it. Afterward I lie on my board, reveling in the fact we did it.

"That was amazing. I totally get that rush," she says.

"You got the adrenaline horny gene like Tank and Samantha?"

She giggles and that's my clue.

I nod in the opposite direction. "Let's get going so we can stop at home before heading to the baby shower."

We paddle back the way we came.

"I think we should ask Sedona to move in with us," she says.

"Why?" I whine like a child. We recently bought a house by downtown Lake Starlight, and yes, it's big enough for Sedona and Palmer, but there's no running around naked if we do that. Her and Palmer are still in the apartment I used to share with Juno.

"Because she's your sister and still needs help when she's traveling."

Sedona's traveling more now after getting a job with a travel magazine, following in my mom's footsteps. Sometimes she takes Palmer, and other times she leaves her with us or Austin or Phoenix.

"Fine. Only because I like that I'm Palmer's favorite uncle and I want to really cement the spot."

Stella shakes her head at my competitive nature. "We'll ask her tonight then. Palmer can have her own room."

"You're really okay with this?" I ask her.

"It was my idea. Of course I am."

We finally reach where my truck is parked and I help her out with her board, then the two of us get to the truck. Unfortunately, the buzz of accomplishing the bore tide has worn off now that we're discussing my sister and niece moving in with us. But whatever.

We get out of our wetsuits and I stare at Stella in her swimsuit. "Want to make out in the back of my truck? Pretend we're in high school or something?"

She chuckles. "Sure." She hops into the back, leaving me to get everything situated.

I hear her turn on the ignition. I'm sure she's cranking the heat, and sure enough, when I climb into the back seat, it feels like I'm in a damn sauna.

She straddles me, and I take the opportunity to tug down the straps of her swimsuit, exposing her tits. "I love these."

I cover her tit with my mouth, and she rocks against my hard-on. We make out like teenagers—except we're adults so we actually fuck in the back seat. It's a little irresponsible since we have to use fast food napkins to clean up, but it's all worth it.

Back at our house, we have plenty of time to get ready, so Stella and I take a little longer, relishing the quiet. As she gets her purse, I stuff the ring into my pocket. I'm not worried that she'll say no. She could, but I doubt it.

"Ready?" I ask.

"I love baby showers."

We walk out of the house, but rather than heading in

the direction of the party at Terra and Mare, I lead her the opposite way.

"Where are we going?" she asks.

"Just come." I guide her to the dock.

She snuggles closer to me, probably remembering our moments here the same way I did. "You're being romantic."

We walk to the edge of the dock, but we don't sit because we're in nice clothes and spring has just arrived with the nicer weather.

"I thought I loved you, but the day you jumped in that lake, I knew for sure you were the one for me," I say.

"It was a moment of temporary insanity. Though maybe I should do it again sometime now that I can enjoy you warming my body up." She steps closer, but I fall down to my knee.

She smiles, tilting her head, and I hold up the ring. "Stella Harrison, you are the love of my life. You stole my heart at ten and have held it ever since. Make me the happiest man alive and marry me?"

"King," she says, her hands covering her face. "Yes."

I slide the ring onto her finger, and she holds it up in the air.

"It's beautiful." She wraps her arms around my neck and kisses me.

"You must be crazy to say yes," I say.

She giggles. "I knew you were a keeper when you shared your textbook with me and asked about my dad. You were always different than the other boys."

She kisses me again, and my heart feels as if it explodes into fireworks. I can't believe we're finally here, full circle, and she's going to be my wife.

———

WE'RE hand in hand when we step into Terra and Mare for the baby shower. Stella asked on the way over if I would mind not announcing our engagement, since it's not our big day. But all eyes zero in on us when we walk in.

Palmer runs to me and I swoop her up in my arms. She hugs Stella and kisses both of us on the cheek. Then she picks up Stella's hand, looks at the ring, and lets her hand drop. I showed the ring to her yesterday.

Palmer looks at me and signs her thoughts. *Pretty*.

Palmer only knows basic words so far, but she's getting there. Sedona started sign language with her as soon as she found out Palmer was deaf. In a way, the entire family has all been learning right along with my niece.

I shake my head, putting her down to sign. *Secret*.

She giggles, and everyone at the party rushes us like an all-you-can-eat buffet, hugging and saying their congratulations.

So much for that.

The door of the restaurant opens again, and everyone turns, because as far as I can tell, we were the last ones to arrive.

A few guests gasp.

Jamison stands in the doorway.

I scan the immediate area for Palmer, but Sedona's already stepped in front of her, blocking her from his view. Sedona rubs her hand over her swollen belly as though she's trying to protect the baby inside who's due in about a month.

"Sedona." Jamison's blue eyes widen and the color drains from his face when he gets a good look at her stomach.

But Sedona doesn't need to worry because all my

brothers and brothers-in-law come shoulder to shoulder with me in front of her, crossing our arms.

Good luck, bastard. You aren't getting through us.

The End

COCKAMAMIE UNICORN RAMBLINGS

Whoa, that story was all kinds of emotion, wasn't it? At one point in the middle of the story Rayne thought to herself, is this even funny? But as any of our faithful Piper Rayne fans know, we try to be true to the characters. Kingston and Stella just had too much of a past, and their love was so deep it felt more emotional than funny a lot of the time.

We've had all the Bailey covers ready to go since book one. Stella and Kingston's photograph is one of our favorites but we're not going to lie, we were worried about the backlash of two white women writing a black heroine. We've seen the comments on Facebook—some people think books should be more diverse regardless of the race of who is writing them and others disagree. But we just didn't feel like the reality would be that out of nine kids, they would all marry in their same race. We had trouble finding photographs of interracial couples but fell in love with Stella and Kingston's photo as soon as we saw it. (Are you listening photographers? Please start shooting more interracial couples!!!)

Because of our concern, we reached out to diversity editor, Renita McKinney, for her help. She's an amazing woman and she helped us tremendously with this book! We also had three sensitivity readers go through the book and we owe them a huge thanks as well—Amber L. Cotton, Isha Coleman and LaToya Toney-Walterhouse. Any issues within these pages are on us, not anyone else.

When we decided on writing this story line, I'm not sure we thought it was going to toe the line of second chance romance. Originally, we thought maybe Stella would work at the local bar but then that would mean she would've always been in Lake Starlight. But as we teased Kingston and Stella's story and brought Owen in, it quickly turned into something bigger. It wasn't just a my best friend's girl trope because Kingston had been friends with her too. Good friends. The best of friends. Add in the fact that they weren't getting their HEA until book eight and we knew they couldn't both live in the same town for that long and never get together. And so Stella left for school and didn't return for a long time.

One of our secrets is, we came up with their past while writing this book. We knew something huge had to have happened for Stella to run but we had no idea what until we started WMBFG. Thankfully, because we kept Kingston and his history with Stella vague in previous stories, we didn't write ourselves into a corner.

Rayne did a shit ton of research on the crazy ass stunts Kingston loves. She watched video after video wanting it to seem authentic because she'd never dream of doing any of them, but she admires those who do. You can go to YouTube and look up speedriding down mountains or bore tide in Anchorage. You can even see the Alaska Adventure Race. Alaska is so beautiful and all the videos show how lucky the Baileys are to live there.

Our team deserves HUGE HUGS, who if not for them, we'd never be able to get these books to you!

Danielle Sanchez and the entire Wildfire Marketing Solutions team!

Renita McKinney for her diversity edit.

Cassie from Joy Editing for line edits.

Ellie from My Brother's Editor for line edits.

Shawna from Behind the Writer for proofreading.

Our sensitivity readers— Amber L. Cotton, Isha Coleman and LaToya Toney-Walterhouse.

Sarah from Okay Creations for the cover and branding for the entire series.

Sara from Sara Eirew Photography for the super sexy picture of Juno and Colton.

Bloggers who consistently carve out time to read, review and/or promote us.

Our Piper Rayne Unicorns who champion this series to others with their whole hearts.

You the reader who took a chance on our book with so many choices out there!

We're already tearing up just thinking about Sedona's book. The last full-length book in The Bailey series. UGH. But Jamison is back and the Bailey brothers aren't on the welcoming committee, that's for sure. We can't wait to see how it all unfolds. Bet you can't either. ;)

XO,
Piper & Rayne

ABOUT PIPER & RAYNE

Piper Rayne is a USA Today Bestselling Author duo who write "heartwarming humor with a side of sizzle" about families, whether that be blood or found. They both have e-readers full of one-clickable books, they're married to husbands who drive them to drink, and they're both chauffeurs to their kids. Most of all, they love hot heroes and quirky heroines who make them laugh, and they hope you do, too!

ALSO BY PIPER RAYNE

The Baileys

Lessons from a One-Night Stand

Advice from a Jilted Bride

Birth of a Baby Daddy

Operation Bailey Wedding (Novella)

Falling for My Brother's Best Friend

Demise of a Self-Centered Playboy

Confessions of a Naughty Nanny

Operation Bailey Babies (Novella)

Secrets of the World's Worst Matchmaker

Winning My Best Friend's Girl

Rules for Dating your Ex

Operation Bailey Birthday (Novella)

The Greenes

My Twist of Fortune (FREE)

My Beautiful Neighbor

My Almost Ex

My Vegas Groom

The Greene Family Summer Bash

My Sister's Flirty Friend

My Unexpected Surprise

My Famous Frenemy

The Greene Family Vacation

My Scorned Best Friend

My Fake Fiancé

My Brother's Forbidden Friend

The Modern Love World

Charmed by the Bartender

Hooked by the Boxer

Mad about the Banker

Complete Set (all 3 books)

The Single Dad's Club

Real Deal

Dirty Talker

Sexy Beast

Complete Set (all 3 books)

Hollywood Hearts

Mister Mom

Animal Attraction

Domestic Bliss

Bedroom Games

Cold as Ice

On Thin Ice

Break the Ice

Complete Set (all 3 books +)

Charity Case

Manic Monday

Afternoon Delight

Happy Hour

Complete Set (all 3 books)

Blue Collar Brothers

Flirting with Fire

Crushing on the Cop

Engaged to the EMT

Complete Set (All 3 books)

White Collar Brothers

Sexy Filthy Boss

Dirty Flirty Enemy

Wild Steamy Hook-up

The Rooftop Crew

My Bestie's Ex

A Royal Mistake

The Rival Roomies

Our Star-Crossed Kiss

The Do-Over

A Co-Workers Crush

Hockey Hotties

Countdown to a Kiss (Free Novella)

My Lucky #13

The Trouble with #9

Faking it with #41

Sneaking around with #34

Second Shot with #76

Offside with #55